ALL I CAN TAKE OF YOU

All I Can Take of You

A collection of short stories

by

LINDA BOROFF

BOOKS

Adelaide Books
New York / Lisbon
2020

ALL I CAN TAKE OF YOU
A collection of short stories
By Linda Boroff

Copyright © by Linda Boroff
Cover design © 2020 Adelaide Books

Published by Adelaide Books, New York / Lisbon
adelaidebooks.org

Editor-in-Chief
Stevan V. Nikolic

For any information, please address Adelaide Books
at info@adelaidebooks.org
or write to:
Adelaide Books
244 Fifth Ave. Suite D27
New York, NY, 10001

ISBN: 978-1-952570-97-1

Printed in the United States of America

Contents

A Brief Organic History   *7*

Home Like a Shadow   *9*

A Season of Turbulence   *26*

A Shoo-In   *72*

The Shakes   *87*

Lowfathead   *94*

Night School   *115*

A Suitable Poison   *128*

Sunnyside   *140*

A Journey From Which Many Do Not Return   *156*

The Big Bash *170*

Euphoric Recall   *180*

The Hundred Thousand Dollar Suit   *194*

Let That Be a Lesson   *208*

The Discarded   *222*

Acknowledgements   229

About the Author   231

A Brief Organic History

"She's no Lolita, that's for sure," I once overheard my mother say about me, with a chuckle; she was as unintentionally and catastrophically destructive as Godzilla's hind end. What her description meant was that at thirteen I had dark, truculent hair, pruned like a topiary or wrestled into a stiff besom of a ponytail, white legs shaped like soda straws, dark accusatory eyes and the petulant mouth of the perennially misunderstood.

I was *that one.* Who forgot. Missed. Started it. Made all the fuss. Saw. Tattled. Lied. Got caught. Spoiled everything. Got in trouble. Got everyone in trouble. Was last. Got lost. Brought it all on herself. Got no sympathy.

The One with the Pick-on-Me pheromone that attracted every bully within a ten-mile radius. The One that even amiable teachers took an instant aversion to.

The One who tried to buy friends.

And the One who got flashed. Because I was indisputedly the champion flasher victim of all time: Queen Schmuck-Spotter. Empress Pecker-Peeker. To this day I think of a man as a sort of sideways Jack-in-the-Box. In fact I can see my whole life in flasher retrospective, all of them lined up side by side through the years like priapic Rockettes, extending mirror-perfect into infinity. Some of them must have traveled thousands of miles, guided by instinct like arctic terns through storm and wind, over trackless desert and featureless ocean to a destination they recognized only when it loomed up before them in a plaid skirt on its way to Latin Club.

Years later, a defendant being prosecuted by my own husband for exposing himself on the Santa Cruz mall managed *during his own trial* to extricate his schwanz from his orange prisoner's jumpsuit and waggle it at me under the table as his jury exited for deliberation. Why me?

Because you're watching for it, Cliff insisted. And that apparently was the crux: I expected to be flashed, ergo I attracted lily-wavers. My *karma*, to use the vernacular of this tree-hugging, clove-smoking, Birkenstock-wearing headquarters, had actually opened all those flies and whipped out all those peters.

"So he had one for the road. You wanna file a complaint?"

No, I wanted to laugh, because Cliff was so funny, and because it really had been a very fine and funny marriage while it lasted.

Home Like a Shadow

"I was born here," Cliff answers. "Nobody *moves* here."

We are racing through the Kettleman Hills, running late for his mother's birthday dinner and heading for trouble at eighty miles per hour. I clench my teeth as the parched, shoulderless curves yank the Camaro through them by sheer centrifugal force, hot asphalt uncoiling before us like a whip. The sky is relentlessly blue, only fading a little at the eastern horizon. Below, the earth is platted into odd geometrical shapes: scalene triangles and parallelograms of umber, khaki, and ochre.

"What is it they grow out here again?"

"Cotton wheat alfalfa."

"You know," I say, clutching the dashboard, "those are the first words you've used that weren't negative."

"Rattlesnakes." But he grins. Alton has been an easy place for Cliff to leave, but not to stay away from. As I scan the landscape, the word "empty" keeps coming to mind, but I have been taught that empty refers only to the imagination of the observer, never to the reality.

A jet swoops into view, flying low, reflecting the sun like a needle in the eye. Cliff jerks his head left. "Lemoore Naval Air Station. Back in high school, I used to work there summers tending the runways. Temperature out on the blacktop'd hit about one-forty." An English major drunk on Keats and Virginia Wolfe, I am trying to envision this place as a sort of boondocks Brigadoon, but it seems more hellish by the minute.

"It has its own harsh beauty," I try.

"And you've read a lot of books." But a moment later, he says, "In the spring, these hills turn into a carpet of flowers overnight. Golden poppies and blue lupine." I lean my head against him. "Gone as fast as they came."

His shoulder is reassuringly hard and warm beneath my cheek. Not that I'm worried about meeting his family; I know by now that I am not the type of girl that parents approve of. I don't even take it personally anymore. "Slinky," one mother had sniffed, as if that were something bad. Anyway, what Cliff and I have, no parent can get between. Not yet.

The town of Alton was built by Standard Oil from the ground up, Cliff tells me, back when the San Joaquin Valley was rumored to be floating on a sea of crude. Once the truth became known, the company pulled out, leaving behind a showcase high school that the town never grew into and a smattering of oil pumps that go on living in death.

These broad-beaked, seesawing contraptions remind me at first of toy birds. But the English major soon conjures each one hosting a luckless spirit, an alcoholic perhaps, condemned to suck away at dry earth until some sin has been expiated, as in Hans Christian Anderson's "The Girl Who Stepped on a Loaf." One day, the souls would fly free at last, soaring up out of the pumps as white doves to disappear into that boundless sky.

You don't really enter Alton; you simply notice the ramshackle houses getting closer together. Piles of sunbleached lumber and crusted paint cans lie about in patchy, weedy yards, as if people had once hoped to renew their lives, but gave up.

I see battered green fiberglass awnings, faded lawn flamingos, and overgrown succulents in cracked terracotta tubs. One street boasts a veneer of prosperity: "Beverly Hills," Cliff scoffs. But most homes have that timeless look of American rural poverty, with their weathered, splintery siding and disintegrating window frames, a crate stuck under the front door as a step.

Suddenly, I ache for him: beneath his lanky, cynical poise, preppy wardrobe, spotless car, and neat file of law school applications lies this sad origin.

And I bite back an impulse to confess that my own family is probably poorer than half the people living in these shacks, only less honest about it; shoring up a middle-class facade with overextended credit cards and grudging loans from relatives.

When I met Cliff on a blind date, I had finessed my life story with carefully crafted fictions: my father's sporadic employment and frequent absences became an executive career path; my mother's clerkship in a toy store an escape from bourgeois boredom. Since I started college, no relationship has ever lasted long enough to reach a day of reckoning.

We grind slowly down the unpaved main street to minimize the dust cloud. "There's Sam n' Eileen!" Cliff waves to an elderly couple who had stopped gardening to watch us pass, heads on a slow swivel, eyes narrowed, mouths agape. "Sam taught history out at the high school, hell of a nice guy. It's probably you they're gawkin' at, nothing personal."

"Alton High, Home of the Rattlers," I read, farther on. Outsize Doric columns are crowned by a stone frieze of warriors and naiads bracketing the etched phrase, "A posse ad esse." Cliff smiles at my polite, analytical frown. "It means 'From the possible to the actual.' No irony intended. Go ahead and laugh."

At half past six, we pull up to a white one-story bungalow whose green shutters matched the Astroturf lawn. We get out and stretch wearily, nerves vibrating. The heat is still fierce but starting to yield, the relieved earth giving off a mulchy aroma. The evening serenade of frogs, crickets and swamp coolers is already getting underway. A wrought-iron banister, leaning askew, conducts us up three steps to a wooden door bearing many casual scuff marks and three serious, penetrating wounds.

"C'mon in." But Cliff opens the door only enough for him to poke his head through and glance around. After a moment he throws it wide and pulls me after him.

Kitchen and living room share a single space. A table midway between them is set with white cloth, candles, and a mob of silverware. I note fake wood paneling and a giant TV. A brass-chained swag lamp with tasseled, mustard-yellow shade hovers low over a gray sofa that seems to be composed entirely of stained, swollen cushions. The dingy carpet was once bright orange.

Two women at the stove turn and squeal with delight. "Cliff! You made it after all!" The older woman takes a quick puff from her cigarette, parks it on the edge of the sink, and runs in her high heels, leaking smoke, to grab him. Her kiss leaves a blot of hot pink lipstick on his flushed cheek. "I swear, you get handsomer every time I see you!" She gives Cliff a searching glance. "Where the hell you been?"

"Ran late. Auntie Verna, this is Meghan Wittman. Meghan, this here is my favorite naughty aunt."

"Oh get out, you big flirt." Auntie Verna reaches across Cliff to hug me. I get a whiff of hard liquor, tobacco and perfume before she holds me away for a better look. Her sharp blue eyes scan me so quickly that I can almost feel the wind of their passing.

"Ain't she pretty, and will you look at all that hair! We used to call it raven's wing back in my day." She laughs, her teeth straight, but stained and missing molars. Her porous blonde hair is falling out of a twist barely confined by two plastic tortoiseshell daggers.

Cliff's mother steps up behind Verna, and I realize instantly where Cliff got his looks.

"Meghan, my mom, Lillian."

"Just call me Lili." She pronounces it Lee-Lee. Her face is radiantly beautiful, but the fragile skin has been no match for the Central Valley sun. Her sea-mist eyes, wide and large, are Cliff's, her symmetrical features translated into the masculine. Wavy hair, dyed honey blonde, hangs to her collarbone, tendrils curling around her damp forehead. She is thin beneath a translucent, full-skirted dress that matches her eyes. Something about her begs for consolation.

"Well, I'm *glad* he's late, so there," Lili says to Verna. She looks at me. "You kids missed the worst of the heat. Lord, we've had a scorcher." She rubs the back of her hand across her forehead. "I couldn't even bring myself to start dinner till an hour ago."

"What's wrong with the air conditioner?"

"Ask your father." Verna and Cliff exchange a look.

"Why are you cooking on your birthday anyway, mom?"

"I wanted to cook, I just don't know why Paul set the time so early."

"Because it's when the hell people get hungry," comes a low growl from the bedroom. Everybody freezes, only their eyes moving from one to the other.

"He's okay once he eats," Verna whispers to me and winks.

"So's Godzilla," says Cliff.

"Well I'm pleased to meet you at last, Meghan." Lili squeezes my hand. "Now let me just get you a little somethin' to take the dust out of your mouth."

"And I'll help Clifford here bring in your things." Verna takes Cliff firmly by the arm, but he stands planted.

"What the hell's his problem?"

"Now, don't you go starting up."

"He's the one starting up."

"Well, he gets that way when he's hungry, you oughta know by now." Verna smiles helplessly at me, and I nod in commiseration, as if I too have been down this road countless times. "He was expectin' you at two."

"And I told the sonofabitch I couldn't make it here by two."

"It's goddamn disrespectful of your mom, is what it is. And they been at that bottle all day, and whose fault is that?" A stubby, graying man emerges from the bedroom in a blue striped seersucker bathrobe hanging half open to reveal a hairy, concave chest above an ample belly. His eyebrows are thick black bolts drawn together by his scowl. His beard is about three days old.

"Get some clothes on," Cliff says without looking. In the silence, Lili leads me into the kitchen and points at a cardboard storage box on the counter.

"I got out my great grandma's bone china in honor of the occasion." Her voice drops to a whisper. "I never did know what they mean by 'bone', do you?" I shake my head, and she crinkles up her nose and laughs. "Kinda don't want to think about it."

"Well?" says Paul to the room at large. "Ain't anybody gonna introduce me?"

"Not till you get dressed." Cliff stares straight ahead.

"Aahhhh, it's been hotter n' a goddamn furnace all day," Paul mutters and turns back into his room. It takes him a couple of tries to pull the swollen door shut behind him.

"Happy birthday, Mom." Cliff grabs Lili around the waist and swings her in a circle.

"My turn, my turn!" Verna capers like a little girl, loses her balance and sprawls across the counter. Lili reaches into the box, takes out an eggshell-thin teacup and pours about three fingers of bourbon into it from a half-gallon bottle.

"Happy birthday to me," she sings, handing me the teacup and sipping from her own.

"Take it easy, mom," Cliff says. Lili holds her cup to the kitchen window, whose light illuminates a silver-wigged swain strumming his lyre to a lady reclining in a garden, a smitten spaniel at her feet.

"Enchanting," I say, the bourbon burning a welcome path to my empty stomach.

"This set of porcelain was to be her wedding gift from her daddy. But she couldn't marry, you see, on account of the Civil War. So he give it to her anyway as a kind of consolation prize for being an old maid."

"Tell her what happened then," says Cliff.

"Oh she married all right and had...."

"Fourteen kids," says Cliff.

"Fourteen that *lived*. And we descended from the second youngest son. He was supposed to be the best lookin' too."

"That I believe," I say. Verna gives my arm a squeeze as Lili sloshes more bourbon into my teacup.

"Gotta catch you up. Cliff?" Lili hands him a teacup, and Cliff takes it, raising his pinky with a simper. We women burst out laughing.

"Thanks anyway." Cliff takes a glass from the cupboard and pours himself a stiff shot. He surveys the half-gallon bottle and raises an eyebrow.

"Oh go on," Verna says. "It's a party."

"Mom's kin owned a lot of land back in Georgia till the Depression came along," Cliff says, running tap water into his glass. "Lotta land."

"You mean they hung onto it through the Civil War?" I say, "Sherman's March and everything?"

"Yup. Worked it with their own hands after all the nigras left," Verna says. "Just like in *Gone with the Wind*."

"They had the biggest still in the county," Cliff says, and Lili wheels on him.

"She don't need to know that."

"It's no big deal, for God's sake." Cliff suddenly sniffs the air. "What's burning?"

"Oh land, I clean forgot." Verna yanks open the oven to reveal a smoking cast-iron skillet of scorched yellow cornbread. "Ain't too bad," she says and picks up a flimsy potholder to seize the heavy pan, which dips in her wobbly grasp and falls, skidding. Lili screams.

"Goddamn it." Cliff grabs a towel and hoists the pan onto the counter. We peer at a swelling red welt on Lili's calf.

"Ain't so bad," Lili says, reaching for her drink.

"Stop it, Mom. We've got to get you treated."

"On my birthday too," says Lili and sips and whimpers.

"It's nobody's fault," I say, feeling the bourbon.

"Get in the car," says Cliff, taking his mother by the arm, but she jerks away.

"We've been cookin' all day," says Verna. "Your favorites, ham hocks n' navy beans, chicken-fry steak, fresh tomatas, mashed potatas n' gravy."

"Hey," says Cliff. "Whose birthday is it anyway?" Both ladies laugh.

"I done buttered it up," says Lili. "See? It'll be fine."

"That's not what you're supposed to do with a burn, Mom."

"Don't go tellin' your mother what to do," snaps Verna. "Mr. Joe College. She's been around a lot longer than you, and she knows a helluva lot more." Cliff salutes his mother with his glass, and we all drink.

"Sally gonna make it?"

"No, Ken had to work," says Lili.

"Sure he did." Cliff turns to me. "Dad thinks Ken wasn't good enough to marry my sister, which is true of course because Ken's a lazy fuckup. But there's no bad situation that dad can't make worse, so he treats Ken like shit..."

"Clifford! You stop that! What's this girl gonna think of us, and she ain't even ate yet? C'mon. Everything's ready." Lili begins dishing food onto the china plates with unsteady hands, spilling some.

Paul reenters, freshly shaved and dressed in a plaid sport coat, a yellow shirt and a wine-colored tie, his hair slicked back. He catches my eye and nods once, curtly.

"Don't we look fancy," Verna teases.

Paul stoops to examine Lili's leg. "What'd you go and do now?"

"Nothing you need to bother over," Lili says.

Paul turns to Cliff. "You know what happens she gets to drinkin' in the daytime. If you'd a got here when you was supposed to, she'd a ate somethin' by now." He continues past the kitchen, jingling car keys.

"And just where do you think you're going?" Cliff says, moving between Paul and the door.

"Play a little cards." Everybody stares. "I'll be back for dinner."

"Dinner's now," Lili wails. "Paul, you set your ass down." But Paul continues toward the door, detouring around Cliff.

"You goddamn son of a bitch," says Cliff.

Paul waves his hand dismissively. "You've already gone and ruint your mom's birthday."

"I'm here, Paul," says Cliff. "You walk out that door, and you're the one ruining Mom's birthday." Paul exits, slamming the door.

"It's a sickness, honey." Verna says as Lili sinks into a kitchen chair. Verna brings Lili her teacup, and we all look at the floor.

"He lost near two hundred last week at lo-ball," Lili says. "I don't know what to do with him." Cliff starts for the door, cursing around the cigarette he is lighting.

"Don't you go takin' after him now," says Verna. She and Lili run out the door, and I quickly refill my teacup before they reenter with Cliff in tow.

My head whirling pleasantly, I polish off a breaded steak, two pieces of the carboniferous cornbread and a bowl of beans. Cliff, too, eats with appetite, but Verna, who is really drunk, just nibbles at her food and smokes, while Lili eats nothing at all.

"Mom, eat something. It's a great meal."

"Cliffer'," Lili snaps, "you jus' mind your own. damn. bidness." Cliff answers with a little boy pout. Lili is not amused and turns away, shaking her head. Decades of disappointment drag her features down, revealing a woman who considers most of her life to have been a wrong turn.

"Where your folks from?" Verna asks me, her head bobbing.

"Los Angeles, by way of Chicago."

"And whuz your dad do?"

"He's a consultant in... systems management. For corporations." I look straight into her eyes and smile. "My mom runs a children's store."

"Such a 'complish family. You Jews," Verna leans forward and narrows her eyes, "are so damn smart! No wonder you own half the world."

"Jews are just like everybody else, Auntie," says Cliff.

"They are not, Cliff." Verna bristles. "How come you always contradic' me? Whatever I say, you take the other side.

Never fails." Cliff gives me a helpless look, and I am beset with a powerful urge to giggle. I look down quickly and cough.

"I always wanted to go to college," says Lili.

"You still can, Mom."

"I'm tired of it, Cliffer', dontcha know? Goddamn tired." Lili sways, the chair tipping, and Cliff stands up quickly.

"Let's get you to bed."

Verna too rises unsteadily. "I'll be headin' home then."

"Hang on, Verna. I'll give you a ride. Meghan can look after Mom." He takes Verna by the arm and walks her out the door, leaving me alone with Lili, who again begins to topple.

"Here, let me help you," I say. She grabs for my arms, and I pull her up off the chair and begin backing toward where I believe the bedrooms are. As I support her wilting weight down the hallway, I have one of those moments in which you suddenly become aware of the extreme oddness of existence, especially your own: the utter improbability and yet inevitability of being in this very place and time.

The bedroom is bright yellow. A set of veneered furniture in some Spanish motif nearly takes up the entire space: a gargantuan chest of drawers with vicious, riveted pewter corners and a headboard worthy of a conquistador. Overflowing ashtrays sit atop massive bed tables with heavy, pendulous drawer-pulls. All leftover space is filled with gimcracky figurines and framed crosstitch samplers yellowed with time or cigarette smoke: praying hands, a bonnet with blue ribbons held aloft by angels.

I arrange the frayed patchwork quilt as best I can and lay Lili on top; after a moment, I take off her shoes. I carry out the ashtrays and dump them in the kitchen trash. When I get back, she is asleep. Fighting an impulse to study her face, I return to the kitchen, clear the table, and wash the dishes, helping myself to more bourbon.

An hour later, I go into the living room, locate the remote deep amid the couch cushions, and turn on the television. At one a.m., I tiptoe down the hallway to the bedroom in which Cliff had put my overnight bag, change into a nightgown, and get into bed.

I am awakened in pitch black by shouting; then a shattering crash, and another.

"Go on," Lili says, "Do 'em all." The crashes continue as I listen, blinking. A child waking into the nighttime battles of adults is an ancient, universal experience, and the dread too is universal and often justified. The dark is pregnant with menace, but also with anticipation. Shamming sleep, you are a clandestine audience, taking in unimaginably juicy and terrifying new information. Secrets are revealed, mysteries solved for better or worse, usually worse. And each uttered word holds the potential to change the landscape of life forever.

You debate whether to stay put in hopes of peaceful resolution, or to reveal yourself and demand explanations, exact concessions. Most of the time though, you lie immobile, fearful of diverting the conflict onto yourself. More than anything, you wish for morning, which lies galaxies away, across the sky.

I rise at last and crack open my door to peek out. The teacups lie in wicked curved shards all up and down the hallway, and as I watch, a couple of dinner plates sail past me and shatter against the opposite wall.

"What the hell's going on?" Cliff comes pounding into view. I can see inside the parents' bedroom across the hall, where Paul is now wielding a large sewing scissors from which dangles a dress, its sleeve nearly amputated.

Cliff twists the scissors out of Paul's hand and hurls them onto the floor, as Lili shout look out, look out, don't don't don't! Paul gazes stupidly at Cliff, and they disappear from view, grappling. Lili rises, only to rebound, seconds later, onto the bed.

"You're going to kill him," she implores above the grunting and shuffling.

"Hope I do. Fucking old bastard."

I leave my room and begin to cross the hallway before I remember the shards. Too late, I feel the bite under my left heel and blunder into Cliff and Paul rolling across the bedroom floor. They knock me over like a bowling pin, and I seize Cliff's hands and try to pull them from around his father's neck.

"Cliff, stop!"

"You're going to kill him," Lili shrieks again and sprawls across the bed, reaching down to grab for Cliff, who finally lets go of Paul.

Paul looks at us all with a blank, uncomprehending stare. "Try puttin' a pillow under your ass," he says to me.

Cliff shakes his head. "Go back to bed, Meghan," he says. "Please?"

But instead, I grab the box of china and carry it into the living room. All of the cups are gone and most of the gold-bordered dinner plates, but a large soup tureen, the saucers, and the soup bowls are still intact. I notice a folded piece of paper between two saucers and draw it out. It is a letter, written in pencil, dated April 10, 1864. The paper, a ruled stationery, is soft and thin, the penmanship precise:

My Dearest Beatrice,

By this time, you must surely know of the esteem in which I hold you and always have done. The uncertainty of our present circumstances gives me no reason to presume that you would look favorably upon a proposal of marriage from one who may not even rely upon seeing another summer. Nevertheless, the thought of you is the sweetest joy to me, and I cannot rest without asking you to consider becoming my cherished wife directly these hostilities should cease.

I do not wish to burden you with my entreaties, but only desire selfishly to carry with me the knowledge that your eyes will soon see, and perhaps look kindly upon, this proposal from a heart that will be loyal and loving so long as it beats and through Eternity as well.

With Highest Regard,
Jeremy Sinclair, Capt., CSA

I stand holding the letter while time seems to swirl around me. For a moment I consider taking it with me, to keep it safe from Paul and Lili's slicing and ripping; their need to annihilate. But I finally replace it and cover the box with a cushion. My foot is still bleeding, though the stains are nearly invisible on the blaring carpet. As I return to my room, Cliff holds up a slashed blouse for me to see.

"Lunatic." He strides down the hall, slippers crunching on broken china, and returns moments later with a roll of large black plastic bags, a broom and dustpan. He rips off a bag, inflates it with a violent shake, and loads the clothes quickly into it. Then he sweeps up the china and throws it into the bag with the clothes. When he opens the back door, a rush of cool night air brings a sweet, mysterious fragrance. I hear him open a trash can outside, then jam the lid back down and re-enter, locking the door behind him.

"Get some sleep, Meghan," Cliff says. I get into bed, and the lights go off, and the house becomes very still. But I crave the cool outdoors so powerfully that I am soon driven to rise and tiptoe down the hall, open the back door, and glide into the yard.

Without ambient light, the sky is so thick with stars that they seemed almost smeared across the black vault: the true, primal sky. I stand rooted with astonishment and nearly scream when Cliff comes up behind and wraps his arms around me.

"C'mon." He takes my hand and guides me across the yard to his car, where I stretch out in the back seat, still transfixed by the sky through the windows. "I can't lie about them anymore," Cliff says. "I had to let you see it."

"It's okay."

"I know I don't have the right to ask you to.... be with me. After that." He holds me so tightly I lose my breath; then he raises my nightgown and we make love, he stroking my hair and breathing my name over and over. "We don't have to end up like them. I'd rather be dead. You and I, we can live."

I awaken to painful brightness. The sun pouring through the flimsy blue curtains of my bedroom has ignited the walls, my limbs, the very air into flaring turquoise. Children's shouts and morning sounds pour in through the open window.

I rise and stretch silently, holding the knowledge of Cliff's and my deeper love gingerly, afraid to think about it, lest it vanish. Perhaps it is already gone. I grab my overnight bag and steal down the hallway to the bathroom, where I confront myself in the mirror like an old, lost friend. The reflection is not true and elongates my face like a Modigliani. My eyes, circled beneath, gaze back at me wide and conspiratorial. What the hell? I mouth at myself.

From a rusty nozzle, I turn on tepid water and brush my teeth amid moaning pipes. The shower is a yellowing plastic

Durastall unit with holes punched for the head and handles. I quickly climb in, soaping with a slimy-soft bar that I find on the moldy rubber mat. I wash my hair with it too, and it turns my waist-length hair into a tangled heap, which I comb through as best I can. I hurriedly apply mascara and lipstick with shaking hands, then return quietly to my room and close the door. The blue conflagration has faded to pastel, but the brief morning coolness is already giving way to the heat, flexing its strength at nine a.m.

I make my bed, only now allowing myself to glance around. When I spot high school yearbooks, I seize one and page through it greedily for pictures of Cliff. I am not disappointed. He is on the flyleaf, crouched in a football uniform, then caught in a candid with gavel poised in a meeting of the student senate. Pages later, tuxedoed, he escorts a homecoming princess.

Outside my room, I hear stirring at last: Paul's heavy tread and the click of a cigarette lighter. In the kitchen, the refrigerator door opens. "Pork chops n' aiggs," Paul sings out. Lili shuffles down the hallway, smoking.

"Meghan," she calls, "coffee's on. You sleep okay, honey?" I leave my bedroom and enter the kitchen at the same time as Cliff, still in his bathrobe. He cadges a cigarette from his father, who lights it for him solemnly. They exchange laconic looks and burst out laughing.

"I thought sure you was gonna raise that little Mexican bastard," Paul says, smoking with relish.

"Nahhh, I figured he was holdin' a full house."

"Sometimes I think you do got half a brain in your head." Paul guffaws, and Cliff chuckles. "Musta got it from me." He winks at me, and I laugh along with everybody. "What you kids got goin' today?"

"I thought I'd take Meghan over to meet Earl n' Marie," Cliff says, looking at me for the first time.

"Oh that'll be nice," says Lili, beating eggs. "They was askin' after you." Paul fills a coffee mug, crosses the kitchen, and sets it in front of me.

"You take cream n' sugar?"

"Black's fine," I say.

"That's ma girl." Paul shakes a Marlboro from his pack and offers it to me. After a moment's hesitation, I pluck it out, and he lights it. "I hear things got a little lively here last night." He winks. "You gotta get used to us."

"Oh, I slept just fine," I say. Cliff comes over and puts his arm around my shoulders, while deep within me something stirs, as if ready to rise and take wing at last.

A Season of Turbulence

I. Precession and Trepidation

The night flight from L.A. to Anchorage had a two-hour lay-over in Seattle, giving the gang of thunderheads lurking on the horizon plenty of time to move in and start wreaking their havoc.

Pummeled by savage airpackets, our plane rhumbas into a midnight sky the color of a deep bruise. Lightning reveals monstrous cumulonimbus towering away on all sides, and electrons seethe across our fragile outer membrane like fire ants. How much longer till this puny hollow tube splits open and dumps its screeching cargo out into the cyclone?

Clutching the armrests, I recall my bonehead physics professor explaining seasonal change to his classroom of slack-jawed liberal arts majors: "the obliquity of the ecliptic." Won-deringly, we mouthed the unfamiliar consonant clusters, imag-ining our hapless planet spiked through and through by its cruel axis, yawing away from light and warmth into the long, black, icebound winter nights.

I shudder, and my seatmate, whose name is Kitty, puts her hand over mine and gives me a little grimace of commiser-ation. She is about thirty-five and busty in a pale blue sheath dress, tight in the hips. Her homemade platinum hair is teased high into a sixties' bouffant, a blue velveteen bow stuck above the bangs. Her black-lined blue eyes remind me of an animal peering from its lair. When she smokes, she rolls the ash off instead of tapping it.

By now, the stewardesses are pouring free wine and helping themselves too. They are dressed as bimbo Cossacks, a tribute to Alaska's Russian past: gray miniskirts and tunics, black boots and karakhul hats. One of them, a blonde with a mischievous ferretlike profile, hoists a half gallon jug of Mountain Red and swigs smoothly to raggedy cheers. Her hat falls off, and the man sitting across from me puts it on and tries to dance the Kozatsky in the aisle and topples over. Kitty applauds him with fingers wide apart like a child's. He lies on his back in his orange paisley shirt and doubleknit bell bottoms, grabbing at the stewardesses' legs.

After several more glasses of wine, Kitty and I make our way up to first class, staggering and bouncing off the seats as the plane jolts. "What're they gonna do, throw us out?" Kitty says, settling herself and kicking off her shoes. "At least we've got enough room now to kiss our asses goodbye." She tells me that she is moving to Anchorage to find work as a "dentical assistant." I reply that I am traveling up to stay with my boyfriend, a UCLA law student who is interning with the Alaska Public Defender office.

"I had a public defender," Kitty says, and drops her gaze. "I did eight months in Sybil Brand, you might as well know." She searches my face, and I smile warmly, as if that were a classical music camp instead of a women's penitentiary. "I coulda pulled two to five," Kitty says, "but I got lucky, that's what the judge said. Some luck."

"Here's to luck." We click our plastic cups and drink. If I am lucky, Cliff, who has been in Anchorage all summer while

I traveled around Europe with an old roommate, has not yet replaced me with a local girl.

"It was coke, possession for sale," Kitty is saying, "but it wasn't mine, I swear to God."

"I believe you."

"I hate the stuff, makes me sneeze." She mauls her buttonish nose with her palm. "The cops pulled us over on Pico for a taillight out, and we knowed they was gonna search us, so Duke, he planted it in my purse. He said it was only fair 'cause he had two priors."

"Fair?!" I straighten my back with indignation, and wine slops over the rim of my cup. Lifting my skirt primly, I suck the fabric. "I hope you're through with him."

"What do you think I'm going to Alaska for, the weather?" We laugh and drink to this, the plane joining in the merriment with an aerobatic plunge.

"Here's to new beginnings," I say around my bitten tongue.

"Did you ever hear of an *old* beginning?" Kitty says. A stewardess comes by and refills us, and Kitty makes her joke about old beginnings, and we all drink to it. The stewardess moves on, taking Kitty's high spirits with her.

"I've made a messa my life. Go ahead and say it." Her iridescent, candy-pink lips twitch downward, and her eyes brim.

"Not at all," I say, though I have been thinking just that. "You're another Moll Flanders."

She stops dabbing her eyes with the cocktail napkin. "Who's that, a friend of yours?"

"A literary character," I say. It comes out 'lirarry'.

"Well I'm not lirarry but I sure am a character." We drink to that, and I write down Cliff's phone number for her, wondering if I will regret it. You always pick up strays, I can hear him saying. All because your mother rejected you.

At some point Kitty and I make a run for the restroom and throw up side by side. Later, the landing gear drops with a shuddering spasm, causing me and one of the stewardesses to scream. By now, Kitty is sleeping across our seats in the fetal position; I pick up my head from her stockinged feet in my lap and watch the alien city rise up to swallow us.

Suddenly, I am stumbling around a glaring, fluorescent arena, frantically trying to decode senseless signs amid the babble of lunatics. One keeps calling out to me—Paul Bunyan in a plaid flannel shirt and jeans, hair hanging lank to his shoulders, eyes crazy blue above a grizzly-colored thicket of beard. I flee, but he catches up and grabs my elbow.

"Brynn! What the fuck?"

I blink. "Cliff?"

He laughs and strokes his beard as if calming a small animal. "Don't worry, I'll shave it off."

"No don't. I like it!"

Grinning, he hoists my suitcase. "So how was Europe?"

"Lonely." This second lie in under ten seconds glides out slick as a soap bubble. Cliff drops my suitcase to enfold me, then holds me at arm's length.

"Whew, you blow chow?" I try to explain about the cosmic cyclone and the fire ants, but the syllables just roll around in my mouth like marbles. Cliff's head keeps duplicating itself, and my efforts to merge the two versions make him laugh.

In the parking lot awaits a battered green Travelall, its flanks corroded with rust, a vehicle so manly that it does not know how to contain a woman. As we carom down the wet-black streets, I slide around helplessly on its bench seat in my silky skirt, grabbing at the dashboard, ending up with my head in Cliff's lap and my heels braced against the passenger window. His elbow pokes me in the side when he shifts gears.

"We're staying with Solly, my boss," Cliff says. "He's the state public defender. His wife left him and went back to Brazil, so he rents out rooms. It's quite the trysting place now for married judges and their lady friends."

"Ick."

Cliff glances down at me mischievously. "If those walls could talk, Anchorage would sizzle like Death Valley." I laugh, and he suddenly yanks the van to the curb. "God, I've missed you." We kiss, and for some reason, probably the booze, I start to cry.

Solly's house is brutally large; a colonial of white brick and wood with Doric pillars and mighty evergreens in the front yard ideal for hiding bears in the branches. Despite the late hour, the lights within are blazing.

"Looks like Solly waited up to meet you," Cliff says, navigating the long, curved driveway. He seems pleased. "Then again, he might just be getting ready to take off." Since his ex-wife Lhosa's departure, Cliff explains, Solly has become a compulsive traveler who leaves town on any pretext, even in the middle of the night or during a storm. When home, he paces like a caged animal.

The internship program was Solly's idea, supplementing his overworked staff with second-year law students like Cliff from the lower forty-eight. Lacking a license, they cannot actually try cases, but can enter pleas or make appearances in a poor man's version of legal representation. Remote native villages welcome even these novices to help them handle crimes too serious for their tribal councils, those that raise the bloody spectre of retaliation and vendetta.

"But aren't those the very cases that need experienced lawyers?" We are standing in the entryway, and Cliff drops my suitcase.

"Why do you say that, Brynn? You think I can't handle a real case?"

"Of course you can. It just seems…"

"You've been here a whole hour, and you're already full of opinions. And just drunk enough to voice them."

"Guilty on all counts," I murmur, and he quickly puts his arm around me.

"Sorry. But believe it or not, I've been kicking some serious ass in court. Just wait and see."

At the opposite end of the cavernous room, a thin, fiftyish man in a suit and black-rimmed glasses sits beseeching a pregnant native girl, who is crying and shredding her kleenex. At a card table near the fireplace, Solly is playing backgammon with a boy who looks about fourteen. I can almost feel Solly's radar homing in on our mini-tiff. He misses nothing, I think.

Cliff had spoken of Solly with the worshipful deference that law students reserve for alpha lawyers who are particularly feared. So I had conjured up one of those flamboyant, womanizing legal warriors with a long gray ponytail, a white buckskin suit, and perhaps a tie tack made of walrus penis bone. Instead, I am introduced to an unremarkable man in his late forties of medium height and blurry physique, wearing a threadbare green wool cardigan, white T-shirt and worn ochre cords. With his curly, receding brown hair, rosy, near-beardless cheeks and mild gray eyes, Solly looks almost cuddly. Within moments, of shaking hands, I realize that the mildness is deceptive.

"Brynn and her ex-con seatmate got wasted on the flight up," Cliff tells him.

"Thanks, Cliff," I say, and to Solly, "We ran into a storm."

"Even the stewardesses got stewed," Cliff says. Solly watches us narrowly, a smile playing around his lips. At the galvanic word "stewardess" the skinny judge glances quickly at me while the pregnant girl hiccups and mops her eyes. I have the uncomfortable sense that Solly's cold lawyer's brain has already classified me as a lightweight. I give him what I hope is a worldly, Simone Signoret smile but must look more like a sheepish, crooked grin.

The house has three stories, one underground, where Cliff now conducts me. The walls of our subterranean bedroom are white and damp. A couple of narrow crank windows look out at ground level on a muddy back yard where forlorn, rugged tufts of sawtooth grass bend in the stiff, wet wind. Blisters of paint on the windowsills crumble at the slightest touch. The carpet is a coarse, loopy shag of artificial fiber in eerie shades of bright blue—royal, aqua, indigo. Its toxicity has not deterred the growth of a healthy crop of mushrooms along the baseboards.

A mattress on the floor, a particle-board chest of drawers bearing many glass stains, and a beanbag chair the color of dried blood complete the decor. Beside the bed sits a clock-radio whose hour and minute notations turn over on little flip cards with unnerving clacks.

"I'm sure I'll love it," I say, without irony. Cliff smiles, proud as a child, and we hit the bed, in which I do not notice the crumbs for a good two hours.

Cliff grew up in the San Joaquin Valley, in a tiny town whose roots as an Okie labor camp persist in the deteriorating wooden shanties on its periphery, used now for lovemaking and score-settling. Cliff's generation had come of age along the deadly two-lanes that string together charmless hamlets with names like Firebaugh and Oildale. They learn very young to hide family secrets and to put their deepest faith in the laws of chance.

The town's rise from its origins has been painfully slow, like an overmatched boxer climbing up off the mat. Cliff was the sole member of his graduating class to attend a four-year college; the too-smart son of the town's surly postman, lugging his mailbag along its dusty streets for thirty years. Cliff's parents managed to be both insanely reckless and stubbornly traditional; devout believers in the power of cards and liquor to fill the empty places.

My own parents' mercurial marriage had recently collapsed in the wake of bankruptcy and foreclosure. These days, happy, peaceful homes feel like a too-tight garment; something is sure to give way, a button or a seam, and reveal the stained, scarred truth of me. It was a relief to be around Cliff's family: Spending the night in his parents' flimsy house, I had been awakened at 2 a.m. by their drunken shouting of years, love and money squandered; I had soon fallen back to sleep, comfortable amid the familiar, bitter heat.

My father, a failed entrepreneur, now advertises his romanic availability with a hairy chestful of beads and a dyed combover bracketed by creepy sideburns. Sometimes he tries to pass himself off as a doctor. My mother's conversation is divided between spiteful tattling and maudlin recollections of a past that never was.

Cliff and I had met on a blind date, set up by our respective roommates, who did not particularly care for us. At UCLA, Cliff walked around with a chip on his shoulder, a provocative smart-ass who arrived late to class and exploded over trivia. When he applied for the Alaska internship, his long-suffering professors had given him suspiciously hearty recommendations.

II. Lhosa's Angle of Inclination

At first, I spend a lot of time alone in Solly's house which, like Alaska itself, gives an impression of space unoccupied, but far

33

from empty. Mornings, I lie drowsy in bed amid the pattering splash and warm fog of Cliff's shower; fragrances of coffee and bacon and aftershave make their way downstairs. The voices above are mostly male, punctuated by the trebles of women overnighters. The phone rings incessantly, the front door slams over and over. Finally, I come to rest in a silence that echoes faintly, like background radiation of the frantic activity just past.

Soon, amid that diffuse white noise, I begin to sense Lhosa's presence. I can almost hear her giggle when I stumble on some piece of dorky judicial underwear; I imagine her basking catlike in the weak sunbeams that steal across the carpet.

An avid student of marital failure, I follow the snippets of information about Solly and Lhosa that Cliff drops like breadcrumbs. Solly, the son of a New York City union organizer, had been called to the law as to primal combat by his father's bruises from the truncheons of strikebreaking goons. At Columbia, he had absorbed the battle words, challenges and tactics, girding himself for a lifetime of conflict.

But suddenly, days from taking the Bar, some crisis of destiny had impelled him to join the Peace Corps, journeying to the slums of Rio de Janeiro, ears still ringing with his father's curses and his mother's tearful pleas.

He had met Lhosa when she tried to pick his pocket one day in the train station. As Cliff told it, Solly had chased the ragged teenager outside in a pelting rain, and she had wheeled to confront him, as glorious as an antelope run to earth, water streaming over her taut cheeks and bosom. And he had known with finality that his mission in life was to serve not his father or the American Left, but this woman and her tribe.

In a country where the beauty of the poor is so little valued it is tossed out as trash, Lhosa's family had somehow scraped together enough money to fulfill their daughter's ge-netic promise; the long limbs and queenly carriage architected for walking in sand and for dancing; the smooth, ample breasts and buttocks—all destined to deliver her either to a poor, drunken husband or to the prostitute's bed. But now Solly discovered his own power and put forth his claim, changing her fate as profoundly as an earthquake does the landscape. Buoyed by her glorious image, Solly returned to America and passed the Bar effortlessly, re-entering Rio as a conquering war-lord to claim his soul mate, the saga complete.

But after practicing in New York for over a decade, Solly's spirit had again grown restless, and he had headed for Alaska, this violent, haughty land he now thought of as his spiritual origin. Here, as Cliff tells it, Solly's family legend grew a little soggy from the countless storms and freezes and thaws. Words, like voracious Arctic mosquitoes, drained it; paper bounded it. More than anything, the routine of family life and the passage of years ate it away. Gradually, Solly returned to his first love, the law, which had only bided its time.

Two years ago, Lhosa had reached the dangerous age of thirty-nine and been suddenly besieged by a swarm of insights and fears. They circled her head, buzzed in her ears; woke her at night. Alaska had never been her home. Marooned, she had only endured the craggy, alien terrain and deadly cold water and frigid, mountain-walled sky. Here, the sun itself was a capricious visitor who sometimes overstayed his welcome until he drove you half mad and other times went missing for months.

Then, whole cities would barricade themselves within ugly, drafty walls, under siege from perpetual night, from the earth itself. If you ventured out, you had to wrap yourself in animal hides like a savage—or worse, in impervious artificial fabrics woven tight as steel. The very air was not life-giving and warm but fierce. Every breath hurt.

Gradually, Lhosa pulled away from her life. Solly hosted frequent gatherings, and Lhosa became surrounded by the transitory, potent beauty of drunken young women fetched up from the lower forty-eight as I had been, or poured home from local bars. She was now a *matron*, expected to make welcome Solly's tiresome students, freshen their drinks and listen by the hour to their tedious, paper-pushing dreams. How she must have seethed, she whose radiant bronze beauty had once flowed through the streets like a river of lava.

No student had the imagination or courage to woo Lhosa herself. Solly, comfortably uxorious, failed to notice his wife's dread or her gnawing hunger; he had *murderers* to defend. So this husband, who had once seemed such a prize, not only ceased to please Lhosa but began to repulse her.

Most of all, she loathed the Law, her adversary triumphant, with its prissy pleadings and precedents, its self-congratulatory arrogance and pride in its own pretentious bulk. Its deference to scoundrels. You are nothing but sinners, she shouted drunkenly at Solly. You defend the guilty, all puffed up with pride. You don't care what people do to each other, it is for you all a game, a wicked sport! *Prostitutas!*

Though nobody believed that legal ethics were Lhosa's issue, it was true that the Public Defenders competed personally and relentlessly with the District Attorneys, their mirror image and evil twin. Whatever transgression the DAs held against a defendant, the PDs instantly, reflexively, denied it. The two offices yipped and tugged at the law like hyenas with a thigh bone. Away from court, they turned into chess teams, spending days trying to outflank their adversaries and negate the opposition's next move.

In the past, Lhosa had gleefully boasted of this dance to her awed family in their Rio tenement, using much legal jargon to impress them. But now, she smoldered with the rage of the misled. She fled Solly's voice and hid from him in her own home, first in bedrooms; later in shower stalls and even closets.

Having seen *Five Easy Pieces*, she considered just climbing into the cab of some logging truck headed for parts unknown, but she feared being murdered and dumped. She imagined her body eaten by animals—or worse, persisting frozen, mummified in some glacial crevasse to emerge thousands of years later and be put on museum display like a mammoth carcass, shriveled and gray, her mouth open in a silent scream, a *thing* to frighten children.

Desperate, she tried to create her own Brazil here; she greeted Solly's friends barefoot, thonged and saronged as if on a Rio beach, but she only felt ludicrous. If her wrap fell open, the men actually looked away, shamefaced. Failing to provoke, she grew bolder, flouting the sacred Code of Criminal Justice itself. First came shoplifting, then hashish was discovered on her person during a barroom tiff.

Solly set his weak jaw and called in favors from the police department and the DA's office. So far, they had obliged, but they still had their jobs to do, and Solly realized that it would not be long until his wife's behavior would begin to erode his fearsome reputation. She was his Achilles Heel.

He inflicted on Lhosa a dry, unctuous little therapist, who perched above her on a long-legged stool, tic'ing and clearing his throat, writing observations precisely with skinny, pale and hairy hands in a small black notebook. He smelled unwashed. After each session, he shared his notes with Solly for hours.

Lhosa knew that If her sanity were to survive, she had to act. But how? To whom could she turn? And then, as if dispatched by some Amazonian magic, her salvation arrived: A gardener knocked at their door—in the dead of winter! That was how she knew he was a magic man; a thief of hearts, but in this case there was no theft. He owned the sultry, homesick housewife the moment she opened the door.

I could envision him in my mind—Aleut and African-American, a graceful, viperine faun of twenty years, with seraphic amber eyes and fine-pored skin whose subtle hues seemed to shift like the sea under the sun. He had arrived to release her from the spell of the dry-rotted, crumbling Law and save her from incipient madness. And finally, to return her to Brazil, finding in the course of this rescue, the home that he himself had sought all his life.

The couple did not leave at once. Lhosa needed time to heal, to reclaim the woman she had been. Her body, replenished with love, swelled and grew young again. Her tears and saliva returned, and her female moisture. She presided now over the nightly parties in her home with a wise and serene sensuality; the heedless young tarts brought in by the interns and randy old judges began to watch Lhosa with the envious side-eyes she had been accustomed to. Oddly, she grew happy now and began to cook and clean and shop again, tallying her household accounts meticulously.

By the time Solly realized that he was in a battle, it was lost. He was not armed for it anyway. Failing to intimidate or shame her, he tried to cast Lhosa off to the other man as used up and crazy, but by then he did not have the standing for that.

When the time was right, Lhosa simply decamped, first to her lover's tacky apartment off K Street in Anchorage, and from there a month later, to Rio. She left long letters for Solly and Matt, which both now carry around in their wallets and pull out at odd times to study, as if to verify some fact or sudden insight.

The divorce had got underway like a lazy monster, a cyclops provoked, lurching into battle ugly and brutal. But Lhosa was ready for everything. She revealed an unsuspected talent for litigation, conducting brisk, tough negotiations over her alimony, defiantly selling off community property and driving hard cash bargains. Nearly every day, somebody arrived to pick up furniture or a household item Lhosa had sold them, including the marital bed. All transactions were conducted now from Brazil, even those phone charges appearing on Solly's bill.

Solly and Lhosa's son, Matt, is a gangly, fresher-faced version of his father; I see nothing Brazilian about him but a slight, fortunate fullness of the mouth. He has his father's shy grin and boneless cheeks. His skin has the ivory tint of a Martindale-Hubbell page. Some of the resident lawyers have remarked to him—by way of compliment—that he would have no trouble passing for white.

Since the breakup, the lawyers have informally adopted the boy, stocking the refrigerator, doing his laundry, and tracking his homework. They monitor his emotional development in their clumsy, confrontive way and assure him that, despite the current turmoil in his life, he can still grow up to be a lawyer. Matt, who already knows how to choose his words, responds to this encouraging news with mumbled platitudes and a noncommittal smile. Sometimes, lubricated by the liquor in Solly's bar, the lawyers segue into tearful confessions of their own infidelities and excesses. They share with the boy the deepest fears of their tribe: of failing the bar, of being overturned on appeal, of an open fly during cross examination.

To compensate for the steadily emptying house, the lawyers have hauled in their own contributions, furnishings accepted in lieu of fees or held for imprisoned defendants. The result has been a melange of lamed recliners, tables, and highboys. Sofas run the gamut from stabbed and taped-up naugahyde with drug detritus among the cushions to "The Goddess"—a massive French antique worthy of Versailles, upholstered in silken petit-point. The Goddess displays a droll Louis XV-era bewigged swain strumming his lyre to a mistress who coyly displays her cleavage, while at her feet, a maltese lapdog attempts to mount a greyhound.

But no matter how much furniture arrives, the house still feels oddly vacant. The vaultlike living room is framed in picture windows that look out on the surrounding upscale neighborhood—there is nothing particularly Alaskan about our cul-de-sac; we might be anywhere. As the days shorten into October, Cliff and I lie before the fireplace scanning the yard for moose that never materialize, drinking heavily and gorging on salmon dropped off at the door every morning like milk.

III. The Nodding Sphere

Cliff finally finds me a job as a legal secretary with a former public defender who had recently left to start his own practice. My new boss, Fred Carroll, has rented a small walkup office downtown paneled in a strikingly phony wood laminate over hollow walls through which the wind sometimes whistles. The roof amplifies the steady drumming of the autumn rains. Movers somehow hoist a mammoth legal desk up the narrow staircase and into the adjoining room, facing me. The waiting room chairs, upholstered in scratchy red burlap, will make sure that no client gets too comfortable.

Fred's peremptory wife Annette, a former legal secretary, comes in to help me set him up. We order stationery and business cards, office equipment, file folders and gummed labels while their three children draw with felt tip pens and fold origami cranes from the yellow legal pads. Bored stiff, I try to weigh whether I would be happy doing this for Cliff.

After a week, I notice that Fred has fallen for me, displaying the labored deference of a man who much prefers ordering people around. Tall and disturbingly strong, he has reddish curly hair and pitted skin; there is something sharklike about his face, his eyes as cold and lightless as the deep ocean.

One evening, when Cliff and I are dining at his house, his eight-year-old son makes some childish joking retort to Fred's order to eat. Without warning, Fred strikes him across the face, sending the boy spinning onto the floor. Wordlessly, Annette kneels and raises the sobbing boy and walks him into his bedroom as Fred resumes eating.

"So who's Solly backing in the city council runoff?" Fred says, deftly slicing himself a piece of rare roast beef and holding it dripping before his mouth. Cliff gathers his thoughts for a halting answer, and after that the conversation resumes. Annette returns and seats herself, looking at nobody.

"Looks like it'll be a close one," she says, settling her napkin in her lap. "The election."

"What the fuck do you know about it?" says Fred, with a complacent chuckle. Annette forks in a mouthful of food and chews briskly.

"You know," I say, "I feel like I'm getting a migraine." Fred's face instantly dissolves into real alarm, the deep creases of his meaty forehead torqued with solicitude. "Nothing," I say, "helps these things but sleep. We'd better hit the road before it gets bad."

"You take the day off tomorrow," Fred says. "With pay. That's an order. Annette'll sub in for you." Annette's mouth opens and quickly closes.

"Oh I wouldn't think of it," I say smoothly. "I'll be fine by morning." I rub my temples.

"Cliff," says Fred. "you've got a very responsible wi.. I mean girlfriend." His cunning little gaffe gives us an excuse to exit laughing.

"He's a very sick man," I say to Cliff in the car as we wave goodbye to Fred and Annette, framed by their front door like any happy couple.

"What are we supposed to do, turn him in?"

"Yes, and soon."

"All that will accomplish is losing you your job and getting me in hot water at the office. He still works there part time, and he's got a lot of buddies. The kid'll be fine."

"You know that's not true." We drive in silence. "And what do you care about his buddies? We're going back to L.A. in a few weeks."

"What if I want to practice here? Besides, it's kind of chickenshit to take the man's pay and then report him."

"What's chickenshit," I say, "is smacking an eight-year-old kid around."

"How about fucking up your boyfriend's job?"

"I don't recall that covering up a crime was included in your job description."

"Don't twist everything around, English major." I wave that blunted old weapon away.

"Your father used to clock you like that, didn't he?"

"So?"

"So that's why you almost choked him to death when you were seventeen."

Cliff looks at me blandly, staking out the calm, professional terrain, a mannerism he has picked up from Solly. "No, I almost choked him to death because he'd lost another week's pay in the fucking Bayview Card Room." Unable to hold the pose, he clenches his teeth, his jaw working, nostrils flaring.

"And because he'd poked his fat, fucking tobacco-stained finger in my face one time too many." Cliff suddenly pounds the steering wheel. "Goddammit. Can we just drop the subject?"

"I don't understand. How could you let that abuse happen to another child?" I see him thinking, not about the question, but how to get out of answering it. "And while we're on the subject, how are you going to deal with defending monsters, anyway? Have you thought about that?"

The question is pure flattery; he is still years away from even defending litterers, but I want to reassure him that he matters, despite his father and Solly and Fred and all the patronizing professors—not only to me, but to the spinning earth itself.

"You'll help me," Cliff says.

"You sound very sure of that."

"Isn't that what wives do?"

I keep my eyes carefully on the road but my breathing gives me away. "Boy," I say at last, "you really do want to change the subject."

"And you really do have a hard time accepting love." But he turns to me looking worried. "You do want to, don't you? Marry me?"

I nod, because I daren't speak. For some, love can't wait to arrive and take up residence, but that has not been my story. Rather, love has been rare and elusive, an anomaly. And conditional. So I've learned to be a tough sell; to greet proffered love distrustfully, like a package delivered to the wrong address or bearing someone else's name.

"A nod, indicating yes," Cliff says. "I'm holding you to that." I put my head on his shoulder and think now about the wonderful, sacred earth precessing on its axis just as it was meant to, everything happening in accordance with divine destiny, the whole crazy universe a symphony of love and hope.

IV. Axial Tilt

Now that I have set up Fred's office, the only task remaining is to hire him a secretary to replace me after Cliff and I return to California at the end of December. I write a couple of want ads for my position and compose another ad announcing Fred's grand opening, specializing in criminal defense.

After a couple of suffocatingly empty days alone in the office, I decide that this is an ideal time to tackle Proust and find *Remembrance of Things Past* in paperback at a secondhand bookstore. The first fifteen pages are filled with somebody's careful, penciled notations, but these soon dwindle away to phone numbers, a shopping list and some doodles of female flip hairdos. The rest of the book is pristine. The story instantly envelopes me like a stimulating second skin; a total escape from the bleak, flimsy K Street office to the world of Fin de Siecle France. I keep the book in my desk drawer where I can feel it glow and pulse like a magic ruby, beckoning me with its riches. Fred must go through my desk, because I overhear him asking an applicant if she has read Proust.

"How tall are you?" Fred asks me one morning when I bring in his mail.

"About five-ten," I tell him. "Last time I measured."

"I bet you towered over the boys in school."

"'Towered' is the word."

Fred leaves his desk and comes around to stand beside me. "Well it all turned out very nicely, if I do say." He looks me up and down approvingly, a connoisseur. I can feel the heat of his lust barely contained, and a wave of contempt washes over me. I am angrier at him on Cliff's behalf than on my own.

"It always seemed to attract bullies to me," I say, turning on him what must have been an icy glare, because he backs away instantly with a slight apologetic cough and pretends to search among the papers on his desk.

I refrain from telling Cliff about this, because in the world he comes from and whose social parameters he still accepts unquestioningly, even a hint of encroachment by another male provokes—if not demands—a violent response. I also understand that this means I can never tell him—not in years to come, not in the heat of an argument or even casually in passing. He will see this as a betrayal of gargantuan proportions, depriving him of the opportunity of reprisal; making him seem even more a fool than if I had responded to Fred's pass.

Love, I am discovering, demands careful management; even casual acts hold the potential to damage it profoundly. And this insight brings with it the realization that I must indeed love Cliff, deeply and helplessly. Feeling exposed and vulnerable as a molted crustacean, I worry that Cliff's successful conquest will cause him to lose interest in me. I try to conceal the depth of my love, feeling guilty and manipulative. Cliff, on the other hand, relieved of restraint, showers me with all the affection of his hungry soul. Fred, embarrassed by his clientless state, now gives me time off to accompany Cliff to appearances and investigations in other parts of Alaska. We take off in the Travelall on trips to Homer, the Denali National Park and the Kenai Peninsula. Ironically, I recall the interiors spaces of Alaska better than I do this scenic diorama, whose beauty easily overwhelms my conceptual memory. In fact, all my outdoor recollections of Alaska are suspect now: the haughty snow-capped vistas and green-gold valleys; azure glaciers and salmon thrashing in their pebbly deathbeds—are those recollections even mine? Or are they pilfered from dentist office travel magazines and TV documentaries, pasted over spaces left empty by my preoccupation with myself?

Instead, what I do recall in fine detail are narrow office aisles and beige fabric cubicles; the dowdy dress and bad haircuts of minor bureaucrats and the hard stares I got from miniskirted receptionists; I remember the sawdust-covered floors of dingy downtown bars where the lawyers went to slum; the cheap storefronts and lunchtime restaurants packed with workers slurping soup.

And the drunks, of course, weaving wearily down the Anchorage city streets, ignored and stepped around daintily. Or sitting with their boots in the gutter holding cigarettes in grimy, mittened paws, their faces darkened, bloated and bloody from last night's brawls, eyes squeezed shut against the dagger sun, awaiting the night—which obligingly arrives earlier and earlier.

Many of the drunks are native; many are not. The men watch Cliff with flat, anomic stares; to them he wears the mantle of unearned power like a princeling. But the women venture their shy, hopeless smiles at me, and I smile back uncertainly thinking of my own growing alcohol consumption with vague unease, trying to conjure up some massive, unbridgeable gulf that separates me from them, my fate from theirs.

I stand in the dim, candlelit bathroom analyzing my shadowed face and body in the mirror, my teeth already beginning to chatter, It is mid-December, and somebody has neglected to pay the utilities bill, causing the company to promptly turn off the power—no warnings, apologies or appeals: this is Alaska. Cash money is now mandatory, along with a punishingly large deposit before we can bathe again in warm water or turn on the heat.

Solly is off on one of his endless excursions, and suddenly none of the regulars has any money or knows how to pay a bill.

Dropping Matt at the home of a school friend, the regulars quickly scatter to back-up locations for conducting their trysts. Only Cliff and I, improvident spenders who have depleted our loan stipends for the month, remain in the massive house, burning logs, zipped into a common sleeping bag before the fireplace in a welcome if frigid solitude.

Now, I hold my breath and plunge into the thirty-something-degree shower, the air exiting my lungs in an indescribable, involuntary sound, a gutteral death-huff. I curse and scream. Teeth clattering, I soap myself and shampoo my already numb scalp with stiffening fingers.

"You are truly nuts," Cliff shouts and ducks into the icy torrent beside me, bellowing curses and laughing at his shriveling male parts. Afterward, we rub each other dry with coarse towels until our skin turns red. I light a couple of candles with violently shaking hands so we can see to get dressed, but instead we see one another in the strange, dim light and fall into bed consumed with ice age passion, warming quickly, entwined in a primal, mutual glow.

As a newcomer and stranger, here solely at the bidding of another, I am finding that Alaska attracts many footloose migrants who believe that the place is their spiritual destiny. These feel a deep and abiding connection with its wildness; there is a place within them that only Alaska can find and touch and make its home. They treat Alaska as some sort of moody friend whom they need only woo or placate with great tenderness and understanding in order to be provided for, even sheltered and protected by the place. They remind me of people who keep ferocious pets because they imagine they have an ancient and ineffable bond with their fierceness.

I don't get along well with these rather arrogant romantics because I radiate the skepticism and irreverence of the city dweller. I had instantly grasped that this place is a killer and not to be trusted or cut any slack whatsoever. Nothing is to be assumed. From the moment of your arrival, Alaska tests you in myriad ways that you never see coming. It lies in wait for inattentiveness, despondency, miscalculation, bad luck; for that careless moment; that forgivable, playful impulse or that weak spot—whether in your tire or in your ability to read a stranger. And that is how it delivers you your fate.

The independent spirits seem to go missing a lot—not always lethally, but often enough. Though they are rarely aggressive and almost never have problems with alcohol, they are attacked by other people with greater than usual frequency. They have a puzzling tendency to die prematurely, sometimes by their own hands. They are particularly attracted to bears, whom they seek out and bedevil on their turf with lofty intentions and sometimes tragic results. They get lost halfway up or down some mountain or are discovered in a ditch outside town with an empty gas tank or a busted hose or a missing wallet or a bloody box cutter.

"What's wrong with this place?" Cliff finally asks me late one Saturday morning. We are getting dressed—these days a race with the sun, which hovers teasingly just above the horizon before ducking out of sight by early afternoon.

"With Solly's place?"

"No, with Alaska. You aren't... content here. "

"Are you asking what I think could be improved?" Or what my problem is?"

"The latter."

"I guess it bothers me that for a lot of people, Alaska is not a beginning, it's... the end."

"You could say that about any place."

"But I'm saying it about this place."

"And I'm saying that it *can* be a beginning. For us."

"I don't think so."

"What if I decide to practice here?"

"Is anybody inviting you after you graduate? Solly?"

Cliff looks away quickly. "Not exactly. I mean, it depends on how well I do." We potter about for a few moments, our mutual irritation swelling like a blister.

"Are you implying that I'm a liability?" I ask, and as Cliff opens his mouth to answer, the phone rings.

"Goddammit," he says, because we both know who it is. Predictably, Kitty has not thrived here. Duke, with his usual sense of entitlement, had followed her up mere days after her arrival, bringing a luxuriant fleece blanket as a housewarming gift for her chilly furnished flat. That blanket alone would have overcome far firmer determination than Kitty's. Their problems had soon begun all over again. Duke found work easily in boat construction, which paid well, but money never had been their issue, as Kitty explained to me in one of her frequent calls.

Cliff extends the ringing phone toward me like a dirty diaper. "Because you care about our relationship," he says loudly, "you're finally going to enlighten Kitty that sitting together on a plane and drinking yourselves into a stupor does not give her a perpetual claim on you or the right to commandeer all your free time."

"She's not 'commandeering' anything, Cliff," I say and pick up the receiver. "Hello?"

"Where were you?" says Kitty, "In the shower or making push-push?"

"Neither."

"You won't believe this," Kitty says, a signal that she is geared up for a nice long chat.

Cliff gives me a glare that belongs in silent films. The change of seasons is having an odd effect on him. While he had relished the endless days of summer and could be found cheerily washing his car or briefing a case at 3 or 4 a.m., he now behaves as if he is being cheated of something vital as the daylight contracts. The faster-approaching sunsets make him increasingly jittery, and he feels obligated to squeeze more and more frenetic activity into the shrinking daylight hours.

Every weekend, he rushes around doing chores, checking the angle of the sun anxiously against his watch in a losing battle. He cannot to seem to realize that 1 p.m. is still only midday, even if it is already growing dark outside. I reiterate this patiently to him, and while he acknowledges the logic, something still has him frantic; the dying of the light, as Dylan Thomas would have it.

"Goddammit, we shot the day to shit again," Cliff grouses, the moment I disengage from Kitty. I have spoken to her for only ten minutes or so, and it is still barely past noon, but Cliff has been watching suspiciously for the shadows outside to lengthen, and now they have. He is antsy to "do something with the day," and my conversation with Kitty is pure theft of his precious time in this zero sum game of light versus dark.

"Come on, Cliff," I say. "Kitty needs a friend." Brushing back the hair from my forehead, I graze my eye and wince in sudden pain that manifests as inexplicable anger. Shut the fuck up about her already, I want to scream at Cliff—and then, as if some trigger has been pulled, go on screaming. But I clench my teeth, and in a few seconds the pain subsides, along with the urge to unload. Sometimes the whole edifice of love rests on just such a slender pedestal as the ability to be quiet at a certain moment.

"You know, she got herself tossed out of the bar at the Captain Cook again last Wednesday. In the middle of the day."

"You told me that already."

"Did I tell you she'd have gone to jail for drunk and disorderly if I hadn't talked the manager out of pressing charges?"

"But Isn't that your job? To keep people out of jail?" Cliff gives me a sardonic look. He is not particularly fond of women in trouble, I am discovering, nor of troubled women. But he shows an almost brotherly compassion toward men in similar straits. Consequently, he has developed an infuriating sympathy for Duke, a handsome, ruddy mesomorph with a thick shock of black hair and the low, dense hairline of the chronic alcoholic. Duke is making a decent living in Anchorage, but of course he cannot stay away from Kitty, nor she from him. They are already known around town as trouble.

Having been in and out of jail for half his life makes Duke compatible with the Alaskan style of lost years and vague resumes. Even when sober, he has a barroom volubility, a confiding, almost touching need to unburden himself to strangers, along with the disarming talent of lying with the utmost self-disclosing sincerity. I have seen others with this amoral, hypnotic charm, and they are not all defendants nor are they all men.

But the package is particularly effective on Cliff, who fears that he is an undeserving fraud in constant danger of being unmasked. For this, he can probably thank his bitter, unappeasable father whose favorite word is liar, pronounced *laar*, from the side of the mouth, like a snarl. Cliff and I had discovered early on that we fit together in all the jagged places.

So Cliff was set up to be easy prey for a true fraud like Duke. "I actually like Duke," Cliff says now—using "actually" as a wedge into my indulgence. "Believe it or not, Duke actually means well."

"Do you have to provoke me like this?" I reply. "Actually?"

"Kitty's just never satisfied unless she's stirring the pot," Cliff says, provoking me.

"And you've been listening to Duke—the ultimate pot-stirrer. He goads her and then puts her down—after she did time for him, for God's sake."

"Don't get mad at me. What can I say? Duke is the kind of guy that only other men understand."

"Stop normalizing him." I add, "you should see yourself smirking."

"It's just, Duke can be a very funny guy,"

"Funny as cyanide." Cliff and I face each other, flushed.

"Truce?" He says, using his disarming ability to fold his tents at just the right moment.

"Why are we fighting so much over Kitty and Duke?" I ask him.

"Because she's taking up so much of our time."

"No," I say. It's because they're some kind of lightning rod for us. Or... a test."

"A test of what?"

"Of who we are."

"Explain yourself."

"I can't. I don't know what that means. Just leave Kitty alone."

"Happy to, when she leaves us alone. And I'll tell you who we are. We're us. There's never been an 'us' before. We're better than any of them—Solly and Lhosa, our parents..." Cliff takes me in his arms.

"That's what every idealistic young couple says."

"Boy are you cynical," Cliff rocks me back and forth. "We're just starting out. We can make our lives what we choose to." I nod, beating back words like luck, fate, heredity that bubble up—and then he adds as if talking to himself, "I thought Kitty was going to be a 'dentical assistant'." We always had a laugh over that, but now his mockery angers me again.

"It's hard for her. You talk about work as if it's the measure of everybody, but it's really the measure of women you don't happen to like. You hold women to a higher standard than men—unless they're young and beautiful, of course."

"Guilty of being a man. Anyway, that should reassure you, since you're young and beautiful."

"So was Lhosa."

"Ouch! Is that what I've got in store?"

"I thought you liked her." Cliff is always going on about Lhosa's 'grit'—out of Solly's hearing, of course—but he really admires her greed triumphant, and of course her overt, contrived sexuality. He also nurses a secret satisfaction from her nose-thumbing at Solly.

But Kitty, poor, plump and a lousy romantic strategist, is nothing but a loser to Cliff. It is his worst label for a person. I turn away, deriving a cold, unexpected comfort from this argument; relief from the gnawing guilt of my own casual infidelity in Europe. Perhaps I was only "claiming my freedom," as Cliff often says of Lhosa.

"Kitty is a simple person. All she really wants is to keep house and prowl the secondhand shops. But she keeps trying to please Duke, and now that he has her figured out, he just keeps raising the bar higher and higher."

"Why did you give her our phone number?" Cliff asks.

"Because she was new here. And alone."

"No," Cliff says. "You gave it to her because she asked for it. Do you see the difference?"

"I see you patronizing me right now."

"She was not with you on that plane for more than a couple of hours," Cliff says. "But she figured out that she had a potential patsy, someone she could lean on to solve her problems."

"That's exactly what Duke has done with you."

"Defending losers is my job. I just don't care to associate with them socially. So—bottom line—can you please unencumber yourself of Kitty? And do it before she ruins our whole stay in Alaska?"

"Fine."

"Just tell her you're busy and stick to it. Eventually, even she'll get the idea." He looks so smug in his cruelty that it makes me want to rip into him with some pointed confession or revelation.

"Whatever makes you happy," I manage.

"She said, dripping with sarcasm."

"What did Kitty ever do to you?"

"It's not what she did. It's what she can do."

"We should just stop right here."

Kitty, however, is not in the least deterred by my half-hearted tactic of unavailability. In fact, trusting me at my word, that I am busy, she calls even more persistently. In truth, I am far from bored by her yarns of Anchorage after dark—and of her life in general, a living fable that she adorns with truths, lies and wishful thinking as needed. For Kitty, the boundary between fact and fantasy is conveniently amorphous, an ever-shifting line that coils around and includes any incident or story that appeals to her, however implausible.

At her best, she delivers bawdy jailhouse and bedroom tales with total disdain for propriety, embellished with her sly talent for mimicry. At her worst, she falls into an irritating and discomfiting boastfulness. She drops the names of movie stars and international playboys who were once infatuated with her; recounts orgies on yachts and anecdotes of Vegas high rollers who draped her in jewelry and haute couture.

"She's a pathological liar," Cliff says flatly when I relate these excesses.

"Not necessarily. Think of her fifteen years younger. Some of those stories just might be true." Cliff snorts. To him Kitty has always been what she is now. But then, Cliff finds the present so intense that he is almost unable to reflect backward—or beyond. People call him a "hothead" but the truth may be more complex, a weakness in his ability to link cause and effect, to anticipate accurately. This trait sometimes makes for casualties—or heroes.

Last week he was nearly held in contempt for calling an elderly judge "a disgrace to the bench." Solly, suppressing a smile, had gone downtown to "defend" him. I even appeared as a character witness, attesting straight-faced to Cliff's frequently voiced "respect for the judiciary" in our personal conversations. Following this, the judge summoned the penitent, scolded him and released him, We departed for the Anchorage Westward, where, for fun, Cliff retained his pose of wholly inauthentic contrition almost until the third drink.

I sometimes meet Solly's colorless gaze after one of Cliff's outbursts and see in it a message directed at me. I look away, feeling disloyal and collusive, because I already know what Solly is trying to tell me.

And then one morning, almost as if two bills have been paid, the electricity in the house, and that between Cliff and me magically returns. We awaken in luxurious warmth, spooned on The Goddess, which we have pushed in front of the fireplace. Outside, the snow sweeps earthward in vast diagonal sheets of undersized, dingy flakes.

Framed in the massive picture window directly above us is a moose the size of a T-Rex. I gasp and nudge Cliff, and we gaze in wonder at the browsing creature, its velvet muzzle dripping with strings of grassy saliva, lugubrious eyes watching us with calm and majestic indifference. It is so close we dare not move, worried that it might come thundering through the glass and trample us into patties. After endless moments, it turns its massive brindle flank to us and then its incredible Pleistocene rump, flaunting its bulk and balls brazenly as it ambles off. Awed, we begin joking about his armamentarium and are suddenly flooded with laughter and the wonder of being here, together in this moment that neither of us will ever forget, the sweet intimacy and hilarity ours alone now, forever.

And I understand too that we cannot help but precess away from this magical time, even as the earth departs its seasons. I vow inwardly to do whatever it takes to remain with Cliff, even if that means becoming worthy of Alaska too. But in the calm that flows through me as we cuddle back to sleep, I suddenly become aware of Lhosa. I can almost sense her watching me, her mouth twisted into a cynical, rather ugly smile.

Days later, I am standing before the same window, but my audience is now a group of the young and not-so-young regulars who spend their nights at Solly's. They have returned with the electricity, and brought a few more of their ilk along with them. I notice a couple of judges, and Solly too is in attendance, standing beside Cliff, who had asked me to come home early from work that day for a "meeting." Everybody is drinking, and it almost feels like a party, but beneath the socializing and shop talk is some mystifying agenda: The men have a proposal to present for my approval.

Standing before them, Cliff looks professional and correct, as if shouldering a major responsibility. He clears his throat and winks at me, searching for a way to begin. I feel like a bug in a jar until I notice that the assembled men are watching him, not me, studying him closely, as they would a man getting ready to leap a gorge on a mountain bike or confess that he wants to start seeing other women.

I have no reason to suspect anything shocking or new. I already met the young women who had been his flirtations before my arrival and reassured myself that they were not serious threats.

"Hey," Cliff says softly to me, as if to steel us both for some ordeal. By now, I am curious enough to put on my sanest and most forgiving face, which consists of adjusting my eyebrows slightly upward, and softening my mouth and eyes. Whatever you have to tell me, this look says, I forgive you in advance because I am that kind of person and because I love you. It is the type of expression that people should be wariest of.

"I... "Cliff looks around. "*We* need a... a bit of a favor." A small sigh of relief passes among our audience: *Iacta alia est.*

"Sure," I say, as if it is already granted. "What is it?"

"You might want to hear it first, before you agree to it."

"She said yes already," one of our auditors blurts with a fatuous giggle. It was probably Matt the kid, because Cliff wheels in annoyance and then catches himself and turns back to me.

"Brynn, there's this woman, this *lady*, who needs a place to stay—just for a few days," he adds quickly.

"Oh. Sure." I say. "Of course. What's the big deal?"

"She's a hooker," Matt blurts, and giggles again.

"Cool it," Cliff says, and to me. "Okay. So? Do you want to take it back?"

"Take what back?" I say.

"Your permission."

"Why would I?" Cliff smiles and reaches out to take my arm as a small cheer goes up. I roll my eyes and leave the room.

"I owe you one," Cliff says after me. I turn and smile like a Washington hostess. And somehow it's that smile of mine and not his disingenuous public gratitude that leaves me with a feeling of nauseous trepidation.

I am alone in Fred's office when the banging on the door begins. I had already locked it because although it is only 2:00 in the afternoon, it is as dark as midnight outside. Some people deal with the premature night by drinking their way into it, and a number of these are now wandering the street good and drunk, looking to raise a little mischief and perhaps snatch what there is for the taking.

"Brynn! Open up." Kitty's whisper penetrates the cheap, hollow door so urgently that I fear her fist or her shoe will follow it. I hurriedly put aside Proust and rise and make my way through the tacky waiting room with its giveaway news-papers and Fred's old *Sports Illustrated* magazines. The minute I slide the bolt, Kitty floods in, smelling of sour wine, her mascara coursing clownlike down her cheeks.

"C'mon." I say, leading her to my tiny office, where she flings herself into a chair and picks up a manila folder to fan herself. She glances at it. "Curland versus Curland." Somebody suing themselves?" I take the file away. "Brynn, he's gonna kill my ass."

Kitty looks up at me, and I battle the impulse to laugh, she is so comically forlorn. I would counsel flight, but she has already tried that. Duke eventually follows her wherever she goes anyway. I feel oddly envious. I cannot imagine a lover— even Cliff—becoming so obsessed with me that he would put his very freedom at risk. That has not been my experience of love. Kitty and I stare at each other in the universal, uncom-prehending dilemma of women trying to access the vortex of the male mind. She looks away and scans the office, as if to fix the moment.

"I should have stayed in Vegas," she says, with a mock pout. Her eyes flatten and assume a look I am now familiar with. "Lance used to take me there all the time. Lance Reventlow, you know who *he* is, of course."

"The playboy?"

"Cary Grant was his stepfather, did you know that? They never got along. Lance died a couple of months ago in a plane crash." She leans forward. "He was a fully rated pilot but he let this... *idiot* student fly his plane. No one will ever know why."

"Really?"

"The kid didn't even know how to fly! Lance could have flown that Cessna in his sleep. So this kid takes off and then flies the plane right into the ground."

"Oh no!"

"I couldn't stop crying," Kitty says, eyes brimming. "I almost had to be hospitalized."

"Really?"

"Lance wanted to marry me, he told me I was the only woman he could ever see himself being faithful to." I smile with my lips closed and look at the ground, blinking rapidly. Kitty sits back and studies her nails. She sighs. "Nobody understood him like I did. That's what he said." She seeks and catches my eye. "I would have inherited the whole Woolworth fortune. I mean, if we'd stayed together. I told him I wouldn't stand for him cheating on me, though. That was the one rule I had. Anything else, well, I could probably be talked into." She giggles slyly.

"I wish..." I begin, and stop. I had been about to say, "I wish people would stop putting me in these impossible situations," but Kitty looks at me with the clear and innocent expectancy of a child, and I blurt instead, "I wish you had married Lance."

She smiles sadly. "When we're sure we're doing the right thing, the only thing we can possibly do, that's probably when we make our biggest mistakes. I read that somewhere." She laughs. "That's what makes life so crazy. Like when I let Duke put that dope in my purse." I laugh too and show her to the restroom, where she reapplies her cornered-subterranean-creature eye makeup, hugs me and leaves.

V. Eclipse

Later that week, I am alone in Solly's house, tidying up, when I hear a timid tap at the door. Imagining that Kitty has found her way out here, I pull the door open with a put-upon expression and am brought up short at the sight of a beautiful native woman in her early twenties looking around nervously.

"I…I'm Erika," she says to my blank stare. "Some of the guys told me it was okay if I stay here a couple days?" For some reason, I had expected a blowsy aging woman with wrinkled cleavage and brassy red hair… but that was absurd, of course. The effusive concern of the men would never have been expended on such a woman. Erika, however, was a different story.

For his part, Cliff had been evasive and laconic, other than to explain that the girl was merely trying to avoid her pimp long enough to get on a plane. The pimp, who was capable of lethal rage over such issues as the temperature of his dinner, was sure to have an opinion about Erika's pending departure and take action accordingly.

"Come in." I open the door wider, and she glides past me.

For the second time that week I hear the words, "He's going to kill me." But the Athabaskan girl speaks with as flat an affect as if mentioning that it looks like snow. Even run to earth like this, she maintains an almost regal bearing. Tall and slim, she moves with an antelope grace not diminished by the clumsy quilted jacket she wears, frayed at the cuffs, held together with frog closings, only two of which are intact. Stuffing protrudes from a tear in the shoulder. Her black, sloe eyes scan the roadway and the woods beyond the property. Her parted lips are beautifully shaped but dry.

Even at my age, I know that terror so abject and lovely can drive a certain kind of man to provoke it over and over merely to enjoy the sight. Her hair courses past her waist, and a thought occurs to me that this shining banner could soon belong to a dead person.

So this is the kind of woman that men kill for, I am thinking; themselves or each other. Or else they kill her, because they cannot bear the idea of her escaping them, prevailing over them, perhaps loving their friend or rival. As the girl moves around the living room, I notice that each and every window offers a perfect shot.

"I'll pull the curtains," I say.

"It won't do any good."

"Shall I call the sheriffs?"

"Ya, sure. Do that." She smiles at me with true amusement. "Sheriff is his brother-in-law. And a couple of the deputies, they all grew up together. They only want to save him."

"Then they should... try to talk some sense into him."

"This is sense to them: If I die, then his spirit will go free. He will be healed of the sickness that I cause." She laughs bitterly. "This is all my fault, you see. It's *cultural.*"

I understand now that the lawyers in this house, those vaguely comic characters, are engaged in a battle to save her, not only from the crazy pimp lurking somewhere outside like a savage predator—but from the fate that such a woman seems to attract. In a way, this isn't about her at all. The men on both sides are each doing what they believe must be done.

And I suddenly realize how very difficult thwarting her fate is going to be and wonder if this rather bookish bunch is up for the job; if all the legal tricks they have memorized will be sufficient to conquer the bear. Their very whiteness makes them seem so weak to me, although in reality, the very opposite is probably true. And while some of them will bend every effort to put the pimp behind bars, others, their adversarial reflex fully aroused, will be scheming feverishly to keep him free. It is all madness.

With Erika's arrival, a silence takes root and grows between Cliff and me. I notice that he and Erika avoid one another, though the other men seek her out and counsel her obsessively, an attention she endures with downcast eyes. I can think of many reasons why I don't wish to start dissecting her odd behavior towards Cliff. Rather, I let the questions hang unasked between us like a fog, telling myself that I he owes me nothing, least of all fidelity. When I can stand it no longer, I choose a topic that he will find irresistible, so that he has to answer.

"What's going to become of her?"

"I told you. We're going to get her out of here on Monday morning on a flight to Minneapolis."

"Why there?"

"A sister."

"Prostitute?"

"I don't know, Brynn," he says wearily and with such finality that I busy myself with something out of the room, and after a while he comes and finds me and puts his arm around me.

"Are you in love with her?"

"No." He looks at me. "It didn't mean anything. Not a goddamn thing, okay?"

"Okay. But I think it did."

"Don't think."

"Actually, I'm relieved."

"What's that supposed to mean?"

My cheeks are burning, and my stomach feels as if somebody has planted a boot in it good and hard. "I'll tell you someday. Maybe," I try to toss off.

"Don't."

"Okay."

All Friday night and into Saturday morning, Erika retains her wistful aura, truncating all efforts to draw her into conversation. Several men I have never seen before drop by and spend time in her bedroom, then leave by the back door. Everybody is drinking a good deal, and arguments break out among the lawyers—brief, sharp and revealingly mean-spirited.

At midday on Saturday, Erika taps at my bedroom door and asks me to accompany her to the Anchorage Westward, where she has a "date." Cliff and a lawyer visiting from Homer have gone down to the office to work for a few hours.

I join her in the living room, and we gaze out into the bleak, frigid twilight.

"I don't think you ought to leave here," I tell her. "Bobby could be lurking right outside."

"You're right. I guess." Erika subsides for about half an hour but paces the living room restlessly. She finally mentions her "date" again; she needs me to drive her downtown in the Travelall since she has no car. At last, feeling crazy, I agree. I too am eager to get away from here.

The moment we are free of the house, Erika becomes talkative and confiding. She seems to believe that she owes me something, in exchange for the favor I am doing her.

Erika parks me in the cavernous lobby of the Westward, one of Anchorage's two upscale hotels, and finds me a *Sunset* magazine to read.

"This won't take long," she says and disappears into an elevator. The clerks and bellmen pay little attention to her but make no effort to conceal their interest in me.

"Don't worry," Erika giggles when she has rejoined me, giddy, her eyes alight with mischief. "I told them you're not a pro."

"Thanks, I guess." We laugh at the thought of it, and Erika feels so good that she stops at a nondescript, green-walled cafeteria near Fort Richardson and has herself another brief date with a serviceman in the Travelall while I wait inside, stirring my watery coffee. Though on the way home she feeds me the conventional orthodoxy about prostitution, that she abhors the life and once settled in Minneapolis will never turn another trick, it is apparent that she is having a ball.

"I'm leaving you my date book," she announces. "And my bed too. You brought me luck. Maybe they'll bring you some too."

"Your *bed*?"

"It's practically new. It ought to go to a good friend." That my tentative companionship qualifies me in her mind for that status saddens me momentarily.

As we pull into Solly's driveway she hands me the worn black tabbed address book. "You might need money sometime. It's like insurance, you know? Everybody's in here... the big shots, you know, the guys who run things here. I knew 'em all."

"Thank you."

"You just gotta remember one thing: Always ask to see a man's penis first."

"His..."

"If he's a cop, he won't show it to you. Simple thing, but it can save your ass."

""Thank you," I say.

There is no midnight on the planet darker than Anchorage at 5 a.m. on a Monday in late December. The lawyers have assembled to accompany Erika to the airport, knocking back shots of whisky with the sharp, assertive whip of the head fitting for men about to risk their lives for a beautiful woman. Revolvers bulge from the side pockets of their business suits.

Cliff looks at me deadpan, swirling whisky in his mouth and something about his expression sets me off laughing, which puts him at pains to swallow the liquor quickly, before it comes out his nose. Erika is standing by the largest window in full view of the world, despite the lawyers' frantic efforts to conceal her. There is no sign of the pimp, which is probably the reason for her sullen silence. She actually has to be coaxed into the Travelall, which is so packed with lawyers packing heat that there is thankfully no room for me. Two other cars follow in a little caravan, and I am left alone in the house to watch the tail lights disappear into black, bone-piercing sleet. Pleasantly high, I wander downstairs to where her bed has just been hauled in and ensconced. After a moment's hesitation, I fling myself onto it, and it is indeed the most comfortable and commodious bed I have ever experienced. I fall asleep instantly. When Cliff returns, we christen it and claim it for our own.

For the next week, Cliff and I get along better than we ever have. Perhaps it is the knowledge that his internship is finally ending, and that we have come through some sort of crucible. We treat each other tenderly, shop for Christmas gifts, leave corny little love notes on the pillows, and exchange frosty kisses while ice skating. We meet for lunch every day downtown and plan to spend Christmas and New Year's in Hawaii, celebrating with luaus and mai-tais.

So when Duke is arrested late one Saturday morning for taking a couple of swings at Kitty, Cliff only shoots me a look of mild exasperation as he throws on his jacket. A freezing rain has been falling since last night, and the weather is too nasty anyway to do much with the rapidly dwindling day. At least this will get him out of the house, he says. He'll stop by the courthouse and put in an appearance for Duke, then go into the office and work for a couple of hours on a brief he wants to finish before his internship ends. Once Cliff leaves, I pour myself a cup of coffee, adding a shot of brandy, and decide to cook up a big pot of chili for dinner while awaiting Kitty's inevitable call.

After a while Solly's son Matt comes into the kitchen and confesses to me that Erika had turned him on to cocaine.

"Why did she do that?"

"She said she wanted me know what it is, so I could, like, avoid it."

"That doesn't make a lot of sense, Matt."

"No, I guess not." He giggles.

"Did you like it?"

"No. It made my nose itch." I smile, thinking of Kitty.

By three o'clock, I am feeling vaguely neglected at not having heard from anybody. I resist the urge to call Cliff at the office. The place, awash in romantic intrigue, is a nest of gossip. Calling one's boyfriend is often interpreted as a sign of weakness or insecurity.

I wonder what kind of a lousy weekend Kitty is going to have now, whether cooped up alone or with Duke, who has been losing steadily at cards for the past month. By the time the phone finally rings, I am a little tipsy from my second—or is it third—coffee and brandy. So it takes me a couple of minutes to comprehend what has Cliff so agitated.

I finally realize that he is telling me he went straight to Duke's bail hearing and argued so effectively that he succeeded in getting him released on his own recognizance. Whereupon Duke, not neglecting to praise Cliff as "the best of that bunch," had returned home and beaten Kitty to death, so precipitously that Cliff was still at the courthouse and had not yet gone back to the jail to finish up the paperwork on Duke's release.

And that is why, Cliff tells me, he thought at first that somebody else must have murdered Kitty, until told by an officer that Duke himself had actually called from the apartment to confess.

"He called you? At the courthouse?"

"No. Aren't you listening? He called that little smart-ass assistant DA Tom Koenig and confessed to him." Tom had been Cliff's adversary at the bail hearing that morning and had returned to his own office to sulk at having been bested by a law student. But even Tom had trouble believing that Duke could have gotten home so fast and carried out the crime, first with his fists, and then, panicked at the gravity of the injuries he had inflicted, "putting her out of her misery" with the lug wrench from the toolchest on the back of his pickup.

Within minutes of murdering Kitty, Duke was on the phone, feeling remorseful, helpless and sorry for himself, as well as hungry. He had gone and done it, hadn't he? And she didn't even have it coming, that was the whole thing, Duke wept. She had even gone shopping for a big steak dinner when she heard he'd been released. What a worthless sonofabitch he was. Duke's tears fell into the frying pan in which he was attempting to cook the steak. His remorse knew no bounds. It was time to just give in and let the system put him where he belonged.

He should never have been let out, Duke wailed to the arriving deputies as they handcuffed him. That inexperienced little shit of a public defender wasn't even a lawyer for Christ's sake. And that was what had actually cost Kitty her life, didn't they see? He had a lot to answer for, that PD.

To their credit, the deputies proceed to simply throw Duke in a cell and manage to neglect to feed him both lunch and dinner, despite his bawling for hours and making such a din with his aluminum mug on the bars that they could hardly hear themselves think.

VI. Solstice

Solly appears magically that very evening from wherever he had been wandering. He declares himself deeply concerned for Cliff's state of mind, as are the other lawyers who gather to spend the night with us. I have been crying and drinking all day. In fact, everybody gets very drunk very quickly, except for Cliff, who keeps to himself in our bedroom, head bowed, bearing his pain in stoic silence, running through the hearing over and over again in his mind.

I tell him that I have never loved him as much as I do at this very moment, and he raises his head and looks at me, probably trying to think of a way to say that he does not feel the same without hurting me. I am warned by the lawyers not to intrude on his grief and not to overdo the crying. Nobody even guesses that it is Kitty I am grieving. In fact, most of them do not even mention her name. She is just "that woman" or"that crazy woman."

At about 11 p.m., the lawyers coax Cliff out of the bedroom and form a protective cordon around him, as if to keep away the guilt. I remind them of the obvious—that their touching solicitude for the beautiful Erika had probably saved her life, while Kitty had been, as I said, "an object of condescending amusement" to them.

"Speak English for once," Cliff says nastily from his seat on The Goddess, where he is drinking from a bottle of Schnapps. "She was the butt of our jokes is what you mean. My jokes." I sit beside him and smile thinly out at them all. I do not dare to put my arm around him because I am afraid he would shrug it off like a stinging insect.

Moments later, I retreat to our room unnoticed and light all the candles remaining from our days of the power shutoff. Kitty had given us a joke candle shaped like a penis, which Cliff and I had been unable to bring ourselves to light. I light it now and stand holding it in the flickering gloom, knowing how Kitty would laugh at the sight of me. And the weight of my loss rolls over me like a juggernaut. I try to tease out my own responsibility for her death: Had we not met on the plane; had I refused her Cliff's number. Had I traveled on a different flight to Alaska or not even gone. Had Solly sent Cliff back to California after his intemperate remarks and mock trial for contempt. While I am puzzling this out, the clock heaves over a flip card and it becomes December 22. The solstice is over. For some reason, I feel vastly relieved.

I intuit by the rash talk now emanating from upstairs that my own inability to keep Kitty at a safe distance was the fundamental problem. They too have been trying to circle back and assign complicity to me in Kitty's death. It had been my ill-starred friendship with her that had set the tragedy on its inevitable course, its axial tilt just right. Moments later, I hear the lawyers, an informal lynch mob now, huffing with indignation as they make their way downstairs to confront me.

If, says Rob, a lawyer who is conducting an affair with a local married woman, I allow every flake to entangle my personal life with hers, it bodes ill for Cliff's career. Even though Cliff is too much of a gentleman to tell me this in so many words.

"No he isn't."

"Brynn, listen to me. Distancing oneself from one's cases is critical (cri'cal), for the very reason that we are now seeing."

"Objection."

"To what?"

"To you being in my fucking bedroom uninvited."

"All we're saying is that you have the potential to hurt Cliff's legal career at a very early phase."

"Thank you."

"C'mon Brynn, We don't mean it that way. Come back upstairs and put out these fucking candles. Cliff needs you right now." Rob extends a bottle of scotch, and I take a drink, blow out the candles and troop back upstairs. Here, correspondingly, the lawyers are all at pains to assure Cliff that "these things" happen; are bound to happen, *must*, in fact, happen sooner or later. Better to get it out of the way early in his career, so he can toughen up. And of course whether Duke had been O-R'ed that very day or served a week, a month, or a year, Kitty was doomed. Her fate could not be escaped.

At about four-thirty, somebody recalls a parable about a man who saw Death menace him in the Baghdad marketplace. And the man had instantly fled to Samarra, the very place where Death, coincidentally, had been traveling to keep an appointment with him. We sit around pondering this for quite a long time.

The next day, as soon as Cliff and I are able to rise, we go out into the rapidly encroaching dark for steaks and more whisky. In the front yard, amid the eerily lengthening shadows, I snap a picture of Cliff standing before the mammoth fir tree, holding his briefcase. His shoulders droop, and he looks sad and small, although he is six feet two and in the prime of his life. His attempted smile seems only to beseech. We end up drinking too much again and get into a spat, over what, I could never recall.

"Cliff, "I always say to him in the fantasy that I have concocted of Kitty's last day, "maybe Duke just needs to stay in jail and cool his jets this weekend." And in my reconstruction, Cliff hesitates and takes his hand from the doorknob, as if something I said has given him pause. I never get farther than that in my mind, just his hand lifted ever so slightly, but that is enough. That makes all the difference.

A Shoo-In

This round-headed guy plucking at the nubbles on our sofa and talking talking talking is Cliff's boss, so there's no getting rid of him anytime soon. Beneath a dark, scanty Julius Caesar haircut, Bill's plump cheeks shine with earnest perspiration; his brown eyes are squeezed into analytical slits. Alarmingly woolly arms protrude from a short-sleeved white shirt, seams and buttons straining. Bill might look like a hairy version of the Pillsbury Doughboy, but I know that beneath this cuddly facade lurks the steely mental schematic of Otto Von Bismarck.

Recently, Bill has been pitching the County Board of Supervisors ("the supes") to appoint him superior court judge—a seat left open by the overdue retirement of old Clark Abschneggar, who was practically embalmed on the bench. Rumor had it, Clark wore a motorman's friend strapped to his leg up there, and sometimes his soft snore would be audible during a trial, like the ebb and flow of a gentle sea.

For Bill, the bench would be an islet of serenity, far from the squabbles of the district attorney's office, where he is chief assistant and likely to stay that way. As a judge, Bill could rule unchallenged and command the craven submission to which he thinks he is entitled. The supes, however, are a capricious and ornery bunch, capable of breathtaking pettiness. Though we keep reassuring Bill that he is a sure thing, we all know there is reasonable doubt.

I retreat to the kitchen, where I remove from the oven a tray of cheesy crackers dotted with bacon bits and bear it into the living room like the head of John the Baptist.

"Hey, eats!" My husband Cliff greets me with a look of cheery desperation.

Bill grabs a handful of crackers and chews them up without pausing. "The point I'm trying to make," he says, spitting crumbs, "is that the court is long overdue for a change. And I'm a breath of fresh air. Whattya think?"

"I think you're a regular mistral," I said, causing Cliff to nearly choke on his massive gulp of seven and seven.

"What's that? A *mistrial?*" Bill's hairy paw grips his sweating drink, his knuckles nearly invisible. "I mean, be straight with me here, Cliff. Do you think I have a shot?" Cliff and I nod in unison, so vigorously that I hear his neck crack.

Gossip has it that Bill's welcome in his own home has worn thin, thanks to a rumored dalliance with one of those big-haired court clerks—notorious lawyer groupies who specialize in unappreciated husbands. So Bill has been banished to seek his reassurance at the homes of various underlings. Guided by some internal compass, he arrived tonight unannounced to perch on our living room sofa like a bulky albatross and commandeer our evening. As the youngest DA and most recent hire, Cliff has about as much autonomy as those chained to the wall of the Doges' dungeon.

Cliff's nostrils flare as he tries to stifle yawn after yawn. A yawn, as everyone knows, will not be denied. Suppressed, it only retreats to gather strength for the next assault, and the next, until the battle saps your physical and moral stamina. Until you don't care anymore about the consequences. Let me out now! warns the yawn. Or I will come back bigger than ever. I will batter at your locked lips and clenched teeth, distorting your face into ferocious grimaces until I finally burst forth in a gape as big as a lion's roar and give you a permanent case of TMJ.

Tonight, oiled with our bourbon, Bill has revisited his childhood as a naive and bookish youth, collecting stamps, ordering real! live! sea monsters from the back of his comic books with his paper route money. As the volume of his talk expands, its substance thins. He grows cautious rather than reckless as the booze takes effect.

"Isn't it funny how our fates guide us?" He now ruminates. "I feel like the bench is just reaching out and... grabbing me." I suddenly imagine a Gumby-shaped bench growing hands to snag Bill's hairy tuchus, and I let out a giggle, because I am drunk. Cliff's quick warning glance reminds me that this is the trench duty I signed up for.

I was barely twenty-one when we arrived in Santa Madre— the average age of the severed heads that this town's most noted serial killer was supposedly storing in his trunk while earning clean bills of health from his psychiatrist. Driving down the Santa Madre Mall on our first day, I noticed that the prevailing fashions hearkened back to Charles Manson.

"Brynn," Cliff said, reading my mind, "they can't *all* be serial killers." But in fact, Cliff had those very killers to thank for his first job out of law school. With senior staff stretched thin, ambitious young lawyers could cut their teeth on lesser felonies they might wait years to handle in a big city.

To me, Santa Madre resembled a cross between the Renaissance Pleasure Faire and a Haight Ashbury swap meet. Citizens not busy dismembering bodies in the redwoods seemed to live by medieval craft—candle-dipping, glass staining, ceramic dragon and wizard manufacture. The Santa Madre Boardwalk and its sleazy beachfront ecosystem regularly fed the DA's office a menu of dope and love crimes. These were tried in the County Building, an angular stack of gray concrete slabs that dominated the banks of the town's sluggish, self-named river. The sheriff's office was located in the basement; from a distance on that first day, it all looked grim and Soviet, the perfect counterpoint to the mall's florid counterculture.

Besides the Boardwalk, Santa Madre's other main felony locus is the Pleistocene-looking redwood forest that surrounds the town. Deep, foliage-choked gorges plummet beyond the skinny roads to trickling streams. These morph into biblical floods during the winter rains, tossing uprooted redwoods around like so many pool cues, slamming them into bridges and roads, bringing the whole region to a soaking standstill.

Anyone who has ever ventured into a redwood forest and lost sight of the roadway experiences, if they are minimally perceptive, the vulnerability that all living things know they were born for. You sense the inescapable burden of life, of metabolism and predation, the best bargain the creator was able to strike with the laws of physics. While you may prevail for a brief, unlikely span, the world that once sustained you is sure to turn on you eventually and devour you, casually, without pity.

As if he has just read something unsettling in my mind, Bill suddenly looks straight at me, though he continues speaking to Cliff.

"So, my man, be honest with me. Do you think the Semple girls are going to come back to bite me?" My attention suddenly sharpens like a Ginsu knife, slicing through the gauzy layers of bourbon and boredom.

"Of course not," Cliff says quickly. "You only did what you had to do."

"I didn't know Clark was going to throw the book at them." Bill looks at Cliff almost pleadingly.

"How could you know?"

"Senile old bastard." Bill shakes his head, and both men look at the floor.

"Who are the Semple girls?" I suddenly have a strange sensation of being in a redwood forest, night falling, and it is not all my imagination. The men ignore me, as men do when women encroach on those deep areas of bad conscience that they guard and close ranks over and lie about if need be; all they must cede in order to love and live with a woman and have something to show for it.

"Worst nightmare," Bill says. The men both nod and shake their heads at the same time. Cliff looks—guiltily, I imagine—at me. Bill's eyes remain down, and I follow his gaze to a little black smudge on the beige carpet caused by a chunk of my mascara that fell off the wand weeks ago. Gotta get that up, I think.

"I just figured," Bill says, "Clark would cut me some slack on sentencing if I just... I mean, the younger one, she knew she shouldn't have, but come on. After all...."

"Exactly," Cliff says.

I've had enough. "What in the hell are you guys talking about?" They jump at my tone of voice, but are still deep into it.

"State prison, what the fuck?" Bill says.

"What the fuck is right," says Cliff.

"For the last time," I say, with an edge, "Who are the Semple girls?"

Bill finally looks me in the eye. "They're a couple of... of really nice girls."

"Yeah," Cliff says. He frowns as if weighing something. Me. "What would you do..." he says to me, then stops. Although

Cliff and I have pledged never to say anything that could risk extending Bill's stay, I now turn expectantly toward Bill, lips parted, head tilted to one side. Just as I calculated, Bill cannot resist.

"There's this old fart, okay?" Bill says, extending his glass, which I seize and fill, generously. "Pillar of the community, married his sweetheart right after the War. They have two daughters in their thirties.

"You can tell her his name," Cliff says. "It's not like it's a secret."

"Cyrus Semple. Heard of him?

"No," I say.

"Well, it happened before your time. It's been years now. Anyway, Cyrus gets out of the... Army was it?"

"I dunno," says Cliff.

"Maybe it was the Air Force," Bill says. "Army Air Corps they called it then."

"For God's sake," I say.

"Okay okay. So Cyrus starts up an insurance business out in Bledsoe Valley, a little hole in the wall at first, but Cyrus had a talent for business, so it grew. Semple Insurance." He waits for my reaction, but I look blank. Bill takes an infuriatingly dainty sip of his drink and nibbles a cracker as if at a Hillsborough cocktail party.

"So anyway, he's married to his wartime sweetheart and they have these two daughters..."

"The Semple girls," I say.

"Right. And they didn't do so well, the daughters. They grew up, and one of them married a real asshole, and he left her with an autistic kid to raise..."

"The other one have any kids?" Cliff asks. "Sarah?"

"Of course Sarah had kids," Bill says. "Two daughters and a son."

"I'm going to scream," I say to both of them.

"Okay, so the years pass, and things go well, for dad I mean. Cyrus makes his bundle, so to speak. He gets ready to retire." Bill looks quickly at Cliff. "And then one day, this girl walks into his office."

"Why don't you say 'this crack whore,'" Cliff says, and I realize he is drunk.

"Oh, she was your worst nightmare, all right," Bill says to me.

"With a kid," Cliff says. "Didn't have a clue who the father was."

"Tsk tsk," I say.

"I hate when you do that thing with your mouth." Cliff narrows his eyes.

"Don't make psycho eyes at me," I say, and then I do that thing with my mouth again.

"Anyway," Bill says quickly, "because old Cyrus is a nice guy, he listens to this girl's tale of sad woe and ends up giving her a job answering phones in his office." I nod. "Now Cyrus was about sixty-eight then, and he'd been looking to retire for years. He and Christy his wife were going to sell their house and go on one of those round the world cruises, really start enjoying life. I mean they had provided for the girls, and there was plenty left over. And Christy was the salt of the earth."

"Uh huh."

"They were from Minnesota originally, and Christy baked pies and sold them on the side. You've heard of Christy's Crusty Pies?"

"No," I say. The booze I drank with Bill and Cliff, plus what I sneaked in the kitchen is starting to wear off, and I consider reinforcing it, but can't think of an excuse to get up at this point in the story.

"Anyway, there's this other guy all ready to buy the business, just waiting, you know, and yet Cyrus just keeps on working. He tells Christy and the girls, one more year and I'll retire. But somehow one year becomes two, and two turns into three. And suddenly one day, Cyrus just keels over dead at work. Massive heart attack."

"Awww," I say. "He should have retired." Cliff is watching me the way people watch the dentist approaching with the drill.

"So everyone's devastated, naturally. I mean, Cyrus was a fixture of the community. Everyone had their insurance with him. They give him a full-page obit in the paper, big fancy memorial service etcetera. Send him off in grand style, half the town goes."

"I'm verklempt." I pretend to mop my eyes and giggle.

"What does that mean?" Bill asks.

"It means," Cliff says, "that she's drunk."

"It does not. It means I'm all choked up."

"I always wondered," says Bill, "did either of your families object to you guys getting married? I mean one being Jewish and one not?"

"Both of them," I say. "But his family forgave me because I have blue eyes, so I can almost 'pass.'"

"Why don't you have a cup of coffee, Brynn?" Cliff says.

"But since Cliff's father thinks the Protocols of the Elders of Zion should be taught as a college course, that may have gotten my family a little bit upset." Cliff looks at Bill and shakes his head. I suddenly notice how ruthlessly attractive Cliff has become; how he has evolved from the appealingly needy kid I fell for in college, into an explosive legal wunderkind with a few criminal tendencies of his own.

"Anyway, to get back," Bill says, "Christy and the girls finally sit down with a lawyer to go over the will and distribute the money. And that's when they find out." Cliff closes his eyes as if before a familiar blow.

"Find out what?" I say.

"That that there was no money."

"None at all?"

"Not a cent. All their savings, gone. Not only that, but the insurance agency was mortgaged to the hilt. And Cyrus had borrowed against the home and their other real estate too, a vacation home in Tahoe, some undeveloped lots. Their IRAs had been drained, you name it."

"But how could Christy not know?" I say.

"Because," Bill says, "they were that generation. She was an old-fashioned wife and Cyrus always handled the money, and...'

"Because," Cliff interrupts, "She trusted him."

"And he had been steadily giving away everything they had, for years, to Amy the crack whore," Bill says, delivering the punch line.

"How much was there to give away?"

"A lot," Bill says. "They never figured out quite how much."

"My God. What did she do with it,"

"Good question," says Bill. "Far as I know, they never did determine where it went. But Amy was no better judge of character than old Cyrus was, because what didn't go up her nose went up the noses of her various boyfriends, or went away in Vegas. There may have been a couple of dope deals went bad, nothing we could find. There was a theory at one point that they bought land in Uruguay with it, but nobody can prove anything. And Uruguay ain't saying. All they know is, Amy didn't have a pot to pee in when the Semple girls went looking for her. They should have just let well enough alone."

"Twenty-twenty hindsight," Cliff says.

"Oh, and Cyrus hadn't paid taxes in I don't know how long, so there was that."

"There were taxes too?" says Cliff.

"There are always taxes. So anyway, the girls decided one night to pay Amy a visit and get their dad's money back."

"Did they kill her?" I ask.

"Don't jump ahead,' says Cliff.

"Not quite," Bill says. "They brought along a couple of kitchen knives, though. And they'd been drinking, of course, to get their courage up. Because they weren't criminals, these girls. They didn't know what they were doing."

"That's how people die," Cliff says.

"Naaa, they didn't do much more than slice up her clothes," Bill says. "Oh, and she had a few little cuts on her arms."

"They call those defensive wounds." Cliff.

"Yeah, right," Bill says. "What are you, a prosecutor or something?"

"What are you?" Cliff says, "their lawyer?" Both men guffaw. "So Amy gets to the phone and dials 911, and the sheriffs come out and save her worthless ass."

"Who worked that case?" Cliff asks. "Was it Andy Scarametti?"

"Him and Dave Byers. They get out there and by that time, the place is a fucking bloodbath, pardon my French, most of it Barbara's. She got a whole lot worse than she gave from that little weasel."

"Jeez," I say.

"But they arrested both Semple girls, charged them with attempted murder, ADW, the works."

"Who charged them?" Cliff asks.

"Who do you think?" says Bill. "Our fearless leader, of course. He overcharged the case and then gave it to me because he knew it was a howling dog, and I would be the monster who prosecuted these poor destitute girls; it'd be all over the papers, and there went my chance to run against him for DA."

"And unfortunately," Cliff tells me, "Barbara had once gone after her husband with a rolling pin or something like that, so she had a prior. Was nothing."

"Cracked his coconut," Bill says.

"Okay, she had a temper but after that one thing she stayed out of trouble for years, raising that autistic kid. I guess she was hoping that when her old man kicked off, life would get a little easier for her. For all of them."

"Oh boy," I say, because I cannot think of anything else.

"Anyway," Bill says, "I get the case, and my shot at getting elected is going up the old kazoo. My one hope is that Abschneggar, that senile old prick, will go light on sentencing. So everybody can get back to business as usual, and the public can forget all about it."

"And?" I say.

"Just my luck," Bill smacks his head. "This Amy character, this crack whore, this cunning little sociopath gets up on the stand and turns out to be the most sympathetic victim..."

"Ever," says Cliff.

"In the history of the law. The jury actually ran out of kleenexes, I kid you not. Poor little thing had a hard life, raising her kid alone. Family straight out of *Deliverance*, been molested from day one etcetera etcetera." Bill sets his glass down and rises, swaying a little. "Here poor little Amy finally thinks, sob sob, she's landed a decent job at an insurance company, and then this old fart starts staring at her by the hour. He asks all these personal questions that she fends off as best she can without telling him every little detail."

"Of course," says Cliff, "every little detail is exactly what he wanted."

"And next thing, he starts leaving cash on her typewriter every week. First just a little, to help her out with the groceries. Well she didn't have a problem with those. But then one day, he leaves her a check for ten thousand dollars. At first she tried to give it back, she *says*."

"She *says*," Cliff says to me.

"But Cyrus insists, it would give him pleasure. Doesn't ask for a thing sex-wise."

"Right," I say.

"No, I actually believe her there. I mean at first, anyway. The ten thousand, well, it's anybody's guess, but a lot more big checks followed. And she's only human, sniff sniff. She takes one, then another. And finally it gets to be a habit. She gets to expect the checks. The jewelry came later." Bill sits down. "Hit me again. "He extends his glass.

"Can you believe, they kept this up for three years?" Cliff says.

"I think the stress just wore on old Cyrus. He was probably planning to leave his wife and be with Amy but he just couldn't bring himself to... and he kept getting in deeper. Because after a while, little Amy expected her money fix every week."

"So it finally just killed him," I say.

"Fucking predator," Cliff says.

"And old Cyrus was blameless, right?" I say.

"He was a goner the minute she walked into his office," Bill says. They both look at me, and I suddenly recognize a plea across the eons from every man whose life was ever hijacked by unworthy love.

"Well, she sounds like she was... sort of minding her own business," I say. "I mean this old guy gets obsessed with her...

she didn't force Semple to give her all his money, did she?" Bill and Cliff look at each other.

"You just don't get it," Cliff says.

"What don't I get?"

"You women," Cliff says.

I say, "I'm sure the money wasn't a gift. I'm sure she 'earned' it."

"What are you, taking her side?" Cliff asks. And somewhere, something cracks, like a redwood in the forest, anchored by frail and inexplicably shallow roots, giving way in a relatively light wind and crashing to the earth without warning.

"You're drunk," I say.

"You're drunk."

"Look," Bill says. "We're all drunk. Now do you want to hear the rest of the story or not? Okay, she's alone in her trailer, just put her kid to bed, and suddenly these two behemoths come charging in, demand money and start cutting her up with knives."

"They were big girls," Cliff says to me. "And Amy was... small."

"I think Abschneggar had the hots for her too, you want the truth," Bill says.

"Oh, you think?" Cliff says. They both laugh with relish, and I join in, at the thought of old Judge Abschneggar in love, with his white tonsure and watery blue eyes and grog blossoms and skinny shanks. It's good to hear Cliff laugh.

"What did she look like?" I ask.

"Like hell warmed over by now, I'm sure," Cliff says, as if to placate me. "Those redneck women don't age well."

"She was kind of... slithery," Bill says. "You'd have to see her."

"You mean slinky?"

"No," Cliff says. "Lauren Bacall in *To Have and Have Not* was slinky. Amy was slithery, like a serpent."

"But with this angelic little face," Bill says. "Go figure."

"So the girls went to state prison," I say.

"They're still there. Poor Christy took their kids to raise. Of course with no money, the autistic one had to go to an institution. The other boy's on dope, I hear..."

"Christy's the real loser," Bill says. "Those girls knew that what they were doing was a crime. Now their poor mom's got nothing. Her husband's dead, her marriage was a lie, her children are in prison. Amy might have been a woman without principle, judge her if you want, but at that point the Semple girls only had the power to make things worse. And that's precisely what they did."

"Was that from your closing argument?" I ask. Bill bursts out laughing.

"That was my closing argument. Hey Cliff, you got a smart wife."

"I know I got a smart wife," Cliff puts his arm around me and squeezes. He whispers in my ear, "You look so hot in that hippie skirt I'm gonna have to fuck your lights out tonight."

"You know," Bill says, "Dan handed me this stinking case so I'd look like a bully. But I learned something about myself. Do you wanna know what I learned?"

"Sure," I say, bumping my hip against Cliff's.

"I learned that I'm a better judge than a prosecutor. I'm essentially a fair-minded person."

"Yes, you are," Cliff says.

"Be honest with me, though. I can take it. What do you really think of my chances for the bench?"

"I think you're a shoo-in," I say, and Bill looks at me as though I have just revealed the route to the lost treasures of the Anasazi.

"A shoo-in!" He rocks back, tasting it, thinking it over, and somehow, it is sufficient. A state of grace floats down upon him, and I imagine a nimbus of light encircling his brachy-cephalic head, as if shining through redwood fronds. In the silence, he stretches and checks his watch. "Wow, I'd better get going." He smiles at me almost shyly. "Lucky I left the car home. I'm a little drunk."

"I'm a big drunk," I say. Bill doesn't live far, he tells us; just a short stroll to Aurora Heights Drive, ten minutes, tops.

"...give you the three steps of decency," Cliff says, rising. He too stretches, joints popping, and walks Bill to the front door and waves him out into the clear night. I shiver at the sudden chill.

"Two a.m.," Cliff says, closing the door, and gives me a meaningful look. Yawning, he picks up the glasses and cheese tray and starts for the kitchen.

From our living room window, I watch Bill wander away down the sidewalk. He wobbles a bit, but his eyes are fixed aloft on the same steady cosmos that lured Galileo and guided Magellan. Through the next door property of Dawn Dedricksen he shortcuts, stumbling once and kicking loose a small divot of Irish moss. He crosses the street, heaves his bulk with surprising grace over the stressed wood fencing of the Cary Mittlers and, although it is dark and the street lights dim, I see him do a little jig down Tweedsmuir Lane before he fades from sight.

The Shakes

It's time. Obediently, Marketing assembles in front of Human Resources and counts noses, then files out through the vast, slick-floored maroon-and-silver lobby. Job-seekers, huddled like troglodytes in cavernous armchairs, glance up from computer journals as the troupe passes.

"Hasta la Vista!" calls out blonde Annabelle Hopf from the reception desk, waving gaily.

Nobody waves back. Silently, Marketing crowds through the front door into the parking lot to distribute itself—grunting, squeezing, joints popping—among three cars. The dutiful caravan wends a short, cramped distance to downtown, parking on River Street to avoid the noon traffic jam.

Then we shuffle—like so many ducklings or kindergartners, I thought irritably, behind Al Cooke, our Director, all the way down Pacific Avenue to the Palomar Restaurant. I notice that I am dragging my feet, just as I had on field trips back in elementary school. And I feel an insistent, annoying urge to hold Bill Pinkney's hand as he trudges along at my side.

A full year after the earthquake, Pacific Avenue still lies strewn about in raw asphalt chunks, as if ripped by an angry behemoth: post-Godzilla Santa Cruz. Deep, refuse-littered canyons that are the graves of buildings yawn on either side. I feel vaguely ashamed peeping down into them, their broken rusty girders and moldy blockite foundations helplessly exposed like the underwear of dead old ladies.

Overdressed and overemployed, Marketing edges self-consciously along cyclone fencing and across broken pavement, past irreverent youth of all styles and commitments, past blowsy older shoppers and Gabby Hayes homeless. The sun glares down unobstructed on the ruined street, startlingly hot. The March of the Toy Soldiers. No, The Procession of the Damned, I continue bitterly. And guiltily too. Because it's really very nice of the company to buy us all Mexican lunch every other Thursday, just Marketing, a chummy little claque, no interlopers from Admin or IT. Our Tradition, Al terms it.

Of course, the cold steel of corporate coercion glints out from the velvet glove dealing enchiladas. And for some, fear is the "especiale" on the menu, since Al often chooses this occasion to call someone aside and mention in his offhand way that someone is "under evaluation"—that gut-piercing, margarita-negating *corrida*, the guacamole curdling beneath a stinging salsa reflux, the beans hitting the stomach floor like a jai a'lai serve. Poor Mac Morgan had gone positively verde on hearing his summons. Or was it only the restaurant's green-tinted skylight that makes us all look like we're lunching in the Gulag?

I catch my own reflection in one of the few storefront windows left unboarded: limp. My hair droops from its center part, too dismayed to curl. The mouth is petulant, impotent. My brown eyes retreat into shadow, peering back at me accusingly like those of a war orphan.

Mac is history now, I think bitterly. No more Gary Larson cartoons on my chair in the mornings, no more Star-Trek festival fliers. "Morgan's problem was, he thought like an engineer, not a marketing pro," eulogize Al, Mac's unrepentant executioner, punctuating his remark with an analytical pursing of the lips that lifts his jowls a good inch and causes him to resemble something that lurks in a coral reef.

Only an hour, I tell myself: this will be over soon. The hardhats, rulers of the rubble, bestride their 'dozers like cowboys, lazy-hipped, their proud torsos gleaming with honest sweat. Beneath them, the marketing group, children again, gape at serrated iron shovels and mighty saurian pincers groaning and roaring as they gnash at massive slabs of concrete and masonry. I become disoriented, as I always do now when downtown, all illusions demolished forever that afternoon. No stability. No shelter. No safety. Not on this deceptive, faulted earth that can suddenly lurch into animistic life and sway like a hula dancer's hips. Not in the treacherous ocean either, with its hidden riptide pythons. Not in the universe itself, only a big balloon after all, heedlessly inflating toward some cosmic pop. Or worse, dribbling back over the eons to a flaccid little virtual particle, all grandeur mummified.

Certainly not in love. The sudden indoor cool, and the remote vaulted ceiling of the Palomar makes me want to kneel and pray, as I did once before in Notre Dame (and during the earthquake too), my atheism expediently discarded. Kneeling beside me in the church had been a Sorbonne student nicknamed Du-Du. On the wall of his Rue de L'Harpe garret hung a Roy Orbison poster. He serenaded me in fractured English with "Running Scared."

Scared. The earthquake had caught Cliff and me bickering over the Visa bill. He didn't give a damn what my lawyer said, why should he have to pay for half of my psychotherapy?

"Cheating husbands tend to drive their wives to shrinks."

"And you had to see the most expensive shrink in the count, that little quack." Cliff's gaze froze me like blue freon. I wouldn't give him the satisfaction of admitting that I had dialed the only therapist whose ad was big enough to read through my tears.

"And what about these charges for that cozy little hideaway in Calistoga?" I counterattacked, waving the bill. "You took her to our honeymoon resort? I'm supposed to pay half of that?"

And suddenly, as if fed up to here, the earth had shrugged, shuddered with disgust. The house groaned, rocking back and forth; massive cracks clove the walls. We stupefied: What manner of divine retribution had our squabbling called down? I suddenly recalled reading of a woman during World War II convinced that her own turds were torpedoes sinking allied ships. Had they been?

Desperately, we grabbed for each other, swaying, praying aloud as the house danced like a Max Fleischer cartoon. With a cry, we toppled together and rolled across the floor, sheltering one another's heads. So must Sodom have collapsed, amid wails of terror and remorse. I didn't mean it, that high school debate, Resolved: God is Dead. I was kidding.

And then it was over. The earth convulsed one last time and lay still, as if spent, handing us back our lives, a miracle. Bursting with gratitude, we apologized, gushed concessions. How selfish we had been, how misguided. Everything was so clear now. Life was too precious, too uncertain to squander in trivial conflict. Yes, yes, cherish the moment, the priceless gift. Chastened and a little smug, we swept up glass, nipping from a bottle of brandy, asking with compassion as news poured from the radio.

But late that night, he had left again after all, dressed silently in the dark and let himself out. I awakened alone at five a.m. to the wail of sirens, sitting glumly amid the aftershocks, indifferent to doom. Let it all end in rubble then. Let the whole rotten world come down on me.

"Hey Brynn, what's your pleasure?" Bill nudges my arm

"Andale andale," prompts Al from the head of the table.

"To your left," whispers plump Kelly Landsman, "don't look now, is the guy who broke my old boss Sally's heart." The heartbreaker is battling for control of an elongating cheese string. Maddeningly elastic, it resists his efforts, dangling stubbornly from his lips across his fork, stretching toward his tie. He looks up, and his eyes met mine. I make a scissors motion with my fingers and he grins. "Watch out," says Kelly.

"When the worst has already occurred," I answer lightly, "one has nothing left to fear. Or to put it another way, you can't fall off the floor."

"I fell off the floor," Kelly says. "During the earthquake my house broke into four pieces, and I fell off the kitchen floor."

"Onto what?"

"The kitchen floor. But it was five feet lower."

"I'm sure there's some fundamental insight to be gained from that." I smile and toss my hair, a fearless coquette.

"So we figured that pricing was the key." Bill hoists a chip trembling with salsa.

"No way, Jose," shouts Al. "You're off base as usual. Think about the margins, sonny. Where have you been for the past six months?" Salsa drops like tears onto Bill's menu. "No way, Jose," Al says again, this time to the Mexican waiter. "I've got the wrong burrito filling." He pouts. "Where's the beef?"

"Speaking of the worst, I saw Cliff yesterday," says Kelly. "He pulled a sad face, said he'll always love you." I roll my eyes.

"A talent for deception." But he had loved me, hadn't he, rhapsodizing over my dark eyes, my mouth, the way the stem of my back curved beneath his hands. In bed, our contours had fitted perfectly, notched in all the right places, a solid marital foundation if ever there was one. Yet, even then I had been preparing for the cataclysm (not if, but when), bolting my love firmly, warily to the (unreliable) earth, holding myself apart. Needing him the more for that.

The beige flanks of my burrito split and erode under my indifferent fork. Entrails of green rice and pork spill out reminding me suddenly of The Sun Also Rises and the gored horses in the bullring. The meal is ending, I see with relief, people rising with conspicuous grunts and groans of satiety. I toss my napkin gratefully onto the table

"I miss Mac," I say. "Nothing's the same."

"That's for sure," says Bill. "He's working in Sunnyvale now. He hates the commute, but he's holding up." And what else can one wish for after all but to hold up? To hold up is enough. It's everything.

Like a bad dream, Al Cooke materializes at my side and Bill melts away. "Brynn," says Al, "Would you step into the bar with me please? We're due for a chat." His face is so close that I can easily distinguish the graphite-colored bristles on his jaw, the frijole smear beside his mouth. His eyes are a colorless glaze. Such must be the last human image afforded a condemned man: a close-up of his own executioner, all details in place for one final, eternal impression. Al takes my elbow and steers me toward the bar, away from the others.

No reliable way to predict: Deep in my molten core, a cauldron of magma heaves and lurches. A plate shifts and suddenly gives way, rupturing swiftly along the fault. Fissures wrench open like rosy gashes. My mantle shudders as seismic waves, amplified by loose upper sediment, make their way toward the unsuspecting crust. My legs begin to tremble, my head sways as the inner momentum builds. Tremors reverberate along my skin.

Al orders two coffees from the bartender, and I take my seat beside him. In my ears is a roaring, and a tinkling not unlike that of breaking glass.

Lowfathead

Contrary to all nature, the pinched little orifice of a BMW grille has found itself stuck up against the rear end of my Buick, where it rides along in indelicate unison, up and down, as we travel south toward Monterey on this two-lane seciton of Highway 1.

The Beamer plainly cannot endure this public indignity; cannot travel another quarter mile behind my waddling gray hippo ass impeding its thrust for *fahrensraum*. My Buick symbolizes for this guy everything that has ever gotten in his way all his life: his passive-aggressive ex-wife, all stoplights and speed limits, the hair gel he swam through in his dream last night, the VP who warehouses his memos, the shopping cart that made it to the register first.

Back and forth he waggles behind me, cowed—but decreasingly—by the steady stream of traffic hurtling past in the oncoming direction. And though it is but a couple of hundred yards until the four-lane freeway begins, he suddenly erupts from behind and jerks out abreast, shooting me a shuttered glare of contempt and triumph from behind his elongated aviator shades.

He sees, he thinks, a thirtyish cubicle-dwelling female, a speed limit personified, a judicious pillar of rectitude, a sustainer of the status quo. He cannot possibly suspect that I am instead a maniac who has lost everything, whose life means nothing to her, who has come to believe the tangible world nothing but a fraud, and who craves fiery oblivion with the intensity of an acolyte craving redemption. He cannot guess how my foot twitches on the accelerator, how I yearn to trap him in the oncoming lane hypnotized with horror as certain death looms in the form of the double-length semi loaded with brussels sprouts which I detect around a gentle curve.

But the maniac is no murderess. Courteous in my rage, I decelerate to allow him room, and he darts in ahead of me just as the truck surges past, a gust of metallic Armageddon, little green brussel balls bouncing playfully in its wake. The pert rump of the BMW recedes rapidly into the distance.

As I pull into the Trinity Diet Plan parking lot, I unwillingly note the large red and white banner stretched between two buildings, undulating gently in a light, foggy wind. It reads, idiotically, "When You Lose, We All Win."

The Trinity Complex is the international headquarters for the Trinity Weight Loss Crusade, modeled as closely as possible after its counterparts of irs futile, genocidal, plague-spaning counterparts of the middle ages.

I check out my distorted reflection in the convex car window: bulbous forehead, receding chin, shapeless nose, sheep's eyes, the scar of the pimple I ill-advisedly picked before my high school senior yearbook picture.

Who in the hell is this? But I know! Gazing back at me from the window reflection is Friedl—a female schizophrenic in a strait-jacket, photographed in 1904 in a German mental institution and placed, for some reason, on the back of a whimsical postcard for sale in Bookshop Santa Cruz. I think the postcard is meant to communicate the sender's appreciation of life's (humorous) futility.

Friedl, a messenger from my own lunatic collective un-
conscious. Of course! Let other women believe they are the
reincarnation of Marie Antoinette or Cleopatra, or the tempes-
tuous daughter of an 18th century Irish landowner shaking her
chestnut tresses from the back of a prancing black stallion held
by a young groom in tight jodhpurs. My own former life was
spent gazing vacantly into concrete drains, breathing carbolic
disinfectant and wearing restraints.

Like all things superficially inspirational and kitschy that
are able to align themselves with true suffering, the Trinity
Diet has taken the world by storm. Those who take the Trinity
Pledge became "Triniteers." Employees of the Crusade itself,
such as I, are referred to as "Templars," another pious myth.

I shake my head with infinite contempt, aware that my
daft body language is probably being observed from the windows above. Of course, nobody here bothered to inform themselves of the fate of *that* unfortunate sect. But I am indeed a
Templar, doomed by chicaneries never fully comprehended.
An anachronism. A fool. A tool.

I reach the door and a gust of warm air greets me as I
pull it open. I work in the Diet's public relations office, which
reminds me of the torture chamber from "The Pit and the
Pendulum." I sometimes fear that these walls too will begin to
glow red-hot and rush toward the center, grilling us all at our
computers like so many lowfat yuppieburger patties.

Amy Fischbein is already working at the desk next to mine.
Typing away industriously, she looks up and grins. Amy is the
small, energetic, busty type of Jewish female, while I am of the
tall, sallow, sepulchral variety. In an earlier era, Amy would have
spent her life tugging buckets up from wells, singing lustily,
scrubbing, sewing, midwifing, and driving hard bargains. She
would have spat in the face of sadistic overseers, faced down

torch-bearing mobs of Cossacks, and finally schlepped her whole extended family to Ellis Island from where they would fan out to become gastroenterologists and founders of ready-to-wear dynasties.

I, on the other hand, would have been kidnapped by dybbuks on the eve of my arranged wedding to waft about the Bessarabian forests for centuries, harassing travelers and spooking virgins. While Amy was propelling her sons through medical school and ending up a Miami Beach real estate tycoon, I would be whooshing endlessly through the birches.

Given that this is America, however, and that Amy is unmarried, she has followed the only course available to her: To labor with demonic industriousness and in her spare time turn out mammoth needlepoint wall hangings, crewel chair cushions, voluminous afghans, quilts, and room-size rugs of Byzantine complexity. Amy also dutifully attends every singles function within a fifty-mile radius and hands out her business card, garnering at best a few tepid coffee dates. But Amy is not the type to give up easily. She still believes that her "beshaert," her destined lover, awaits her at the very next singles event.

"Welcome to the bullshit factory," she greets me without looking up. Walking past, our boss, Jackie, acknowledges Amy with a brisk, tight little smile. Before being recruited by Trinity, Jackie had been the national editor of a women's magazine that featured a nude male centerfold each month. So she spent a great deal of her time peering at schlongs, which is probably the one thing she and I have in common, although Jackie had been a willing viewer.

"Don't drink that crap," Amy shouts as I raise a beakerful of Trinifluid to my mouth. "It'll turn your kishkas to concrete. Don't you read the mail?"

"Amy," pounces Jackie, "Brynn is barely on board, so please modify your negativity at least until she's through orientation." She gleams at me sympathetically, condensing her smile for Amy. "How's that article on the Five Hundred Pound Miracle coming along?"

"On your desk."

"Bottoms up." Jackie salutes gaily as I gulped down the granular, sod-tasting Trinifluid, then turns her own neat little rump on us, striding away briskly.

"Modify my negativity," Amy mimics. "She's dying to fire me, but she can't. I sling this crap by the ream, nobody's better at it, and that's why they put up with me. Of course they'll can me the minute they find someone who can pile it higher and deeper."

"Jackie *is* the boss, Amy. She has to pay lip service to Trinity, for God's sake."

"Don't mention God and Trinity in the same breath. You have to look in the other direction, you want an explanation for this Dietary Disneyland. Check this out." Amy waves a four-color glossy magazine called *Trinitalk* in front of me. Its pages are packed with first-person testimonials to miraculous and everlasting weight loss against all odds, interspersed with inspirational homilies and snippets of wisdom — all in the style the public has come to associate with the Trinity Diet: a breathless, orgiastic spirituality. She turns back to her computer. "Men," she mutters vaguely, off on some tangent.

Doubtless, she is thinking of my fate. Although I have been at this job only two weeks, everybody knows that my husband recently dumped me for a younger woman. I radiate marital failure the way Renaissance madonnas radiate holiness; my head is surrounded by a glowing nimbus of rejection. I am the personification of everybody's abandonment and betrayal fears, practically an urban legend. I attract pity, familiarity, and overwhelming curiosity, the office Mercy Date. People promise to find me a "nice guy," revealing that they find me about as desirable as a tepid brussels sprout.

Even as my co-workers cluck sympathetically. I know they are also watching for The Real Reason He Left: To see me suddenly, on some trivial provocation, forsake my slightly downcast veneer and metamorphose into a snarling she-demon spitting invective over a missing paper clip. Perhaps if they study me closely enough they can inoculate themselves against my fate.

And of course they are watching with soap-opera prurience to see in which direction my shattered life will now wend (down, of course, but how far?): Will I lose my mind, age visibly, or, most likely, open up at last and subject them all to bitter and boring recountings of his every lost sock, missed dentist pickup, bad spectator sports behavior?

My predicament actually seems to be an ice-breaker, like the cast I wore one summer in high school: Not so bizarre or tragic (in fact, a little comical) that it could not be mentioned; rather encouraging of commiseration. Just as strangers spontaneously shared their own broken leg stories that summer, I have become at Trinity a repository for the shattered love lives and abandonment fears of chance restroom acquaintances. I cannot pass a single day without hearing of some romantic perfidy.

The telephone on my desk rings. "We're together in Trinity, how can I help you?" I answer, as instructed. If possible, I am to handle things on the spot and to pass on the call only if the matter is particularly knotty. Most of the calls come from Triniteers, the national sales force/owners in the field. The Triniteers are mostly concerned about the negative press the Diet has been provoking recently — television exposes, newspaper warnings and other revenue-reducing obstructions.

The Diet is currently locked in a life-or-death struggle with the medical establishment, which is uniting to convince the public that the Trinity Diet will make them sick, poor, and/or dead. We in Public Relations, of course, insist to the contrary that Trinity will make them slender, wealthy, and immortal. And, of course, the Diet has hired its own medical advocates, of varying degrees of legitimacy.

After handling each call, I am to compose a follow-up letter thanking the Triniteer for phoning in, reassuring him or her as to the safety of the Diet, adding as much of an inspirational message as I can dredge up from my own joyless perspective.

Since its founding less than two years ago, the Trinity Diet has risen meteorically to national prominence, covering the country like a locust invasion. The Diet, as it is now simply known, is being called a major sociological revolution. Civilization has awakened from its solid-centric nutritional viewpoint to the blazing revelation of TriniFluid nourishment.

At this moment, nearly everybody in the world seems to be talking and/or selling the Trinity Diet. Whole communities, church congregations, corporations have gone on the Diet, as well as political leaders, sports teams, columnists and celebrities. It is even rumored that residents of the White House are taking Trinity. Hollywood parties feature Oscar-winning movie stars, a little crocked, chorusing off-key the Trinity song. A Trinity version of a popular luxury car is being planned by a European automaker. featuring the Trinity logo, a stylized triangle, as the hood ornament.

It is difficult to calculate the exact number of Templars and Triniteers, because the company has been expanding with the urgency of the Big Bang. Here on the Monterey Peninsula, Trinity has taken over building after building, all linked by Trinitaxis and by a computer network whose power and complexity rivals that of the Pentagon. Yuppie Templars flood the local fern bars after work. A characteristic ruddy sleekness and semi-reverent TriniSpeak have become de rigeur.

Predictably, everything at Trinity is based on the number three. The Diet itself consists of three hundred calories per day. It is consumed in three meals. The location of the Diet's manufacture is a closely guarded secret. I have heard that it is actually concocted in underground silos in a remote, formerly atomic laboratory in the New Mexican desert.

The three members of the founding Arp family are Theodosia, Garth, and their son Theodore. Theodosia Arp is a former beauty queen, a woman of pitch black tumescent hairdo and legendary bustline, whose exact age is only slightly less of a secret than the Strategic Air Command attack code. Her husband, Garth Arp, said to be a reclusive genius who developed the Diet following a revelation during a fast in the desert, is rumored alternately to be terminally ill, absconded with billions, or nonexistent.

The son, Theodore, appears to be in his mid-thirties. He is a smoothly handsome, mustached man with his mother's black, bouffant hair, meticulously barbered. Theodore exudes sincerity and modesty leavened with a certain amused detachment that women find irresistible and which actually heightens his credibility.

Theodore lives surrounded by the kind of messianic adoration that can only attend one who promises what even the major religions of the world dare not: permanent weight loss. He is a masterful and tireless public speaker, appearing on talk shows, attending publicity rallies, cutting ribbons, emerging from limousines. His form, his head seems to appear magically on the print when important news photos are developed — those taken at Summits, key congressional votes, even when the President tours natural disasters, there is Theodore in the act of writing out a check or cradling an infant. His inseparable assistant is a dapper sycophant, also elaborately coiffed, rumored to have been a massage therapist in former incarnation. Together, they run the Trinity Crusade.

But the TriniDoctrine lets it be known, change isn't easy. After all, didn't we sit around for years developing food, marital, health, economic, and attitudinal disorders, culminating in a severely unbalanced metabolic/spiritual existence? After searching vainly for meaning at the altar of the hot fudge sundae, or within the superficially hot and juicy but spiritually desiccated fast food burger, we had finally hit rock bottom. So deep was our malaise that something as drastic, as all encompassing as the Trinity Diet was needed to rescue our species.

Garth Arp's cosmic vision of mankind reaching its full potential through Trinity is summarized in a pamphlet called the TriniFesto, a new world order based on the tenets of the Trinity Crusade. Only Garth could have realized in a moment of divine inspiration that overweight and starvation were actually *one and the same thing!*

It is so elegant: The same Trinity Diet that cured legions of the obese suffering under masses of unwanted schmalz, could turn around and guarantee the nutritional integrity of those starving in Ethiopia. All, fat and thin alike, could now rest assured of nutritional perfection merely by taking Trinity three times daily. All the earth's billions would march arm in arm, with firm stride and fearless eye, into a rosy Trinity sunrise, imbibing their potions. Right now, there seems no limit to what the Trinity Diet could accomplish.

Trinity is much more than a mere diet. It is a plan for eternal life. Once people lose all the weight they need to and achieve the income they always dreamed of, they can embark on the Trinity Infinity Total Maintenance Program. This involves eating a "normal" diet supplemented by a huge line of Trinity Maintenance Foods called the Trinitaste line which even features such indulgences as Trinitruffles. All the while, of course, continuing to drink three or four times a day the Trinity Shake (Trinifluid) referred to simply as "Taking Trinity."

The powder comes in a vast range of flavors. It can be mixed with either milk or water, supplemented by wafers and even by "solids" as conventional food is condescendingly referred to (being on "solids" is considered a bit of a fall from grace by the legions of true believers.) An entire range of diet plans is available. The flexible, custom aspect of the Diet is considered its greatest strength. The "Trinitrim" program permits a slower rate of weight loss by allowing supplementation with one or more conventional foods.

Conversely, if one goes "Trinipure," one lives only on Trinifluid, an exalted and rather holy state. Every morning at 8 a.m. exactly, the entire headquarters work force Takes Trinity in a rather stirring, mass-like ritual. Thus, we are all assured that our nutritional requirements have been met, and also, that we have imbibed not only the spirit but the substance of Trinity.

Although employees are not actually required to Take Trinity, we are looked upon approvingly for doing so. When a Templar decides to go TriniPure, his or her workload might be lightened and some "comp" time considerably tacked onto the weekly work schedule. Whereas anyone who consistently refuses to Take Trinity earns a sort of benign managerial curiosity and perhaps a gently exploration of his or her attitude toward the Crusade. Employment policies are liberal here at

Trinity, benefits superior, with travel to other TriniTemples en-couraged, womb-to-tomb benefits, and free merit vacations to international hot spots as well as ample employee discounts from grateful local shops.

Every morning the Templars also receive an update on the number of pounds lost nationally on the Trinity Diet. This morning, I learn, the total stands at sixty-two million, eight hundred thirty-four thousand four pounds of American schmalz, vanished into thin air.

Since Trinity is a Way of Life for All of Life, Triniteers soon begin building their TriniTriangles. The Crusade itself is built from the ground up on what is called "people marketing." In order to become a Triniteer, the proselyte purchases a be-ginning TriniKit, which includes all sales materials, as well as a complete commercial supply of Trinity. Although this ini-tial investment can be heavy, the Triniteers, once they have achieved a critical mass of sales, are eligible to create their own distribution network. They then become TriKnights of the first, second, third, etc. degrees. A percentage of each novice's in-vestment goes immediately to the TriKnights of each superior degree, so as one ascends, one's income can increase hundreds-fold. They call it "making math work for you."

Only two words are forbidden at Trinity Temple. One is "starve." The other is "pyramid." (Amy tells me that some women have even ceased referring to their periods just to be on the safe side if they are overheard.) She also related to me that a stressed middle Templar, while chatting with Chief Templar Theodore about a recent Egyptian vacation, suddenly found no way out of mentioning the pyramids. After a desperate mental search, he quick-wittedly identified them as those Egyptian Triangles. Theodore, displaying the magnanimity that is his hallmark, merely chuckled and congratulated the anxious

Templar on his sensitivity but commented that he needn't go to extremes except in his pursuit of good health.

It has not taken me long to master the Trinity jargon. I can now dash off glib responses to the barrage of negative press about the curative and health properties of the Diet or its efficacy as a long-term solution to obesity. The other part of my job involves working with the staff of the medical department next door, to try to answer personally the letters that pour in from all over the country.

Most letters acknowledge that the user has indeed lost weight on 300 calories a day but has suffered, in addition, a few negligible and certainly transient side effects. It is up to me to reassure and encourage these Triniteers, and most importantly, to express the deep and personal concern felt by all Templars, from the receptionist up to Theodore himself, towards each and every Triniteer.

Dear Mrs. Foxworth, I write dutifully, Congratulations on Your Recent Weight Loss!!!!! Now in regards to the article in the *Des Moines Register*, let me assure you that the Trinity Diet is a food — not a drug. TriniPowder is composed of only the purest and most natural ingredients. Since nothing in the Diet can even remotely be labeled a drug, the FDA knows full well that it cannot legally ban or otherwise restrict the sale of the Trinity Diet. With the best of intentions, our friends in the FDA seem to be conspiring to keep America obese!

I was sorry to learn of your chronic [diarrhea, constipation, malaise, weakness, fatigue, missed heartbeats, nausea, trembling, dizziness, syncopal episode, feelings of disorientation or depersonalization.] Remember that drinking large amounts of water is essential to good health at all times, but especially when you are taking Trinity in any form. I strongly advise you to consult with your physician AS SOON AS POSSIBLE [emphasis mine], so that you may be reassured as to your increasing good health and control over your life.

Remember, we here at the Trinity Crusade care about you deeply. That is why we are urging you to visit your physician AS SOON AS POSSIBLE. You may be assured that our highest hopes and kindest thoughts are with you always. We enjoy hearing from you, so keep in touch with us. And please do remember to see your physician AS SOON AS POSSIBLE. I look forward to hearing from you soon. Yours in Trinity.

In fact, I am ideally suited to work for a diet scam. I was born for the job. My family is a wicked gang: the food criminals, the kitchen Cosa Nostra. Let others sin with guns, sex, drugs, numbers. Our contraband is food. Our crimes are of consumption, the punishment a life sentence of guilty gorging.

We didn't gorge on just food, either. We feasted on emotion too, until we were swollen with it. Eyes, bellies. We ate and cried and shouted at each other until we were ready to explode. And explode we did, all the time. We lived at ground zero. Oh, we were angry all right. But about what? What was the big deal?

My sister Francie banged her head on the floor until she passed out. My father took barbiturates until he passed out. I drank till I passed out. My mother never passed out: That was her problem. She had not slept a wink in fifteen years, spending countless lonely hours spent pacing like the ghost of Hamlet's father while the world snored away in blissful indifference.

In fact, neither of my parents ever actually *confessed* to sleeping. In my family, sleep was an index of aggravation deficit. We accused one another of sleeping. We vehemently denied the misdemeanor of sleeping with the righteous indignation of one of my husband Cliff's shoplifting defendants.

"Look at her, she slept like a rock while I ate my heart out all night from the curses she used on me (one goddammit)." The primordial gneiss of Greenland that has been sleeping since the earth cooled could not have slept more soundly than I supposedly did after a rousing night of disrespect and ingratitude. For a daughter such as I the suffering of a mother was a soothing soporific, better than Nembutal.

And despite the fact that we were always too aggravated to eat, we ate like horses. We were constantly on diets, always cutting down, and always eating more than ever. We ate the most of any starving family on this planet. My family's name for chocolate-covered peanuts was opium. We conducted a huge, illicit traffic in it. Opium wars were fought. Oaths were sworn.

Food was not just a substance, meals no mere social ceremony. Food was magic; mealtime was a mythical, poorly understood ritual. Our fearful reverence for the power of food approached that of the ancient Aztecs for Quetzalcoatl. Insatiable, inconsolable, we were always waiting for the Answer, the Diet, the Cure. Always turning over new leaves, reaching new epiphanies, making new vows. Tomorrow was another day to begin the diet that never ended.

And never worked. Nobody tracked the battle against overweight more closely than my family. Food was consumed not by choice but by demonic possession. Our mantra was "nobody forced you to stuff yourself". But something did: the Helping Demon. The God of Gorge. For a Jewish family, we invoked Jesus a lot too: "Jesus Christ, why did I eat so much?" "Jesus Christ, take it away already. No, wait! What are you doing?"

But in fact when it came to food we were as pagan as Druids or Saxons. Or early Greeks: a whole gallery of deities presided over our eating Iliad. And, like Homer, we memorialized the past with mythic sagas to its glory. A truly great meal was immortal, never forgotten. My family had a poultry archive, a spoken history of great chicken dinners. Not to mention a steak archive, and stuffed cabbage, chopped liver, and kugel archives.

"That chicken you made back in March," my father would suddenly rhapsodize from in front of the TV and a restaurant scene had reminded him of chicken past. At the mention of chicken, we were all ears. We knew instantly which chicken he was referring to. We would probably never find out who had committed the murder.

"The chicken this last March? So so." My mother sat up straight. Fran and I held our breaths: a chicken tournament was in the offing.

"Not last March," my father corrected impatiently. "March of 1962."

"Ohhhh, that chicken. That was some chicken, I have to admit."

"The best."

"What are you talking about the best? What about the chicken I made in June (of '63)? That wasn't great chicken?"

"That was the best paprika chicken. The best chicken of all time was March 1962 and that's final." This sparring might continue all night, fueled with handfuls of opium.

Compulsive eaters, we were proportionately spartan and disciplined on one another's behalf. We pushed carrots, the miracle cure for overweight as well as a host of other afflictions. Nervous? Eat a carrot rather than taking a pill. You'll live longer. Craving opium (contemplating aberrant sex, bank robbery, or a career of terrorism)? Eat a carrot. A carrot is the perfect answer to whatever ails you.

"When you come home from school, eat a carrot," suggested my mother helpfully to two starving young lionesses who could have hunted down a wildebeest and devoured it still twitching. She might as well have suggested we eat a rock. To the best of my recollection nobody in my family ever ate a raw carrot.

In my parents' bedroom was secreted a pound of opium. One day after school Francie and I broke in and ate ourselves silly. My parents could not have been more devastated if we had knocked over a Seven Eleven.

"Why oh why why why," mourned my father, tearing his hair. "My own daughters come to my room and steal." But my mother, the peacemaker, produced a huge Hershey bar that she had been hoarding in case of just such an emergency. We were forgiven, the family endured.

The worst, the most unspeakable, heinous and unforgivable crime in my family was to make somebody lose their appetite. Food refusal was the doomsday machine, the atom bomb of family weapons. To blow up a meal was an act of staggering consequences. (Of course non-eating was a double-edged sword. If you declared appetite loss then went ahead and ate anyway you lost credibility forever.)

"I'm too upset to eat," my mother the queen of renunciation would declare, rising regally from a dinnertime tiff. "Your language made me lose my appetite. Go away," as Fran and I hovered guiltily, "my stomach is churning." When I was younger I imagined her stomach as the interior of a volcano, an angry, crimson cauldron boiling with molten maternal secretions brewed up by disrespectful daughters.

"Aw mom, you can so eat."

"C'mon Bernice, have a bite at least or you'll get sick."

"I'm too upset. Maybe later." This was cute. We knew that "later" meant never, ever again, as long as she lived, would she take nourishment, thanks to me, usually. She would be fed intravenously in front of the whole horrified neighborhood until she eventually starved from the aggravation I had inflicted upon her.

"I can't eat either," I parried, clutching my own stomach. This earned only contempt. Go ahead and stuff myself because it was already too late for my mother.

Once my husband Cliff arrived on the scene these little dramas lost some of their impact: Unperturbed, he refused to play along, zeroing in on our lunacy like a U-2 camera.

"You Wolfs are the angriest people I know. That's why you eat like that. If you ever explode, all that pent-up rage will destroy the solar system. You're always getting carted off to the emergency room (true) with stomach pains and shortness of breath and headaches. You get tested for brain tumors. But it's really garden variety rage. You never say what the real problem is. You stuff your faces instead."

Cliff was certainly an authority on rage, garden variety and otherwise. It was only his response to it that differed.

"Cliff dear," said my mother, logic itself, "did you have to call the waiter that name? "

"He's Chinese. He doesn't know what schmendrick means."

"But it was your tone of voice, Cliff." (Zeus enraged).

"I thought he brought you cold food for the third time."

"Ahhhh, we should have just paid the bill and left." My father, a former Air Corps pilot, had courted death throughout the Pacific for years through blizzards of flak but couldn't summon up the nerve to complain. When he opened his own bomb bay, all that ever dropped out was an apology.

"That's what I mean, that's the attitude that got you all killed." Cliff was unable to understand why the Jews of Europe had not died fighting. He, who was capable of dying fighting over his place in a theater line.

But the truth was that no earthly heat source could ever have gotten restaurant food hot enough for my mother. She invariably sent everything back, two, three, even four times. A fragrant dish of bubbling lava would have been pronounced "so-so." Soup cooked on the sun's surface would have grown "ice cold" on its way to our table. The moment her plate was set down, she would reach out and touch the food before her with the flat of her hand, as if feeling for a pulse. The rest followed like responses for a catechism.

"Ice cold."

"So send it back."

"I can't eat this. God knows how long it's been sitting there."

"It's not even safe. We'll all get sick. Send it back."

"I don't even want it any more."

"What are restaurants coming to, you can't get a hot meal any more."

"Remember when you got served and the steam used to rise right up off the plate?"

"I don't see any steam here."

"Brynn, do you see steam?"

"No, mom."

"When this food was cooked, man still walked on all fours." Meanwhile I writhed under the curious glances of our immediate neighbors. And at some point our waiter would be struck blind and deaf, leaving us looking around in all directions like a family of meerkats while the offending food sat untouched on my mother's plate.

In my mind it was already beginning to teem with visible microbial life like a time-lapse study of a petri dish. Or perhaps it would actually rear up pulsating from its plate like The Blob to envelop us: "Family Devoured by Ice Cold Meal." Dateline,

Santa Monica, California. A family in search of a hot meal now joins the ranks of other doomed visionaries who tried to defy the odds but failed in their quest — heroes such as Scott and Earhart. Within sight of their goal, the family fell stricken under the fierce and unexpected onslaught of a massive serving of frigid food.

"Waiter, this food is ice cold."

"I'm sorry. I'll take it back."

"And take all these others back too. They're cold too."

"Mine's okay," I ventured once, perfidiously. I was hungry. The breach thus cleft between me and my family has never fully healed.

Summertime. Three years old, I saunter from the back door of the Elmo Park Apartments, Hopkins, Minnesota, skinny in suspendered blue corduroy pants, swinging my arms vampily from the shoulder. My water-slicked hair is caught just above the right ear by a tortoiseshell barrette, destined to serve for another sixteen years before being lost at a UCLA fraternity party.

Suddenly, I stop short. Looming before me in the driveway is my father's new Buick Roadmaster, massively at rest on four tumescent whitewalls. The car has the benign, streamlined ponderousness of a Disney whale, and with its cetacean grille, chrome baleen, it looks as if it could literally suck up the road. Four incredible tunnels in its side, leading to God-knew-where, are its pedigree.

The neighbors have flooded out to gawk, as impressed as if my father had taxied up in the very B-24 Liberator he had flown over Saipan. The women, pregnant in cotton house-dresses, with bright scarves wound around their pincurls, approach timidly and stroke the monster's greenish flanks. The men, beer bottles in hand, wear pleated pants into which white undershirts are tucked. They stride up and spank the Buick commandingly, nod at the engine statistics, call it "she."

All turn with tolerant amusement to savor my response. I am gaping at the intruder, eyes smoky with suspicion. Attempts to pull me near for an introduction fail. To everyone's delight, my confusion soon resolves itself at last into a drawn-out wail. Later that afternoon, having been coaxed into the car, I slam the right rear door on my thumb, understanding once and for all the concept of solid construction. Within a week, the nail will turn black and fall off, enshrining me as a nursery school celebrity, initiating a lifelong craving for the limelight.

Outside the back door now, I gaze into the kitchen, where my father is sitting with an old Army Air Corps buddy, his former bombardier, at a green formica dinette. They are laughing with their mouths full, celebrating new cars, peace, youth. It is twilight, the air fragrant with the warm raspberries that grow wild behind the project, and also with the fetid odor of the swamp beyond that is not to be drained until a toddler has drowned in it later that summer.

The screen before me sags in its frame from the battering of my countless entrances and exits. A swarm of insects besiege its shaky ramparts. Their brethren have struck up a summertime concert out beyond the Buick, which looms darkly, poised on its concrete slab like some brooding god of highway thunder.

The bombardier's ruddy young face shines with perspiration under the single kitchen bulb; his eyes are flirtatious and blue, his teeth flashing in the arc described by his nodding head.

My mother's face glows. Her own approach is level and steady as she lands dish after steaming dish on the crowded table. She calls and bibs me, then settles herself in a flushed tempest of curly auburn hair, tanned arms and cleavage. At last, she reaches into a bowl, withdrawing modestly the neck of the chicken. Daintily she begins to peck away at it, giggling between bites, lashes fluttering.

I sit transfixed: How perfect the size and shape of it; and oh, the little brown shards of flesh that pull away so thin and savory. The warm, dripping curve lies across Mama's cheeks, leaving a trail of pale gravy which she pats away primly with a pink napkin. Possessed by envy such as I had never known, I nearly fling myself into my mother's lap to grab the neck away. The three adults stop eating and gaze in mild wonder.

Night School

The Monterey Naval Postgraduate School is located on the grounds of the elegant old Del Monte Hotel, purchased by the Navy and converted into a defense university for cold warriors. Once a gracious, charmingly decadent watering hole for industrialist gentry and depression-era glitterati, the place is now home to serious, linear young engineers in uniforms or Mormonish civvies, earning degrees in clandestine one-upsmanship.

The Navy also rotates pilots and navigators through here for six-week "Aviation Safety" courses, and these regular influxes are like some kind of grunion run for women. With luck, I am told, one can meet an officer and conduct a thrilling, if abbreviated, love affair, replete from eye contact, infatuation, and seduction, through grande passion, jealous tailspin and pregnancy scare, all the way to gut-wrenching cinematic farewell—and still have a few days left to mope around before the next class cruises in. Some of the men are married; some even cop to it. Sometimes you want to know; more times you don't.

Actually, this scenario appeals irresistibly. After eight years with Cliff, the madman attorney, I am thoroughly disillusioned with the perennial fencing match known as marriage, with its tortured metaphors of commitment: There is the path-lab model: Are we benign or malignant, operable or terminal? The meteorological model: Is our weather rough or smooth? Are we Westerlies (calm, warm, moisture-laden), or Easterlies (fierce, stormy, blizzard-bearing). Or the mechanical contraption analogue: Is this working, ticking right along? Or are we breaking down, clashing gears, wearing out? For tonight, the hell with all that. Just give me a chance to dance, laugh, and forget. Let one midnight slide by unnoticed; let one morning bring a tasty wince of remorse.

Emily and I leave work and hang around downtown Monterey to strategize. When you are single, Friday night holds a significance far beyond its mere ordinal position at the end of the work week. Friday night is potentially a conduit to the parallel universe of couples that we, veterans of bitter outcomes, nevertheless crave to enter.

The rapidly darkening street holds a magical portent. Monterey's omnipresent fog has cleared to make way for an impressive brass-and-coral sunset, fading now into pale salmons and magentas, the eastern sky deepening to starry blue. Out toward Seaside and Del Rey Oaks, lights emerge, scattered around the curving black void of the Bay like a broken necklace. I feel the familiar ache that this place engenders, deeper than the pain of my present circumstances; a yearning for those beautiful, ineffable possibilities, receding like the tide as I watch impotently from shore.

Like Druids at the sacred hour, we daub our faces with shadow and paint in the ladies room of the Doubletree. I pencil the corners of my eyes hopefully upwards, powder their lids mauve. Seated amongst potted palms and golf-shirted tourists in the lobby, we counsel seriously; the wrong decision here can result in a hopeless night of lukewarm drinks and idle chitchat. We consider our alternatives: We could head for Carmel and hang out at handsome fascist Clint Eastwood's Hog's Breath Inn, trying to mine romance from its boar-bedecked caverns full of boozy regulars and frat-rat golf caddies. We could drive to Pebble Beach and invade the Lodge, trying to chat up the millionaires and far more numerous poseurs. We could head for the bars of Big Sur and watch the hairy locals guzzle cheap liquor and deal dope. But in the end, we decide to navigate the turbulent but bountiful waters of the Naval Postgraduate School.

At the last moment, I balk: it is too soon after Cliff's departure. My fractured ego certainly doesn't need analytical gazes, especially from a roomful of swaggering flyboys.

"Cheer up." Emily dismisses my hesitation. "The worst has already happened — your husband ran off with a Jazzercise instructor. After getting dumped like that any other rejection is going to be child's play. Besides, in the Trident Room, a newly single woman gets more attention than an abandoned zebra foal on the Serengeti."

Emily is our departmental receptionist at the diet scam I work for. And despite the fact that we are nothing alike, we have a lot in common. Emily is plump, linear, and miserably displaced from Los Angeles, while I am tall, thin, neurotic, and miserably displaced from Los Angeles. Both of our husbands have had affairs and left us, defying the hopeful fallacy that most extramarital affairs leave the marriage intact if wobbly, sort of like a harpooned whale that escapes.

Emily and I both have brown hair and eyes, and three-year olds; hers a boy and mine a girl. Our lives have take similar paths in terms of betrayal. Emily's estranged husband Ted (nicknamed Boomer) is a Marine pilot who had traveled here from Miramar in San Diego. By the time Emily arrived with their son and some household furnishings, Boomer was already having an affair with one of the many pilot groupies who infest the officer's club and whose ranks we ourselves are now about to join. This almost instantaneous metamorphosis from cast-off wife to dangerous predator buoys my spirits somehow. Cliff's own girlfriend Lisa was a cop's wife; when the cop began an affair with Cliff's secretary, it freed up Lisa to go after Cliff himself and converted me from slightly smug but vulnerable insider to invidious sex shark.

Emily and I have handled our divorces differently. Never the type to let the dust settle, she immediately retained a lawyer she nicknamed Cujo and sued the living bejesus out of Boomer. Although at this time he is still living in the Bachelor Officers Quarters, his affair is rapidly losing momentum. His air speed is slackening and he is heading into a dive. He is making overtures about bailing out of his adulterous relationship and parachuting to a bumpy landing in Emily's vengeful clutches.

Meanwhile my own husband Cliff is settling in comfortably with his Jazzercise instructor, secure in the knowledge that I am too numb and self-blaming even to consult a lawyer. Emily exhorts me constantly to go on the offensive. Cliff's very name provokes a murderous primal reaction in her.

"Brynn," she scolds from the front seat as if talking to a toddler, "You are letting Cliff and this muscular bimbo just walk away with everything you worked for, including custody of your daughter."

"You don't understand." What she did not understand was my former drinking problem, the custody torpedo which I was concealing for obvious reasons.

"What's to understand? You're getting screwed and you're trying to figure out some way to blame yourself for it." She air-throttles my neck.

"I wish I had a more dramatic name," Emily says seconds later. "Emily sounds so… pale blue. So high-necklined."

"What would you rather be named?"

"Don't laugh, okay? I'm just speaking phonetically. Purely for the *sound.*"

"Gotcha"

"Okay. Diarrhea. Or the other name I like is Cholera."

"You want to be named Diarrhea or Cholera."

"Or something with melody. Tell me those names aren't romantic."

"Emily, I just want you to know, even if you become rich and famous someday, I won't blackmail you with this."

"Thanks, Brynn. I mean, I was just saying."

"Really, thank you. It's reassuring to know that you are definitely crazier than I am."

"Don't put money on it. The night is just beginning."

The Navy School is off Del Monte Avenue. I cut my car lights as instructed and approach the guard kiosk. A squat, middle-aged security guard peers in at us.

"Good evening, ladies. Are you meeting somebody here? he asks with faux sternness. "You need an escort to get on post."

"Yesss," I stammer guiltily, feeling as if I am concealing a terrorist bomb in my purse instead of three Trojans and enough makeup to provision a beauty pageant.

"And who might that be?"

"Captain Linus Pauling," answers Emily sweetly, leaning across me and batting her cleavage at him. Impressed, the guard nods and even salutes us through, touching his hat. I switch on my car lights, suddenly savoring this whole cocka-mamie ritual. I am now a hunting woman, the Diana of the Disco. Why then do I feel as if I am selling the U.S. Navy a bill of goods? It isn't my fault I'm in this situation, I tell myself. I didn't leave Cliff; he left me.

I follow a ribbon of asphalt uncertainly as it weaves among dark, mute buildings and curving velvet lawns draped in shadow. The moon flirts down from among the clouds and treetops as I move past arrow signs pointing to cryptic locations whose names are letters and numbers.

Nostalgia permeates this place. Once the playground of Depression-era glitterati, of Cary Grant and Tallulah Bankhead, the old hotel is now home to serious, linear young engineers in Mormonish civvies and uniforms. The sad, faint ghosts of lives briefly past still lingers palpably in the corners and the shadows. I sense traces of the linen and damask, their Dusenbergs, highballs and croquet, their wisecracks and losses.

I park in a dark lot. The Bachelor Officers Quarters looms before us, five stories high. Emily gets out and glares at a remote window on the fifth story as if calculating the trajectory of a grenade.

"That's where they live. He swears he kicked her out, but I don't believe him." Impressed, I study the dark, patch of a window, the repository of such guilt, lust and sin. It looks nondescript enough.

Feet crunching on the gravel, we find the double doors leading into the main building that houses the officer's club, the Trident Room. Emily knows exactly where she is going while I, on tiptoe, glance around doubtfully, a little worried at her firm, knowing stride.

We pass through several sets of these deep mahogany double doors and down a long, white-painted hallway with color photographs of fighter planes on the walls, flying high above anonymous cities, the empire of the air. Filipino and Mexican kitchen staff gawk at us as we saunter along, trying to look sexy and confident.

The building maintains several banquet rooms. Retired Navy brass and their stolid survivor wives are just finishing up their prime rib among wall hangings and portraits of Naval heroes. They sneak a glance as we camp followers trot past, an ancient idiom. Feeling disreputable, I make tentative eye contact with one or two of the wives. I was once as you were, I try to communicate.

It seems we are early. The mantanned disco deejay, hair sweating Vitalis, is fiddling with knobs on a machine that projects green and purple bubbles onto the walls and ceiling. Men sit around by the tableful, scouting the action. Few women are visible, a fortuitous development. The men have the clean features, short, shiny hair, and bright, analytical eyes of young officers. They eye us openly, emboldened by the beer they have been consuming since five o'clock Happy Hour.

We seat ourselves with insouciant efficiency, checking our chairs for spilled beer, wiping the table prissily with a cocktail napkin. Here, I am a queen of sorts, proudly wearing my gloss of disreputability. Back home, everybody knows about Cliff. I am a neutered object of pity: my best was a bore.

Suddenly, I am assailed with self-consciousness. The humiliation time machine ratchets me back through the years. Once again I am thirteen years old and nearly six feet tall, with the kind of thin face and large eyes that are better suited to gazing out from behind barbed wire, hands extended.

Here, in physical education class of William Tecumseh Sherman Junior High in Minneapolis, we are about to begin the dreaded co-ed ballroom dancing segment.

Today's lesson is the Polka. The students have paired off, the popular kids already holding hands in anticipation, while the less socially adept, who have been foisted on one another, stand dumbly side by side. But I am not even eligible for this clumsy coterie.

I am the tallest girl,. And though I assure God that I would sincerely prefer leukemia, I have nevertheless been tapped to demonstrate the polka with Mr. Ford, the boys' coach, a muscular little knob of a man whose bald head bobs at the level of my Littlest Angel cupless bra.

The music begins, a scratchy, rousing version of *Roll Out the Barrel*. After a few tentative missteps, which inspire a widespread snickering, Mr. Ford and I surprisingly achieve a mutual rhythm. Though I am mildly discomfited by the vague awareness of a new equation here (what other rhythms will become possible with men?) I begin to feel more confident. Mr. Ford too, is emboldened by our initial harmony. As our confidence increases, so does our panache: He dares to execute a few modest dips and flourishes, which I follow.

By unspoken agreement, we begin to gather speed and — ominously — centrifugal momentum, pushing the edge of the envelope. We lift our legs higher, he skips me once aloft. A blur of faces turns to follow our progress around the floor. Mr. Ford's hairy arms grip my waist tightly as we slip the surly bonds of earth. Although he resembles Mr. Clean, I am beginning to have the kind of fun kids have on an amusement park ride.

Suddenly, unexpectedly, we lose synchronicity, a minute medullar miscalculation. Our legs entwine. Like an egg beater that has hit a walnut chip, we come to an abrupt, unexpected stop. And down we go, our energy diverted from vertical to horizontal but hardly diminished. Prisoner's of Newton's Second Law, Mr. Ford and I roll across the floor, ancient Celtic behemoths locked in a cosmic tumble; a mastodon and a sabre tooth in mortal combat, bearing one another toward the tarpit, first he on top, now I, now he again. From the corner of my eye, I notice Alan Perchik, the obsessive crush who inhabits all of my clumsy, bodice ripper-driven fantasies, doubled over with laughter, gripping his crotch…

Two young officers finally detach themselves and meander casually to our table. "Smoker" is a Marine, an F-4 pilot. "Skeeto" flies an F-14 Tomcat. Their 'tags' conceal two all-American names, Bill and Tom. Emily's eyes meet mine briefly and triumphantly above her daiquiri. Smoker is from Atlanta, Skeeto from one of the Carolinas. Both have Rhett Butler grins that look as if they had been practiced a lot, contrasting with a shy, almost courtly propriety. They insist on calling us ma'am until we tell them our names. A paradoxical, irresistible essence of risk-taking and rule-following emanate from them.

Bill seems to find me as exotic as a Melanesian maiden. He is a southerner who had hardly left his home town until he joined the Navy. He is both confounded and fascinated by California. He can't believe I actually attended the notorious Berkeley. When I remind him that scores of thousands of other students did the same, he ponders this with wonder, as though I had insisted that other earthlings had accompanied me through alien abduction. For my part I can't believe he really lands a jet on aircraft carriers. We agree that we certainly, really, have virtually nothing in common. This gives us something to agree on, so we don't have to get into all those little maters we doubtless disagree on, such as gender, abortion, genetics, politics, sociology, anthropology, child-rearing, education, economics, religion, power….

Something is working well here. We manage to chatter incessantly about nothing, shouting this drivel above the music. He is twenty-six, graduated from the University of Georgia, joined the Navy, got jets. I was married to a lawyer, I shrill. My three-year-old daughter is with her father tonight I mention offhandedly, (and for the rest of her childhood too, if he has his way, is what I omit). Bill and I start to laugh at something stupid and, significantly, cannot stop.

"Would you like a tour of the place?" He finally asks, a connoisseur of old hotels having been here a whole twenty-four hours. He promises to show me the favorite window seat of Orson Welles and Rita Hayworth. I cannot wait to see it, I tell him, aficionado of Orson Welles that I am.

Sneaking around the main building, I again feel like a teenager, the important difference being I now have tits instead of toilet paper in my bra. This is my chance to be the Bad Girl Who Made Out.

The corners are pitch dark, and we find a chair outside the chapel, obviously placed there for pre-worship petting. Predictably, the takeoff is a success; the chair beneath us bucks and tosses like an aircraft carrier on a choppy sea. This will not do, of course. We could fall, he insists with a straight face, who thinks nothing of barrel-rolling forty thousand pounds of fuel-bloated hot steel at a height of six miles. Somebody could get hurt. We stagger outside wrapped around each other, toward the Bachelor Officers Quarters, stopping every few feet to maul each other's mouths and grope until our knees turn to licorice and we stagger and fall on our knees and stretch out full-length. The tailored, curving lawn is soaking with dew under the moonlight. Bill's body is hard and lean, a confection after months of chilly starvation, intellectualizing in my shrink's office, writing journal entries about sinking into morasses, weighted by the inertia of depression.

Up in his room, we fuck for hours, babble and doze, watch the lights of downtown Monterey from our window, as Greer Garson might once have. He plays me his favorite music, tells me how, the first time he soloed, he got lost in trackless space and time. I tattle to him about Cliff, his trials, defendants, plea bargains.

"But what about you? What do you do?"

"I work for a diet scam, I mumble, embarrassed for the first time all night. Confessing this makes me feel even nakeder. "Trinity."

"That pyramid scheme?" I wince, fearing he will now eject me from his cockpit-bed. Instead, he laughs, "My aunt is getting rich selling that stuff." I laugh too. It feels good to laugh about the Diet.

"Well tell her to get out of it because the pyramid is about to implode."

"I will."

"Don't tell her my name, though."

"Okay. What is your name?"

"Don't you know?"

"Brynn, Brynn Brynn..." and suddenly he is asleep. I am alone beside him. Far away, somewhere beyond the moon, lies Santa Cruz, my home. The town seems part of somebody else's life.

Like a sleepwalker, I leave the bed and wander the deserted halls, which after dark abandon their artificial military starkness and reclaim their coved ceilings and ornate balustrades. In the large common bathroom, lined with mirrors, I wash my face and do the best I can with my crushed and matted hair, still damp. It is nearly two a.m. and the party below is ending. All around, I hear men's and women's voices trundling upstairs or dopplering down the hall. I wonder how anybody ever gets any sleep here.

Downstairs, the officer's club has transformed itself into a bacchanalia. Music blasts. Women of all colors, shapes, and ages are everywhere. The floor is awash with beer, and pilots are lined up, jostling and pushing, for what they call "carrier land-ings." These consist of a mad dash across the room at full speed to careen, belly-flat, onto a series of pushed-together tables. Although they resemble otters at play, the men are treating this activity with the utmost seriousness, discussing angles of approach and critiquing one another's performances.

I discover Emily at a table of young officers. She is sitting in the lap of one. At the sight of me, she sighs with relief and rises unsteadily.

"Okay, boys, we're out of here." There is a chorus of con-tradiction and disappointment. which suddenly stops when a tall man materializes beside the table: Boomer.

"What the hell do you think you're doing?" He too is quite drunk, and the other men rise and close ranks, ready to grab him.

Emily retorts, "isn't your little friend Debbie getting lonely up in your room? Hadn't you better get back and cheer her up?"

"She's not in my room. I told you I broke it off."

"Sure you did." Boomer takes Emily's arm, which she yanks away. "Don't think you can just reel me back in. Just snap your fingers," she tries to snap her fingers in his face but loses her balance, slips in the beer, and stumbles against him.

"You ought to be home with Eric. You aren't doing any of us any good by coming here, hanging out like a..." his eyes rest on me.

"Don't you tell me what I ought to be doing," Emily shouts. "You picked up that little whore and left me and Eric to..." She becomes incoherent. The men move off clustering uncomfort-ably at the bar. I have already given my phone number and he has promised to call me tomorrow. If he does, I can look forward to my very first Naval affair. If not — I look around — there are many possibilities here.

Emily looks up, face tear-stained "Can you get home okay?"

"Of course. Are you all right?" She shakes her head.

"The big jerk says he's quitting the Navy. He can't do that. All he knows how to do is fly." She actually sobs boo-hoo, blub blub. In sad movies, Emily wails so loudly that the audience turns to crane and peer.

As I leave, I spot them walking unsteadily toward the BOQ, arms around each other. I feel suddenly as if I am stranded on an island. The fog, as if to remedy its earlier negligence, has traveled in swiftly, cloaking the ground in moving misty rags. Under a white sky, I twirl and caper on the empty lawn. I greet the ghosts, strolling amid the faultlessly gardened grounds, and now they are welcoming, inclusive. Somehow, I have joined them.

A Suitable Poison

It wasn't her I noticed, that first time; it was the car. Shockingly red, it flashed in the corner of my eye like a spurt of blood as it pulled into the parking lot outside my office. A Porsche.

Almost before it had spun to a stop, the driver's side door flew open and legs emerged: long, slender, tanned. Naked.

Oh hell, I thought. My rigid posture and jealous, tracking stare must have alerted my office mate, Brian the proofreader, because he got up from his desk and came around to look out my window, leaning against me as if I were a wall.

"Oh, it's just Alexis," he said, feigning indifference, but his voice was raspy, as if his mouth had dried. The skirt of her gleaming white tennis dress lifted in a sudden gust of wind, and a slender arm swept aside a mane of varicolored blonde hair, revealing a straight nose, full lips barely parted and gleaming teeth.

"That's a 'just'?" I was trying for detached.

"Ted's daughter. Age 22. Stanford, Pebble Beach, dressage, the whole enchilada. She works here every summer."

"Aren't we lucky. What does she do?"

He shrugged. "Whatever she wants to, I guess. Ted is a doting father."

"As are many tyrants."

I watched Alexis glide down the petunia-lined entranceway with an odd and queasy sense of audience, a suspicion that the movie running was not the one I had bought a ticket for. When she passed my window, our eyes met briefly—mine brown, sunken and smudged beneath after a night out from which I had barely returned in time for work; hers as blue and white as the Carmel winter sky. A shy smile wavered on her rosy lips, crashed against my stolid gawk, and fled.

Her father, our boss was Ted Braddock, a self-made millionaire turned publisher, a choleric perfectionist who dominated our waking and sleeping hours, which he insisted were essentially the same state. Ted was convinced that his dream of creating a global publishing empire had foundered on the incompetence and laziness of his staff. His monthly magazine, The Business Express, advertised itself as "a finger on the pulse of commerce." It was actually a boilerroom hell whose employee turnover nearly matched its subscriber base.

To me, the reason for Ted's ire was simple: He was living in modern-day California when he really belonged in 14th century Florence, where he could have indulged his whims and rages through war, vendetta and artistic excess. His wife, Lillian (nicknamed Librium) worked part time, staggering under some massive title like Executive Vice President of Operations. She had the bland coloring of a creature whose defense is camouflage. Somehow, her nondescript features had tamed Ted's blazing blue eyes and powerful bones to produce the balanced elegance of Alexis.

"What am I running here, a remedial class for Neanderthals?" It was our weekly editorial staff meeting. Ted hurled the galleys onto the table, and we drew back snarling, a tribe of paleolithic untermenschen, skulking, deceitful, brutal and dull. As usual, the magazine was behind schedule; Ted was simply impossible to satisfy. Articles were written and rewritten until words become only symbols in an arcane code that must be sequenced flawlessly in order to unlock the secret of his approval. After a few weeks, I began to doubt that I could read or write at all. I was also learning that the English language, manipulated beyond endurance, can run amok like a genetic experiment and produce linguistic monstrosities.

"Ted's obsessive-compulsive," Brian said blandly. "like that lady who built the Winchester Mystery House in San Jose. She was afraid that if she ever stopped building, she would die. I think Ted worries that if he ever just signs off an issue and we go to press on time, something terrible will happen, like 'How the erection of Bush changed the business landscape.' And he'll be a laughingstock and lose everything."

"How do you stand him?"

"Are you kidding? How could I stand this job without Ted for comic relief?" I glanced at the article he was proofreading, "Thirty Seconds Over Oakland." The subhead: "Suddenly, a flame from our number one engine illuminated the whole fiscal year."

"Those are the sane ones," Brian said, indicating a new hire who was gathering his belongings to leave after only an hour. "You've got to have something wrong with you to stay here."

In fact, most of us did have some overriding reason for enduring Ted's abuse—massive credit-card debt, a strict Catholic upbringing, or the misguided sense of duty of the Light Brigade. There were, of course, plenty of sycophants who would flourish under Stalin or Idi Amin, and some, like Brian, that I mentally termed euglenas. These were easily pushed around and gave way when prodded, but a tough outer membrane usually preserved the creature intact.

I hung on because my husband had recently left me, and I couldn't even consider the ordeal of interviewing. My hands shook, and I often stared into space in a stupor of conquering or suffering hero fantasy.

Early in life, I realized that our merciful lack of precognition exacts its price on the other end in shock. Looking back, of course, we can revisit any scenario and see the killer lurking plain as day; the car veering from its lane; the metal fatigue on the jumbo jet. The leopard crouching in the sedge.

Cliff had come home early that afternoon. He popped a beer and faced me on the sofa, as if ready to propose a plea bargain.

"Brynn, there's no easy way to say this. I've been seeing someone." He took a pull on the beer, his gray eyes narrowing to assess my response, as if I were an uncommitted juror. Even confessing this duplicity, he still looked as if he represented truth and justice.

Which he did, in a way. I, whose high school nickname had been Olive Oyl, had somehow been allowed to marry a former football captain and student body president. These cosmic illegalities, if not set right, can fracture the fundamental architecture of the universe and bring it careening back to its primordial soup.

The following scene has taken place so often in human history that I believe it is neurologically scripted. I knew what to say next for the same reason that I knew how to point or throw a rock.

"Who is she?"

"You don't know her."

"How long?"

"That's not important."

"Does this mean you're leaving me?"

Cliff sighed and shook his head. "I don't know." He rose and left the room, shoulders bowed with the responsibility of recalibrating the universe. "Probably," he called from the safety of the kitchen. I heard him take another beer from the refrigerator, although I would not have been surprised to see him reenter with a gun or come back as Dracula. All rules of probability seemed to be suspended.

Cliff moved out that night, and my life soon became regulated by legal precedent. I had "fallen into the system," as he used to say of first-time offenders. It means that you always have the power to make things worse.

Soon afterwards, I became the object of gossip and pity at work, radiating marital failure the way Renaissance madonnas radiate sanctity. My situation was actually an ice-breaker, like the cast I had worn on my broken leg one summer: painful but a little comical, inspiring of commiseration. Just as strangers had once shared their own broken limb stories, I now heard tales of marital duplicity and sexual incompatibility from chance restroom acquaintances.

"I have a confession to make," Brian said suddenly one afternoon. When I did not reply, he blurted, "I'd give ten years of my life for a date with her." So this explained his long silences; his hyperawareness of her location in the office, his color change and averted gaze whenever she passed.

He and I were lunching in the courtyard behind the magazine offices, surrounded by bougainvillea, rose bushes, azaleas, and begonias. The place belonged in a Graham Greene novel, its atmosphere of dictatorial menace framed in lush, exotic foliage. Across from us, Alexis chatted with our managing editor, a large-eyed young man with the face of a Byzantine mosaic, whom we had nicknamed Saint Will for his patience; a rare employee able to get along with Ted.

Now I looked at Brian as if for the first time: dark, intelligent eyes, a fragile thinning hairline and a slack, disillusioned mouth that held a certain sensual promise. He was of medium height, with a slight but not weak build. Alexis could do worse, I thought.

"Go for it, Brian," I said, feeling like an old DeSoto with four flat whitewalls. What good was it? Even though I was tall, not too heavy in the thighs, and sported a skillfully reconfigured nose, I remained the wisecracking gal Friday; the loveable, leavable confidante. I understood why Dorothy Parker had felt the need to reduce her anguish to ditty.

Alexis held herself apart from the employees, probably because she was embarrassed by her father. Sometimes I noticed her hanging out with our new managing editor, Thea, a thin, lizardly young woman of flat, flaxen hair and bad skin. Thea's managerial style of unctuousness toward superiors and offhand cruelty to those beneath her had made her a favorite of Ted. Alexis must be extremely lonely, to spend time with Thea. I shared this observation with Brian, who hung on my words as if I spoke in the tongues of the forefathers.

"I'm nobody to Thea." He frowned, calculating his chances at joining her inner circle. "I'm a stage prop."

"I wish I could say the same," I replied. At a meeting that morning, Thea's casual executioner's gaze had lingered on me for a fraction of a second too long. "I'm history," I said.

"Don't be silly. Who'd do your job?"

"Alexis, of course. She's too smart to just hang around adorning the place. I'll bet she thinks she can get the copy past her father on schedule and rescue the magazine."

"If anybody could do it, she could," Brian said, fatuous as a sitcom swain.

"Maybe you'll get to share an office with her after I'm gone," I said nastily.

"You think so?"

"Fuck you, Brian."

That evening, I was to interview the concierge of a Cannery Row luxury hotel for an article. Commercialized and defiled as she is, Cannery Row still recalls for me an era when it was honorable to be a failed writer and hard drinker; to have bitter memories and self-inflicted wounds. Still, I could not help envying the lovers on the hotel balcony overlooking the water, for whom Cannery Row was a place to sip wine, shiver in the dark wind, and awaken warm together to the cries of gulls.

I stood beside the concierge in the lobby of Italian marble and Brazilian teakwood, gazing out onto the ocean. The fog had cleared to make way for an impressive brass-and-coral sunset now fading into pale magentas. Panoramic windows spanned the beach, and wavelets rolled in all the way from Asia just to charm the guests. Out toward Seaside and Del Rey Oaks, jeweled lights followed the curve of the Bay. Here and there, the skeletal remains of defunct sardine canneries, preserved as quaint nostalgia, jutted disturbingly into view.

A small group approached; with a start, I recognized Ted, Lillian and Alexis. They were with another family, talking and laughing. I quickly melted behind a pillar; I had no standing to be greeted by them, nor did I wish for them to have to snub me.

"You know these people?" asked the Italian concierge.

"My boss. And his family."

"Then it is a coincidence," the concierge said. "This too is my boss and his family. The owners, the Rinieris." We watched the two families seat themselves by the window. Drinks arrived. "The girl is very beautiful," said the concierge. Alexis wore a clinging black dress that fell to just below her knees, the neckline cut like a diamond. A bracelet that looked like platinum clasped her upper arm.

It was a few moments before I noticed the young man beside Alexis. He was handsome in a precise-featured way, with dark hair that kept falling over one eye and slender hands that drummed and roamed over the tabletop as if impatient with visibility. Alexis stole a glance at this boy, but he seemed pre-occupied with something beyond the horizon. My heart sank for Brian.

"Who's that?" I asked, and the concierge knew who I meant. He frowned and shook his head slightly.

"The younger son, Peter." An understanding passed between us that we would say nothing more about the families.

Since only those in dire financial need would work for Ted, our office parking lot was the scene of frequent vehicle repossessions. Which is what I assumed was happening the next morning when I heard shouting behind me in the lot as I arrived. "That bastard. That bastard."

I peered discreetly over the top of my car. To my shock, I saw Alexis standing behind her Porsche in impossibly white pants and a red tank top. She stomped her foot in its flat red dance slipper. Her long fingers with their unpolished nails covered her face. When she removed them, she was looking at me.

"I'm sorry," I said stupidly.

"What am I supposed to do now?" She shouted.

` "You could always quit," I said, and at her blank look, I realized that she was referring not to her father, but to some other man.

"You think my father is a bastard." She laughed with mischievous relish. But a moment later, her face clouded and she stomped her foot again. "Why are men like that?"

"Oldest question in the world."

"With some bimbo he met at Doc Ricketts' lounge." She said, answering my unasked question. The stupefying unfairness of existence suddenly crashed upon me; the cease-less march of outrage: every caterpillar infested with its Ich-neumon larva; every abandoned infant; every stock swindle, every sneak attack.

"Join the betrayal club, I'm president." I said. She looked at me with sudden recognition.

"Oh, you're the one whose husband left her."

I have never been able to resist making people feel better at my own expense: "Yes, I am the said rejectee." She walked over and hugged me. I glimpsed an artifact of the spirited, gawky child who must have been tamed and channeled very early in life.

"Your ex is a D.A.," she said, "didn't he just try that murder case?"

"Brennie Harlowe," I said. "He strangled his girlfriend and stuffed..."

She shuddered and made a motion to stop me. "We were afraid he might get off."

"Not a chance. That was one of Cliff's easier cases."

"He's very attractive, your ex," said Alexis. "Of course what he did to you was awful."

An idea wafted into my mind like a spore and instantly took root, sending its devious tendrils spiraling. "How would you like to meet him?" I said. "After all, he's single now."

Alexis threw her head back and laughed too hard, the magnificent hair rippling.

"I thought he left you for another woman. Why would you...." I smiled at her with my lips shut. "Oh. You'd like me to break them up."

"I'd like you to try."

"But that's just... sowing discord," Alexis said.

"Sweet discord." She laughed again, lips curving with relish. "It would serve Peter right."

"It's a perfect way for both of us to get even," I said. "Cliff is coming here at two to drop off some divorce papers; you could just casually stop by my office."

She paused. "I'll think about it. Not out of vengeance, but... "

"Out of curiosity," I supplied, knowing how irresistible to Cliff the curiosity of a girl like Alexis would be. She put her keys into her purse and kicked a pebble away from her car tire. We walked in together, I smirking at the effect this news would have on Brian.

When I reached my office, Thea was standing at my desk. "Brynn, we regret," she said in front of Brian, who was indeed a stage prop to her, "that your work has failed to live up to our expectations. Consistently."

"Is that so?" I said, my stomach dropping. "The only consistent thing about this place is the abu..."

"Ted and I truly hope you find a position that's a better fit for your... talents." Thea flapped my final check at me, and I seized it nimbly on the downflap, telling myself that being the victim of petty office scheming does not diminish one.

Nevertheless, I felt a cloud of asininity cover and conceal me like octopus ink. So now I was desexed and dejobbed. With as much dignity as I could muster, I retraced my steps out to the parking lot. Only in my ongoing internal movie did Brian burst from the building to pursue me in slow motion, whirl me around, and kiss me passionately to the accompaniment of Schumann's Träumerei. In fact, he barely said goodbye.

Early that evening, Cliff called. "Thanks a lot," he said, "for not telling me you were canned. Did you forget I was bringing down that addendum for you to sign?"

"I must have."

"I drove all the way down there for nothing."

"I'm sorry. Really."

"I'm giving you the piano. Don't you even want it?"

"I do," I said.

"It took me over an hour to draft that up."

"I believe you."

"And another two hours on the road, all uncompensated."
I said nothing. "Well you can just come to my office yourself
now and sign it. I'm not going out of my way again."

"All right."

"I'm trying to be fair about this whole thing, Brynn."

"I know. Who did you talk to?"

"What?"

"At the office. Did you speak with anybody while you were
there?"

"Only the receptionist. She told me you were let go. Why?"

"Are you asking why was I let go?"

"I can guess that. Why do you want to know who I talked to?"

"No reason."

When I received a call from Saint Will the next day, I had
an irrational moment of hope: perhaps Ted had come to his
senses after all and wanted me back. I would now have the
pleasure of delivering the scathing farewell speech I had given
to my rear view mirror as I left the parking lot.

"'Brynn, Alexis died last night at Community Hospital.
Her car hit a tree." A silence opened between us, a widening
abyss that I could not reach across. Peter was driving." Will
finally said. "Nobody knows why she let him drive, he was
drunk as a skunk. They were doing about sixty."

"And him?"

"Oh, you know how it always is. He walked away with a
few bruises."

"Oh no," I finally got out.

"It's weird, but Peter apparently told the police they were having some sort of a fight. And... well, your name came up."

"I can't imagine." I said.

"It's all very hazy, he doesn't remember much. I just wanted to tell you that Alexis had nothing to do with your being let go."

"I know that."

"It was me," said Will. "I was the one who suggested you might be happier... working somewhere else." He was breathing rapidly.

"You? I thought it was Thea."

"Thea didn't exactly go to the wall for you. But Ted actually argued for keeping you. He liked you in his own odd way, you know." He paused. "I feel like hell."

"Don't on my account."

"People are being very cruel. They're saying Ted's karma came around and got him." An image that I had been fighting for the last several minutes finally bullied its way into my consciousness: that hair, soaked with blood.

"How's Brian?" I asked.

"Inconsolable. They can't get him to leave the hospital. Who knew he was so devoted to her?" Will paused. "Maybe it would have changed things if ..."

"Nothing could have changed things."

Peter Rinieri was initially charged with vehicular manslaughter, but in the following months, the criminal case receded into the back pages of the paper, dwindled and finally vanished. There must have been a civil suit too, quietly settled.

Last week, Clifford and his girlfriend were married at a church called The Little Congregation of the Human Spirit in the Redwoods. I have not seen Brian since I left the magazine, but for some reason, I keep running into Thea in downtown Monterey. She always greets me warmly, like a long lost friend.

Sunnyside

Three of us checked in, that weekend in November, and found ourselves the only patients in the place. It had been a slow month, we were told. Nobody seemed to know quite what to do with us, and yet here we were, shaky hands, bleary eyes and all.

At last, the director, an amiable fortyish man with a sleek black pompadour and the eager gaze of a Disney rodent, decided to let us rest on the simmer for a while, in the hope that more patients would trickle—or stagger—in. When our numbers reached some kind of critical mass, then they would begin rehabilitating us.

Soon, despite countless games of Trivial Pursuit, unrestricted television and counseling on demand, we were bored silly. The nurses too were bored, shuffling file folders, drinking coffee, and observing us dully from their glassed-in station as we ambled about unsteadily in bathrobes.

Five people had phoned that very morning to reserve beds, confided BettyAnn the head nurse on my third day—two of them actually drunk! Hefty and officious, she wore full white nursing regalia; her cap, an inverted muffin cup of pleated white organdy, perched atop her frizzled gray hair. With the holidays fast approaching, she assured us, we could anticipate a bumper crop of drunks hastening in after DUIs or office-party blackouts. Or coaxed in by concerned family.

I could not imagine such a conventional scenario. Fed up with life at the Trinity Diet, I had fallen off the wagon and gotten drunk in the ladies room at work, sitting glumly in a stall and gulping syrupy blackberry brandy that I had bought on my morning break. Even then, I might have beaten a judicious retreat, but booze makes me sociable. Smiling foggily, I sauntered back to my desk, clutching a cup of coffee as a stage prop. Apprehensive eyeballs seemed to roll in my direction, following my progress to my cubicle, where my computer screen blinked gibberish about bytes and proms.

I thought sadly of my senior prom, to which I had not been asked. I had been a dork, a bookworm, a wanna-be: five-feet ten, with a rump like a Siberian babushka and the galvanic tresses of Frankenstein's bride. What did it matter that I now maintained my weight at a needlessly precise boundary and tortured my hair into a faux glossy mane? I was dishonest and artificial. Everything was. Tears filled my eyes, and I bumped into something, spilling half my coffee.

My boss's door stood temptingly ajar. "Hey, Jackie, I shouted in, "I lead a life of mendacity (mendashity). I can't write whass in my heart." When I pounded my chest with the half-filled coffee cup, I knew that all bets were off.

I knew enough to get out too.

"Bye," I told Gary, our account executive with the schizophrenic brother who had, after a psychotic break in basic training eight years ago, never again spoken a coherent syllable.

"Bye," I offered Tatiana, whose father had been arrested one night in Moscow when she was seven years old, never to reappear in her life.

"Bye," I bid Bill, whose wife had, after he nursed her multiple sclerosis into remission, run off with his best friend.

"Bye," I told Amy, who shook her head sadly at the thought of a fellow Jew going this *goyische* way.

And "Bye," I told Dr. Bertoni, my psychologist, a day later, as he dropped me off at Carmel Sunnyside Hospital, his brown eyes round with alarm above his neat gray goatee. Sensing trouble when I missed my appointment, he had swung by, to spot me through my back door, hugging a box of vin rose and weeping at a TV auction.

While he called Sunnyside to reserve a bed, I had grabbed the wine box and locked myself in the bathroom, extracting its interior mylar sack and squirting wine into my mouth like a bota bag. Ole!

Ole, all you drunken writers—Hemingway, Fitzgerald, Donleavy, Cary, Joyce, Bukowski, Faulkner, Kennedy, Parker, Williams.... here's to yet another soused scribbler, holed up in her personal Pamplona.

"Tony brought us a live one," smiled Caroline, the plump blonde admitting nurse, to Floyd the counselor as she handed me a pen and clipboard.

"Ole!" I responded, and "Bye," heading for the exit sign.

"You're not going anywhere, dear," said Caroline, hooking me deftly into a chair. "Just read the admission form, then sign at the bottom." I peered up defiantly as BettyAnn loomed above me. The sight of all that additional bulk pressed me down into submission. Closing one eye, I made out a dotted line and scratched my name across it.

From the corner of my open eye, I noticed two male patients in bathrobes observing the scene with interest. I waved a greeting: Ole! The nurse strapped a blood pressure cuff around my arm and shut me up with a thermometer. "Where is everybody?" I hissed around it.

"We are everybody," replied the taller of the men. Gray-haired and clean-shaven, he wore a pressed shirt and tie under his bathrobe, an arresting blend of professionalism and dereliction. "I'm Stuart Crossley and this is Reyes Ramirez." I shook hands primly, as if at a Chamber of Commerce mixer.

"Are we glad to see you," said Reyes. "Do you play Trivial Pursuit?"

"Wanna sleep." I lowered my head toward the chair arm.

"Sit up, Brynn," said Caroline.

"I lost my job."

"I have my own business," said Stuart and frowned. "I think."

"The union sent me here," said Reyes. "Too bad about your job, but it's all in the past now."

"I told off the boss."

"Things will get better." Reyes.

"You're right where you belong, dear," said Caroline, patting my shoulder. And I certainly was, from her perspective. As a fully insured patient, I was bread-and-butter to the staff, who fussed over me like a preemie. I was given a bathrobe, a room in "Skid Row," the detox ward, and a tray of chicken soup and crackers.

My room was neatly furnished, with Durer's praying hands in needlepoint on the wall next to the Serenity Prayer in blue cross-stitch. I fell asleep instantly. At 6 a.m., I awakened, exited through a side door and was retrieved, striding briskly along Highway One in my hospital gown, by Reyes and BettyAnn.

Sunnyside Recovery Haven was set among the quaint, woodsy streets of Carmel-By-the-Sea. It must have sounded like a good idea—a "tastefully appointed and discreet sanctuary" for the brandy-quaffing bourgeoisie to sober up, in an atmosphere "rich with California culture, inspired by the soothing song of the ocean mere steps from your window." But times had been tough lately, what with insurance companies tightening up on coverage and a couple of upscale new centers in the same neighborhood. Quite simply, Sunnyside was scrambling for patients.

Stuart turned out to be an insurance executive whose girlfriend had grown tired of picking him up off the floor. Twenty-two-year-old Reyes had three children and a good job in construction, if he didn't get himself killed staggering around the site after lunch.

"You all have a great deal to lose and much more to gain," Floyd the counselor assured us. Floyd seemed to spend a lot of time on the phone yessing his real estate agent wife. His flag of independence was a truly massive handlebar moustache that counterbalanced the hairless dome above it. He passed out three-ring binder workbooks etched with a smiley faced rising sun.

The first section asked us for ten ways that alcohol had made our lives unmanageable. What had our drinking caused us to lose?

"Think what you've lost, Brynn," said my ex-husband Cliff over the hospital phone later that day. Cliff, an attorney, enjoyed interrogation.

"I've been doing little else."

"Your husband. Custody of your daughter. Your house. Your car. Your job. Your self-respect. The esteem of your family and friends."

"My health." I had just returned from Community Hospital, where blood had been drawn. I was surprised to see it still flow red, rather than wine-colored, or amber like scotch. "My clothes." Silence. "I need something to wear, Cliff." I was still in my business suit. The grey-on-black weave seems to undulate like a plaid sea. My hose were gone, and I was still shuffling around in the smart black pumps I had worn to work on that last awful day.

"Brynn, I'm in trial. I can't get down there this week. Don't you have someone else to do this?" If only I had. But even the friends I hadn't alienated with 2 a.m. confessional phone calls were keeping shy. Why board the apres-iceberg Titanic?

"What about Laurie?"

"Don't even ask. I won't let her see you in that place. Dr. Forsmann said to just tell her you needed a rest."

Later that day, the nurses brought me a laundry basket full of the discarded clothes of previous patients. I chose a bubble-gum pink jersey and beige polyester capris with a baggy seat. Chartreuse slippers with pom-poms completed the effect. At last, I looked like a real alcoholic.

And I was one. It was just my luck to beat the odds, to be the exception. Popular belief held that alcoholic Jewish women were as rare as the white Sumatra rhinoceros, but somebody had to do it. I found the word for drunk in my Yiddish dictionary, where people went to look up their grandparents' quaint expressions, not their own epitaphs: Shicker.

I sneaked my first can of beer at six years old, my family preoccupied in the living room with some televised crisis. Later, a crisis myself, I guzzled Listerine and watered my parents' gin. In high school, I drank Southern Comfort ("Sudden Discomfort") and Rainier Ale ("The Green Death"). Well on way now to becoming a Great Drunken Writer. I attended Berkeley because it was a forgiving environment for people going off the rails. And I met Cliff, who liked to drink too. In fact, we drank him right through law school and into private practice.

When I got pregnant with Laurie, the nine months without liquor felt like crossing the Sahara. Pouting in well-monitored sobriety, I fantasized about booze as often as I did about the birth itself. Once Laurie was born, I didn't breast feed her because alcohol would pass into my milk, and I wasn't about to give up drinking for six more months. I stood in the shower crying as the polluted milk ran from my breasts down the drain.

Finally, Cliff had taken the opportunity to leave me for a Jazzercise instructor, taking two-year-old Laurie with him, her sleepy, bunny-covered feet hanging down from her blanket. "I won't watch you kill yourself anymore," Cliff said, "and neither will she." Ever since that night, my life had been a crazy quilt of drunk and sober: two months on the bottle, two months off. Now, drunk again.

During the next week, Andre, a Filipino paramedic, Brent, an Italian real estate broker, Kathi, a blonde punk hairdresser, Eric, a handsome young bush league baseball player, and Frank, a wealthy retired entrepreneur all came in.

Frank, who was six feet six and three hundred pounds, came in horizontally, borne by his son, his grandson, Mike the male nurse, Reyes and Eric. They had trouble maneuvering him around the corners of the narrow hallway since he refused to bend, intermittently roaring and struggling. He had the room next to mine and snored all night like Jovian thunder. "Frank's okay," said good-natured Eric, his roommate.

The acute tremors of detox finally subsided, to be replaced with overwhelming fear, despair and exhaustion. As a chronic alcoholic, I was headed for an early grave—if I were lucky. If not, I could anticipate spending some years raving in diapers. Perhaps I would expire in one apocalyptic hemorrhage, as had Kathi's mother, or deteriorate from progressive liver disease as

Frank was doing. It was all ugly, and I had heard it all before. None of it made the slightest difference when that impulse to go for the bottle hit me.

Eric had permanent tremors from the cocaine and other drugs he had taken along with the booze. His career as a short-stop finished, he wanted to go back to school. Whenever we had soup, he would turn away, to hide his struggle to get each spoonful to his mouth. Late one night, he knocked on my door to escape Frank's snoring, and we made love.

In creative group, we were instructed to model our families in clay. At a loss, I molded my nonexistent family—Cliff, Laurie and I. We lay drying on a large piece of corkboard, gray and macrocephalic, with hollow eyes and identical smiles made from a bottle cap. One day we all fell off my dresser and broke into a jumble of powdery limbs. Every night, the street light shined through my window onto the shattered family. I never slept. Sometimes, as the night wore on, I would doze and murmur, only to awaken with a jerk, heart pounding. When the clock read six, I got up, took a shower and dressed.

Midway through my second week, Pearl Silberstein arrived. I spotted her as I came from morning group. She was sitting in the reception area with its mauve velour chairs, plush gray carpet and rosy lighting. Pamphlets with discreet titles like "Who Am I?" and "A Family Matter" lay neatly arranged on the glass coffee table.

A frail old man in a black suit and hat was shouting at the admission staff in a Yiddish accent, interrupting their answers with "Vas?" and "Zo!" He yanked on his frizzy grey sidelocks and smacked himself on the forehead. Pearl ignored all this, gazing stolidly at the wall. She was fair and plump, with a freckled, bumpy nose, straw-colored hair cut bowl-atop fashion, and a double chin that sagged toward her collarbone like the crop of a hen. She was wearing sandals and a dowdy flowered skirt; a sleeveless black T-shirt exposed formidable hammocks of flesh on her upper arms. Every so often, she took a deep breath and exhaled noisily.

At last the old man shouted, "Genug!" He picked up a pen and scribbled across the forms. Then he walked over to Pearl and grasped her by the shoulders; she shrugged him off like a stinging insect. The old man shrugged his own shoulders and left, muttering and shaking his head.

I was both intrigued and distressed by Pearl's Jewishness. I had felt myself well on the way toward exchanging my troublesome Jewish identity for that of an alcoholic, which seemed a much better fit. Judaism, with its morality and family tradition, had always confounded me, and while I felt insufficiently Jewish, I had certainly won my spurs as an alcoholic.

Besides, our patient group was beginning to forge a common identity. As diverse as California, we all lived under the same umbrella—young, old, Italian, Asian, Wasp, Black, Hispanic, Okie, straight and gay. And Jewish. We had suffered together, witnessed one another's humiliations, confessed our secrets, revealed our rage. We faced great challenges against daunting odds. We needed one another.

So we welcomed Pearl with open arms. It's going to get better, we assured her. She surveyed us with blank, yellowish eyes.

"When do they serve lunch? It better be soon or I'm leaving. I'm not supposed to be here anyway." She glared at me. "And don't tell me this joint is Kosher."

We drew back, and I suddenly realized that Pearl was right. She did not belong here. She belonged in the nuthatch. After loading her plate at the lunch buffet, she took one bite and pronounced the food inedible, demanding that they send out for a decent pastrami sandwich.

There was, soothingly explained Jack the director, no other food service. And after all, she was here to get sober, to learn about her disease.

That, he quickly realized, was the wrong approach.

"Disease? I'll show you disease, Mister. Is starvation a disease? Is rickets and scurvy a disease?" I flinched and tried to focus my chagrin on matters more manageable, such as the pile of bills that had just been delivered to my room, revealing several thousand dollars of arrearages on such items as car, rent, electricity, telephone and credit cards. But even that sinking moment had been preferable to this. "Forget it," Pearl bellowed. "This place is unfit in my book. U-n-f-i-t. I'm leaving." Everyone gaped.

Why, oh why, I wondered, was this happening to me? Because Pearl instantly singled me out and attached herself to me exclusively.

"So what kind of makeup are you wearing, Miss Jewish America?" she demanded that afternoon at group, plopping herself into the seat beside me that I had reserved hopefully for Eric.

"Uh, well it's waterproof for one thing," I responded weakly. "Doesn't run when you cry." Several people chuckled. But Pearl was dead serious.

"Come do my face, will you?"

"Sure," I replied to shut her up, angrily compliant. I would have preferred a week in detox, but this was the story of my life: Other peoples' demands, no matter how onerous or unreasonable, took precedence over my own needs. Until I exploded in drunken outrage, or worse, passive aggression—leaving my phone off the hook for weeks on end, lying about my age, background, feelings.

I needn't have worried about making Pearl over. She appeared at free time with huge black circles penciled around her eyes, her brows shaped into the same angle as mine, her lips drawn into the bow I so carefully outlined. She looked like my lunatic doppelganger. A few people burst out laughing, but she ignored them, seating herself beside me with coy dignity.

"So how do I look, tsatskele? Beautiful as you?"

"Fine, fine."

"You're not just saying that, I hope."

"No, really, you look better than me." Pearl preened. The others were tittering, and I began to sweat. I felt like grabbing Pearl around her fat neck and choking her.

That night, footsteps came pounding down the hall. Shouting erupted outside my door. "Brynn, Brynn, they're killing me. Vay iz mir Brynn, help me. It's a pogrom."

"Eric, wake up!" I nudged him.

"It's that crazy Pearl. How'm I gonna get out of here?" I heard more footsteps and the doorknob turned. In desperation, Eric dove under the bed just as Pearl burst through in her nightgown, huge pendulous breasts waving as she struggled with Mike, the black male nurse, who was holding a paper cup and trying to defend himself. He was also trying not to touch her, but those breasts were everywhere.

"Help, rape," she screamed. And "They're trying to poison me. To shut me up." Mike looked at me helplessly.

"She won't take her medication. Pearl, you is supposed to take this and go to sleep. Your father say you take this every night." Pearl approached me. Her toes, with their long yellow nails, must have been only inches from Eric's nose.

"He's not my father. My parents died in the camps. Brynn, don't let them kill me too."

"Pearl, nobody's trying to kill you," I said. "Take your medicine if it helps you sleep, for God's sake."

"You promise it's not poison?"

"I promise."

"Can I stay with you a while?" Suddenly docile, she drank down the medicine and sat on my bed. A moment later she got in, pulling the covers around her face and giggling like a little girl. Mike waved gaily at me as he hurried back to the nursing station. It took me nearly an hour to coax Pearl into her room, permitting Eric to emerge, covered with dust bunnies.

"How do you stand her?" he said. "She ain't any more interested in sobriety than Brad is in Allison." I laughed, albeit with a sinking feeling. Brad, who was young and gay, was nervously dodging the advances of Allison, a bouncy, blonde teenager. "Her parents didn't die in any camp, either. Jack says they put her in an asylum because she was crazy, but the place closed. The question is, what is she doing here, screwing up our groups..."

"Screwing up our screws," I added, to change the subject before he blurted out something anti-Semitic. I suddenly thought of Pearl as my cross to bear and wondered how I had gone from being the madwoman of XRT Software to Jesus Christ in just one short week?

"She was driving her parents crazy," volunteered Caroline the next day. We were sitting in a chummy little claque in the nurses station. Somehow Pearl's obnoxious behavior had broken down any remaining barriers among us patients. Even the nurses were our allies. "Her grandfather brought her in because her mother is about to have a nervous breakdown herself."

"Sunnyside needs the dough," added Stuart, always the businessman. "Pearl is insured, so she's worth ten thousand bucks. The owners of this place'll can poor Jack if he doesn't at least break even." Everyone clucked sympathetically.

"I still think they ought to send her somewhere they can treat people like her. She don't belong with us." This from Russ the biker, who had spent nine years in state prison for armed robbery. Bearded and pot-bellied, he was our self-appointed arbiter of honesty, our bullshit detector, as he called himself. He had been on and off the wagon for the last thirty years and felt that this made him an authority on sobriety.

"What do you mean services are on Sunday?" It was Friday afternoon. "I beg your pardon, Kommandant," Pearl shouted at Jack, clicking her fat, sandaled feet. "I happen to be Jewish, and so is Brynn here, and the Jewish Sabbath starts on Friday. So what are you going to do about that, hah?"

"Well, I can give you and Brynn time off from family hour if you need to pray..."

"Pray shmay. I demand to go to temple where I can worship with other Jews." She turned to me. "Right?"

"Pearl," I begged, "don't make trouble, okay?"

"It's trouble to want to light a candle? To worship God like our people have done for thousands of years?" Oh hell, I thought. Why don't you just leave me alone? I'm mentally, physically and spiritually sick sick sick.

Late that night, the nurse came into my room with a pile of clothing. "Your ex-husband dropped these off. He said to tell you good luck." The clothes had been grabbed haphazardly. Several cocktail dresses had found their way into the pile, along with the sexy negligee I had bought for our attempted reconciliation, a gruesomely uncomfortable weekend in San Francisco at the Fairmont, trapped in the midst of prom night. The elevators and hallways had been packed with teenage boys in tuxedoes and their satin-clad dates, giggling late in the coffee shop while Cliff and I did a post mortem on our marriage.

"I never went to the prom," I announced at group the next day.

"Bullshit," said Russ. "That's not what got you drunk."

"I never went to the prom," I began again.

"Let's have a prom for Brynn," said Eric. "She's neurotic about high school."

Neuroticism, the third ism in my triumvirate, along with alcoholism and Judaism: At age twelve, I discovered the Merck Manual in the library: I had glaucoma, I realized, in addition to leprosy, acromegaly and just possibly, sleeping sickness. I was riddled with tumors, all inoperable. Turning to the mental illness section, I identified my manic depressive psychosis, schizophrenia and progressive megalomania. The only disease I never imagined I would catch was alcoholism.

"I had a dream last night," intoned Pearl. There was a general shifting and rumbling of discontent. Pearl never made sense and never shut up. "I was naked, riding a giant rocket into space." She held her hands three feet apart.

Eric's smirk cracked open a chink in my self-control that rapidly widened to a fatal fissure. Deep within me swelled the Great Tsunami, building upwards past my cirrhotic liver and inflamed pancreas, gathering speed and rising beyond my varicose esophagus, my raw larynx and trembling uvula, over my tongue to crash, with one final, mighty surge against my desperately locked, grimacing lips. And to rebound violently, exploding partly from my nose, hurling me backwards in my chair so that I grabbed for the edge of the table. An indescribable sound escaped me, something between a thunderous sob and a sneeze. The group turned in amazement. BettyAnn, who had come to dislike me, fixed me with a stony glare.

"Brynn, I don't think you're in any position to laugh at somebody else."

Pearl resumed in her flat, disconnected tone, "The earth moved…" I kept my eyes on the floor, not daring to breathe for fear of another detonation. Several hiccups escaped. "Brynn," said BettyAnn, "take time out, and I'll see you after group." Face burgundy, I stumbled away and returned to my room, where the clay family sobered me instantly.

Some time later, BettyAnn entered and sat on my bed, hugging her clipboard. Outside, the others shuffled past to exercise class.

"The prognosis," said BettyAnn, "is poor."

"Mine?"

"For somebody in as much trouble as you are, Brynn, you show great indifference toward your own recovery. And by the way, I know what's going on between you and Eric, and that is going to stop. In group, you either stare at him or out the window. And you have not, as far as I can see, even begun your writing.

"I have trouble writing if I'm not getting paid," I giggled weakly.

"Well think of it this way: Unless we see some progress toward recovery, the staff and I may be forced to recommend a guardianship."

"What does that mean?"

"It means you are incapable of looking after your own interests competently."

"What happens then?"

"I don't know, Brynn, but you will not be making that decision. Right now is the time for you to make a decision." I pictured myself in the cuckoo's nest, padding around in a nightie with Pearl as a conversational partner.

"Okay. I'll buckle down." BettyAnn shook her head at me as if I had just promised to pay the national debt.

"I want you to talk your head off in group. I want you to tell everybody why you hate yourself so much that you're drinking yourself to death."

"If only I knew."

Another restful night, and we assembled for morning meditation. I was slated to lead a group discussion on the topic of self-obsession. In preparation, I had taken an hour to put on my makeup, changed clothes twice and missed breakfast to style my hair.

"Where's Pearl?" I asked.

"Your problem is over," Russ announced grandly, as if he had just solved it. "She's gone."

"What did you do?"

"I didn't do nothin'. They put her on a bus this morning."

"I know Pearl has been, well, a problem for all of us," said Jack, "especially you, Brynn." With his blubbery cheeks and receding forehead, Jack reminded me of some sea mammal, an otter or a porpoise. "The staff has to consider the well-being of everybody here. Pearl will be better off in a different kind of program."

I thought of Pearl walking alone out the door, duck-footed and bedecked with makeup. "You might at least have let me say goodbye."

"Brynn," said BettyAnn, "I think you'd do best to concentrate on your own problems, which there is no shortage of. Besides," she looked at me almost comfortingly, "Pearl brought this on herself."

Brought this on yourself: why, that was my own theme song. A massive sense of loss suddenly bore down upon me, and a dread so profound that I could scarcely breathe. With difficulty, I rose and walked into my room, closed the door and sat stiffly on the bed. The clay family stared noncommittally. I folded my hands in my lap and closed my eyes. Please help me, I said, to nobody in particular.

A Journey From Which Many Do Not Return

At some point, April began to hang out with Pam, and they soon attracted the nosy interest that surged and crackled around the Club like atmospheric electricity before a storm. "Bad comp'ny, she is," intoned old Ken B, referring to Pam, of course. "But it ain't for me to judge, not with the life I done led." He winked a bleached blue alkie eye at me and grinned. Ken was a cowboy from Salinas, cured by dry heat and whiskey to the shade and texture of a bronc saddle. Deep wrinkles crisscrossed the back of his neck.

I smiled and edged away, not caring to hear Ken's drunk-alog again; how he and Jack Kerouac used to toss them back in the dive bars of Prunedale and Chualar. How, at the end, Ken realized that Jack was going to ride that pony all the way down, so he had shaken Jack's hand one last time and gotten himself to an AA meeting and lived.

"April's only trying to have a little fun," I said, and added "in sobriety" because that was de rigeur. Actually, I was not sure what "fun in sobriety" consisted of. Since my early teens, fun was what I hoped I had had, after coming to. And so far, sobriety only fit the definition of war as ninety percent boredom and the rest pure terror.

We joined hands in a circle and bowed our heads for the Lord's Prayer that ended the 5 p.m. AA meeting at the old Monterey Alano Club. The devout would lower chin to chest and squeeze their eyes tight shut, but I am a peeker, so I could see Pam's large, stormy gray eyes staring defiantly at something lurking out beyond our circle that only she could see. Pam's beauty was in the category of big flowers and fireworks and prom queens—a brief, stunning trajectory with a relatively steep and swift descent. Her tousled, tawny hair still looked drunk. I probably stared a little too hard, because she caught my eye and gave a little simper of annoyance. I quickly shifted my gaze back to God and my feet.

Monterey has always been hospitable to drinking writers, Steinbeck at the top of the pile, of course. A couple of old-timers at the club swore they had fucked some of his women. And speaking of fucking, young "newbies" such as I, fresh from rehab, attracted the same intense interest from the men that limping zebras on the Serengeti receive from lions. Other men would appoint themselves our guardians, and naturally there was a leonine element to that as well.

When we discussed "acceptance" in the meetings, I did not think about alcoholism, but rather about fitting into this new culture of sobriety. "Out there," as we termed the drinking world, my marriage had drowned before the wedding gifts were broken in. My job in public relations had soon followed. I could no longer look forward to closing out the bars in tony Carmel-by-the-Sea, slipping and staggering hilariously down its dark, cobbled streets with some middle-aged golfing swell. Any friends who still called had an annoying tendency to re-mind me of dares accepted, tirades delivered. To them, the

Alano Club, a watering hole for sober alcoholics, hosted only losers, paupers, and oddballs, but I fit at least two of those categories. That I could accept.

In those years, the Alano Club occupied an ancient building on Alvarado Street; a stolid, square story of adobe with a single barred window. The building had settled, so that taller members had to duck through its canted front door. Within, shapeless old armchairs and tape-patched naugahyde sofas embraced a sooty fireplace. Dingy green walls were papered with sobriety slogans and bumper stickers in gothic blackletter: A New Pair of Glasses, Friend of Bill W, and other code by which we drunks could spot one another. To enter the Club, one must not have had a drink within the last twenty-four hours. This steep hurdle kept the place fairly decorous. Employee/members served short orders from behind a pearl gray formica bar. Preserved for some reason under yellowed shellac were a two-dollar bill and a seven of diamonds.

Just as alcohol brings together unlikely people, so does its mirror, recovery. At the Club, dowagers from Pebble Beach rubbed elbows with housemaids and hookers from Seaside; Naval Postgraduate School officers with Confederate pedigrees poured out their anguish to black Army privates from Fort Ord. Whether you had swilled Everclear beneath a freeway overpass or quaffed old brandy at the Concours d'Elegance, you were "right where you belong," the traditional greeting. The Club was our refuge from a world of people who left their drinks half-finished when they paid the tab; who thought "let's have a couple" meant cocktails not bottles; who were reasonably certain, when they took their first sip, where they would awaken the next day, and with whom.

When April greeted me one afternoon in a drugstore on Del Monte Boulevard, I had to force myself to stop and chat.

Though we had never met, we knew, thanks to the meetings, details of one another's lives that might have taken "normies" years to confide.

"You're Brynn P, aren't you?" she said. The initial distinguished me from Brynn B, the addicted nurse, and Brynn N, the old truck stop waitress from Memphis. My reticence didn't faze April. She was in her early forties, blonde and pert. Her plaid skirt and brown pumps were as respectable as any parent could wish in a sixth grade teacher, which she was. Her white cotton blouse was tied at the neck with a bow.

Get me out of here, I thought,

"I think we need to get you out of here," April said.

Early that morning, the phone had summoned me into the lucid terror that was my usual waking state.

"What do you want, Cliff?" I tried not to think of his face.

"You didn't call me back last night, so I figured maybe you didn't get my message."

"I got it, all right."

"So what's your answer?" I said nothing. "Look, Brynn, a divorce doesn't have to be a vendetta. I'm trying to work with you. I made a simple, reasonable request."

"You're supposed to pass your requests through my lawyer."

"That grubby little shyster will want a thousand bucks for divvying up a hundred bucks worth of crappy furniture."

"What do you want with fifty bucks worth of crappy furniture?"

"Karen and I need something to sleep on, for Chrissake."

"Who's Karen?"

"None of your business." I hung up.

That conversation and the images it spawned had led me into bad emotional terrain, so I was browsing the liquor aisle—not with intent, I assured myself—but merely to sightsee.

Nevertheless, I let April guide me out of the store, into the fresh ocean breeze whipping sand across the road from the beach dunes nearby.

I said, "My ex-husband has found somebody."

"Good!" April nodded as if I had just grasped long division. "He wasn't right for you. And hopefully he won't bother you anymore." She took my arm playfully but firmly. "I live just up the street. I'll fix us lunch, and then we can go to a meeting."

Her tidy home was filled with high-quality furniture that looked inherited. The omelet she made for me was perfect. "I've never been married," she laughed. "Just a spinster school-marm. Why don't you spend the night in my spare bedroom? I think that would be wise. You don't need to be alone right now."

"I simply cannot imagine you drunk," I blurted.

"People say that a lot. But oh my, it got bad." She grinned, as if at a sinus infection or a sprained ankle. "Come meet my mice."

If a mouse could visualize paradise, it would be April's mouse resort, where she cared for them with loving officiousness. Something in the uniform perfection of their moist ruby eyes, kinetic whiskers, and snowy, shivery little bodies, completed her. They lived in spotless cages filled with exercise contraptions, mazes, wood shavings and sumptuous mousechow.

"The world is so cruel to mice," April said. "It makes me feel good to give a few of them a safe, happy life."

That night, lying beside them in the guest bedroom, I became aware of nocturnal scuttles; of tiny paws in frenetic motion, burrowing into the cozy dark as their tribe has done for millennia. I felt like a proto-mammal myself, huddled deep in my tunnel, awaiting the Asteroid and my call to destiny.

As the daughter of a minor diplomat, April had grown up in courts—not the type that you slink into and plead to drunk and disorderly, but real ones, like the Court of St. James. Yet, beneath her politesse I sensed a glow that never flared up but never quite died out either, like that of a peat fire.

The next evening, as the meeting began, I crossed the room to sit with April and Pam, under the intent gaze of Old Ken and his buddies. I felt guilty. The emotions of these lonely, self-appointed protectors ran high; I knew that I was moving in their estimation from lost to astray, probably well on my way to reckless and wanton.

But after the meeting, I again sat beside Pam at the fireplace, where the younger men congregated. They oriented towards us in their female-tropic way, like plants turning to the sun.

"Hey Justin!" Pam beckoned a young man with smooth, dark hair parted in the middle. "Come meet Brynn." She whispered in my ear, "check *out* the bulge in his pants."

"Hi Brynn," Justin sat down beside me. "It's nice to see you laugh. We were starting to wonder if you even could."

I had been dumped into rehab from the Community Hospital emergency room after passing out pulseless at a celebrity party I had crashed during the AT&T Pro-Am golf tournament. I later learned that some caddies had dragged me outside for the paramedics to find.

After being resuscitated, I was caught climbing down from my gurney to prowl for drugs. "I can't watch you every minute," the night nurse said, yanking leather cuffs tight to my wrists. "People are fighting for their lives here, while you're trying to throw yours away." It was four a.m. Her eyes were red and watery.

Chatting now with Justin, the black curtain around my feelings unexpectedly lifted. I tried to fix the moment in memory, because I was pretty sure the shadows would quickly return. But to my surprise, a full twenty minutes passed before I suddenly recalled the failed aspirations; the bruises and fractures of mysterious origin; the charcoal leaked into my hair from the nasogastric tube.

Justin had grown up poor, white, and tough in Detroit. He had joined the Army from the streets, where he had been living since his father shot him in the chest at age fourteen with a starter pistol. At Ford Ord, he had reached the rank of corporal before drinking triggered his discharge—honorable, he was at pains to tell me.

"Pretty hair, like copper," he said later that night, running it through his hands. "Pretty blue eyes. Why won't you look at me?"

"You'd better go," I said. "The neighbors will tell my ex I had a man over."

"Who cares?" I could not think of an answer.

Justin and three newly sober friends had rented a furnished house in crime-riddled Seaside. They parked their motorcycles in front, stuck sobriety slogans on the walls, worked at dead end jobs, and went to AA meetings. All wore knives. The music they played was so loud and furious that the cheap sheetrock walls creaked and wobbled beneath its onslaught.

When April, Pam, and I dropped over one day with a couple of female mice as a housewarming gift, Justin's former sergeant, Gavin Brantley, was sitting at the kitchen table, drinking a cup of coffee.

Gavin was twenty-two and the handsomest man I have ever seen. In his uniform, he had that sort of Rupert Brooke, World War 1 beauty that almost made you want to cry. His looks actually buffered me against any real attraction; I prefer lovers who do not take my breath away or outshine me. So I was able to gaze dispassionately at the clear hazel eyes, the broad, smooth forehead and dark brows perfectly aligned; the clear, planar cheeks and the curving young mouth just shy of feminine.

Pam was only mildly impressed; her taste in men ran to the felonious—blank, wanted-poster stares and greasy mullet hair. But April was watching Gavin in a sort of otherworldly trance. For her, everyone else in the room had simply ceased to exist.

April had spent her childhood touring the famous museums of Europe; her degree was in art history. So she must have spotted those rare classical dimensions at once in Gavin, a straightforward kid from Coeur d'Alene, Idaho, oblivious to Renaissance aesthetics. He was a tanker, and his conversation focused on guns, sports, and Fort Ord trivia. April couldn't have been more rapt if he were discussing the lost treasures of the Anasazi.

Despite Gavin's angelic looks, he had the morals of the average noncom and speedily helped himself to what April freely—insistently—offered. He soon began to spend nights, then weekends at her place. I suspected she was giving him money; Pam was certain of it.

"April," I said tentatively to her after a meeting, "I hope you're being...careful."

"Why, whatever could you mean?" She flushed, her eyes darting about.

"At least," I begged, "don't fall in love with him." Even as I spoke, I realized how idiotic I sounded. "For some people, sex is just . . . recreation."

"Are we projecting here?" April said frostily, arching her brows.

"No! I just worry that. . . ."

"Nonsense! Everyone sees the world through their own lenses, Brynn. Try turning them on yourself." Eyes closed, I nodded.

I soon discovered that within Justin, despite his years of conning, lying, seducing, and score settling, dwelt a tender, constant heart. Who knew? He admired my college degree and enrolled in night school. On my birthday, he borrowed a robin's egg blue, three-piece doubleknit suit from his roommate and escorted me to lunch at the Lodge at Pebble Beach, parading me into a roomful of startled millionaires, calling the Maître d' "my good dude."

"Don't fight it," Pam grinned with lecherous relish. "He's exactly what you need."

"If Justin is what I need, then what is Gavin to April?" We had saved her a seat at the meeting as usual, but she had failed to show up.

"The next worst thing to a drink."

"That's what I was afraid of."

"I take that back." Pam said. "Alcohol she knows is poison."

"What should we do?"

Pam shrugged. "Pray for her."

"No, really. I owe April. She saved me from going back out."

"God saved you." I rolled my eyes, and Pam stared at me, horrified. "Why, you don't believe in the Program at all!" People moved away discreetly; around here, apostasy was a high crime.

"All I mean," I said, knowing I had crossed into perilous terrain, "is that we shouldn't just abandon her."

Pam's eyes brightened with tears. "Don't you dare judge me. I've got a son I can't even visit. Parents who want nothing to do with me. I was a hooker by age thirteen." She began to sob. "The Program is all I've got. What do you expect me to do? Sure, April's making an ass of herself. You've done it. We all have." I thought back on my history of arid, superficial relationships; my shunning of the commitment I distrusted and the intimacy I feared, avoiding not only rejection but all potential joys as well.

April soon traded her dowdy dresses for miniskirts and tight shirts. She began to wear makeup and let her hair grow wild and curly. At the Club, she spoke of Gavin by the hour; how his love was freeing her from the stifling expectations that had warped her life.

"Oh wasn't I the perfect little lady, always trying to please parents who couldn't be troubled to notice me. If only I made high enough grades, if only I dressed or sang perfectly, then maybe they'd love me like they did my brother. No wonder I drank."

I hardly knew how to respond. Few rules existed that I hadn't found a way to break. It only went to show alcoholism's amazing ability to destroy the overly compliant and the rebel with equal efficiency.

"And won't the eyebrows go up back east when they find out I'm with a younger man. An *enlisted* man!" April cackled with glee. I forced a chuckle.

Her world now revolved entirely around Gavin: photographing him, mapping out education and employment strategies for him after he left the Army. She could not comprehend his choosing to be with anyone but her in the coming years.

"April's burnt," said Justin, shaking his head.

"I'm not defending Gavin," I said, "but April can be hard to turn down. And if she thinks he needs money, she'll practically force it on him."

"It don't take much forcing," said Justin. "Gavin, he don't earn shit."

The Club frequently held dances, and it was an open secret that these were the best parties on the Monterey Peninsula, though not a drop of alcohol was permitted. People traveled from as far away as San Francisco and even L.A. The hunger to live and love again, to resurrect romance from the wreckage, contrasted vividly with the Babbitty country club mixers I used to cruise for lovers.

Dancing now with Justin in the Club's twilight amid shabby decorations—the theme was "The Fifties"—I spotted old Ken and Brynn N, my truck stop waitress namesake, gliding wrinkled cheek to cheek. I felt a sudden rush of affection so intense I nearly stumbled. Perhaps it was the woeful teenage music, the valiant approximations of ducktail hairdos and ponytails and bobby-sox; the struggling but irrepressible human spark. A sob caught in my throat, which I quickly concealed with a slight cough. Held tight in Justin's quiet grasp, I let myself settle, tentatively, into what I can only call love.

When the dance ended, we poured from the Club in our dozens to stroll around Monterey, euphoric under the clear, cold sky: It was two a.m. on a Sunday morning, and we were not puking, fighting, or comatose. The sirens we heard were not coming for us. Miracles!

After that night, Justin began to spend more time at my place and finally moved in his possessions: a couple of cardboard boxes containing tattered T-shirts and jeans, motorcycle magazines, coffee mugs. A worn Army certificate attested to his skill at jumping from helicopters. In a Polaroid snapshot, his obese mother waved from a blue sofa. I reminded myself that his life was only beginning, but it still seemed like a scanty showing.

One afternoon, April and I dropped by Justin's house and found the place full of Seaside girls, the type that Justin dismissively referred to as "hams." I recalled a Dorothy Parker short story, her depiction of the type ringing as true now as it did in the nineteen twenties: the drugstore makeup and black-ringed eyes and pale skin; the elaborate hairdos, sweet perfume, cheap high heels and tight, pastel skirts. These modern flappers had taken the place over by some innate territorial entitlement, sitting at the kitchen table and stuffing themselves with cake, prattling about movie stars, beauty school, and how drunk they had gotten over the weekend. Gavin was sitting beside a girl in mauve lipstick whose long, streaked hair tumbled over cleavage tattooed with a butterfly.

"I'm studying to be a dental assistant," she told me.

April stood stiffly at my side. "Gavin," she finally broke in with strained lightness, "I think it's time we left." Gavin did not respond. I looked imploringly at Justin, who rolled his eyes and tapped Gavin on the shoulder.

"Hey Gav, your lady's talkin' to you."

Gavin did not look up. "Mind your own fucking business," he said evenly. "And keep your fucking paws off me." I saw the cords tighten along Justin's arm and the sudden fist. I drew in a breath and closed my eyes. In the silence, one of the hams popped her gum.

"You got it." Justin turned away. In his room, he sat on the bed, rose halfway, then sat back quickly. I knew how he longed to charge out and smash Gavin's pretty face to a bloody pulp. Somebody was going to do it eventually.

Over the next several weeks, April seemed to implode and crumple. The more distant and aloof Gavin grew, the more obsessed she became. She forgave him all, yet he stayed away and ignored her calls. After the meetings, April would seek me out for agonized, repetitive post mortems: How could he act so contrary to his own interests? The tramp was blowsy and coarse; he must soon come to his senses. I asked if Gavin had repaid any of her money and instantly regretted the question.

At last, I told myself to obey Pam's dictum and let go. April would have to get over Gavin in her own time. I made excuses to leave the Club early: Justin, struggling through freshman English composition, needed me, I told myself. But in truth, I was busy frolicking in bed with him, styling my hair, shopping for makeup; gorging on the mundane preoccupations of normalcy, no different from the hams.

It was late afternoon, and a chilly winter haze had descended on Monterey. April's street was quiet; remote and foreboding.

"Something ain't right," Justin said. He knocked at her door several times, then took out his knife and disabled the dead bolt with a sharp jerk. The door swung wide into frigid silence. There was an odor that I did not recognize but that raised the hair on my arms. We found April lying on the living room sofa under a tartan blanket. To my relief, she opened her eyes and held out her arms.

"Oh my dear, dear friends," she said, in the tone of a society hostess, "I am so very glad you've paid me a call." She had colored elaborate red horns and goatees onto all of Gavin's photos. "Such a beautiful boy," she said, looking at them sadly. "But so very, very wicked."

"Shit, the mice," said Justin from the guest bedroom. "Don't come in here." But I did, and I screamed.

April was admitted to an inpatient recovery program somewhere in Arizona, where she spent several months, emerging in a state of medicated serenity. She was welcomed back warmly to the Club as a survivor of relapse, a journey from which many do not return.

Whatever they had done to her in the hospital, it had not been enough to dislodge Gavin. When I glanced at her during meetings, her eyes were shining beatifically; her mouth quivering and her head swaying gently, as if to some sweet, inaudible song. I knew that she was thinking of her errant lover, reliving their transitory hours of ecstasy and nurturing the fond hope that was all he had left her.

I heard around the Club that old Ken B and his cronies held Pam and me accountable as the chief architects of April's collapse, and that may have been true. Yet, for a brief time, her life had glowed with an eerie and thrilling luminescence, like the seashore at night, beyond which lurks the cold, dark and drowning deep.

The Big Bash

It had begun as a celebration, but how on earth had it ended? As Brynn tugged open the double glass doors of the ad agency, heavy with portent, a warm gust of stale garlic and bacon struck her in the face. Confetti lay in the entryway. Beside the deserted reception desk, empty champagne bottles protruded from the wastebasket, their rumps insolently turned toward her.

As she passed the conference room, Brynn glanced in from the corner of her eye, then stopped short to gawk. She bit her lower lip. The long, polished cherrywood table was crowded with smudged glasses and empty liquor bottles—gin, scotch, wine, and those designer potions with names like hair conditioner. Somebody had spelled out 'fuk me' with swizzle sticks. Puddles reflected the sky beyond the panoramic windows; hors d'oeuvres platters sat on the chairs: stale sushi, desiccated cheese wedges; flattened dolmas. Cocktail wieners bulged obscenely from bread rolls, fat congealed around their folds. A greasy pizza box gaped. Nothing, thought Brynn, says kaput like a used pizza box.

The evidence was irrefutable: They had thrown the Big Bash without her! Even as the realization dawned, a part of Brynn wanted to start cleaning up, like the compliant employee she had once been. But that other persistent self—the anxious outsider, the eighth-grader who had prayed for party invitations that never, never arrived; that Brynn writhed again on the sharp thorns of rejection. Twenty years gone, and nothing had changed!

She searched her recollection: Had anyone mentioned a party yesterday as she closed down her computer? No, not a breath. She, the senior copywriter, linchpin of the agency, had been purposely, premeditatedly excluded from the celebration of the Ataxia Software account that she had helped win! All of those concepts had been hers: the distorted dinosaurs, the missing tooth, the exploding phrenology head.

Brynn recalled herself hydroplaning north last night on Highway One in pelting rain, brakes mushy on her old Ford Fairmont. And all the while, this party had been taking shape like a succubus. Of course they had no reason to conceal it now. All this garbage, this rancid affront had been left for her.

She must be stoic now; deny them the satisfaction of seeing her pain. With an anguished effort, Brynn composed her features as Eric, that puppy of a graphic designer, slithered through the heavy door and stood beside her, peeking in at the mess.

"Morning, Brynn" He winced, rolling his eyes. "Our bad."

Why, you talentless, creepy little sycophantic pissant, Brynn thought. "Oh, I've seen worse." She flashed him a tremulous smile. "I hope everyone got home okay." 'Her faux concern provoked a shrug and a head shake at the incomprehensible opacity of fate.

"Me too." Eric opened his mouth to say more, but Brynn strode forward briskly, grabbed the pizza carton, and tried to stuff it into the trash. The overflowing can rejected it, and the carton slid onto the floor, releasing a leathery hunk of cold pizza upside down on the carpet. The warped crust reminded Brynn of a manta ray.

"Oh don't bother with that," said Eric. "The janitors'll be here."

...a dish best eaten cold, thought Brynn, looking at the pizza. She walked unsteadily to her desk. On her chair was a folder of busy work that somebody had not been too inebriated to plop there. Coils of purple crepe paper dripped onto the folder from the chair back. Atop her computer was more crepe paper, and her keyboard was littered with little colored paper dots. She turned the keyboard upside down and shook it. The dots pattered into her shoes.

So this is how it felt to be superseded, Brynn thought, passed over, phased out. It was physical pain dispersed throughout her very pores and molecules—a primal, atavistic dread of exclusion that must hearken back to the australopithecine band, hooting and posturing in the cracked mud of the Olduvai Gorge. Poor Uk-Uk with her 800 cc brain case had felt the same bottom drop out of her world, abandoned to the hyenas over some inadvertent violation of primate protocol.

But wasn't she inflating this simple oversight, this party, beyond its true significance? Hadn't she herself dashed out at five o'clock to pick up Allison at day care, precluding herself from after-hours socializing? They probably didn't bother telling her because they were so sure she could not stay. Of course she could have called Cliff and had him pick up Laurie. But maybe they thought that would cause waves in her custody arrangement, so to spare her further dysfunction... Oh stop with your flimsy band-aids, she told herself. The truth is in your nostrils.

Brynn clenched her fists, looking in mild disgust at the knobby knuckles and greenish veins interlaced vinelike amid protruberant tendons; the blunt-nailed fingers that typed away obediently day after day, manufacturing hyperbole, provoking artificial desire. Polluting the collective human spirit.

Nothing to be done about it. At least, Brynn calculated, they hadn't fired her. No, and she must not give them an excuse by storming out. Steady on, she thought, you can't control what they do, you can only control what you do about it. Or was it how you feel about it? Or was it you can't control how you feel about it, but only how you feel about what you do about it? And here came Eric again, probably wanting to rub it in a little more. But no.

"Can you write some copy about this vest for the Summit winterwear catalog?" he said, shoving under Brynn's nose a tiny photo of a gray vest that reached new levels of nondescript. "A snippet." He held his fingers an inch apart.

As he leaned over, the folder he was carrying gaped open like cleavage, and Brynn reflexively peeked in. From a page inside exploded a luminous purple-and-chartreuse printed retro-psychedelic headline: "Thump It!" A realization hit Brynn:

Why, that was the main theme for the whole Summit ExtremeGear WinterWear campaign! The concept Brynn had been waiting to be asked to create.

"Thump it?" She could not resist blurting. Eric flinched and snatched the folder away, holding it behind him as if concealing a biopsy result from a terminal patient.

"All we need right now is that vest copy," he said.

We, thought Brynn. Now they were "we." And she, Brynn, was non-we.

Meanwhile she of Thump It!, Gaylinn Pratt, junior copywriter, had secretly been invited to concept the theme for their biggest client's most important campaign. Brynn's head swam. Soon, skiers worldwide would Thump It! At Aspen,

Vail, Biarritz, Gstaad. T-shirts by the millions would Thump It! Billboards. Posters. TV commercials and celebrities; a new Everest ascent or South Pole trek would Thump It. And next year would come the follow-on campaign, Thump It Harder or Thump It Higher.

An article in Advertising Age would highlight the daring strategy behind Thump It. The article would focus on how smaller, fast-moving west coast agencies were seizing the creative vanguard from the ponderous behemoths of the past, the DDB Needhams and BBD&Os, brontosauruses munching their clueless cud as the mammals Thumped It.

Gaylinn Pratt would be featured in San Francisco Magazine, a worldly gamine in faded jeans, hugging her knees before a manual typewriter. Having her hair chopped short by a crusty old barber. Chatting with Clint Eastwood at a Pebble Beach charity gala. The article would be titled "Today's ad-femme—not your mother's English major."

And Brynn the English major would write a snippet. She felt the slow burn creeping up her neck to ignite the hair follicles at her temples. Tears welled. "Not a problem," she said with a catch that Eric must have noticed, but ignored. He flapped the forbidden file bye-bye at her and turned away. A weight pressed on Brynn's thorax. The keyboard blurred.

Hadn't Sid himself reassured Brynn only last week that her position was solid? He had hired Gaylinn only to relieve the heroic burden that Brynn carried so well. Now Brynn could do more with her life than write copy. Why, she could begin her novel at last!

But …Thump It. What a lousy theme. Brynn thought of the bunny in Walt

Disney's Bambi. Wasn't he Thumpit? And what about Things That Go Thump in the Night? Rhymes with Lump It, had they considered that? What kind of theme was Thump It for a high-performance adventure gear company that outfitted Everest teams to the summit? Why, the words even sounded like a fall, right down the Hillary Step, thumpit thumpit thumpit.

It was now eight-fifteen, and the agency, after its riotous debauch, remained eerily silent and deserted. Peeking out at the reception desk, Brynn saw that unanswered calls were blinking on the phone, still on auto-pilot. Here was an ethical dilemma: should she pick up the phones until Pam dragged herself in? Oh, don't be a schnook, Brynn told herself. They didn't tell you about the party, it's their problem if Pam got so drunk she couldn't make it in this morning.

Brynn's reflection loomed translucent in the glass door, a lonely, metaphysically solitary figure, curly dark hair escaping its haphazard twist—unlike Gaylinn's blonde Veronica Lake, sweeping her shoulders. The minute I see her, Brynn thought, I start to lumber instead of walk. Even my writing becomes obtuse and Victorian. I am the hulking shadow on the mountain—the Yeti. While Gaylinn skis effortlessly down the other side.

And now Brynn noticed that the door to Sid's corner office was shut, but the lights were on. They must be within already, meeting early—Gaylinn, of course, and Randy Papen, the creative director, that pretentious ass with his gray hair flowing over his black turtleneck, who declared "I'm weak, weak," every time a cute teenage girl walked by. Once, Brynn had once echoed freak, freak, had he heard that? Cheap shot Brynn, her own worst enemy. Never could resist doing herself in.

Oh stop it, she told herself. You really are clinically paranoid. But the thin, bright line of light beneath Sid's office door burned her eyes like a sliver of white-hot metal. They were in there talking about her, phasing her out, shrinking her job to a snippet, or even canning her. What a pleasure it would be to abandon her ersatz poise and just let go like a magnificent animal. Hurl inkwells, kick over wastebaskets.

Brynn looked at the vest and began to type her snippet. Her fingers on the keyboard looked like cocktail wieners. The tiny mirror above her desk reflected a face inflamed, swollen with suppressed pain. The corners of her eyes and mouth canted downward. The Sulk, she thought, my answer to The Scream.

Brynn recalled suddenly an American girl she had once seen pitch a perfect, seamless, flawless scene in a restaurant in St. Tropez. Brynn had been backpacking across Europe with Miriam Katz, that teetotaling bore. The waiters had been pointedly ignoring all of the American students for the better part of two hours. Suddenly, from a nearby table, an empty wine bottle sailed through the air and shattered at the feet of a waiter. The girl who had hurled it was tall, beautiful, and very drunk—almost cartoonish. A long blonde ponytail protruded from the side of her perfect head. It had taken three waiters to wrestle this Amazon outside. All the while, the girl, fearsome and fiery, continued to shout strings of admirably specific ep-ithets into the restaurant until friends arrived and hauled her away.

"Some people have no class," said Miriam Katz, pursing her lips.

"That" said Brynn, "*was* class." A well-executed sundering scene would be an event to treasure. Brynn could become, for one defining moment, a magnificent, rampant animal, heed-less of consequences. The moment was all, but was she equal to it? Whatever words came to her, she would shout, before the entire office. The alternative was to seethe for the rest of her life—not over the outrage, but over her own timid, craven response.

Brynn rose, smiling beatifically, a servant of destiny. She recalled vaguely that assassins were said to see themselves from the outside before their own defining moments. She shivered a little, yet her legs propelled her toward Sid's office. Had she the sand? She stood for a moment, looked behind her, at the past, and flung open the door.

"This is a fucking travesty," she shouted in, tossing an imaginary ponytail.

The first thing she saw was Randy's bare buttocks facing her. He was lying on his side on the floor. Spooned cozily against him lay Sid and before Sid, Gaylinn. Even at this juncture, Brynn felt a tinge of envy.

Almost in slow motion, Brynn watched the three awaken in a sort of horrified chain reaction. Then the room erupted in a mad scramble as limbs and bodies and heads tried to bolt out of sight. But there was no place to hide. Brynn, frozen with disbelief, was witnessing universal, primal panic: the hominid band ambushed by smilodon at the tarpit, sleeping Britons roused by the plundering Danes; speakeasy flappers barreling past cigar-chomping dicks.

In less than two seconds, the world had changed. Brynn slammed the door and turned her back and braced herself against it as hard as she could, as if afraid that they would come stampeding out and flatten her. But behind the door was now only silence. She could not hear even a whisper. An unexpected sense of exhilaration and power suddenly overcame her, as if they were her prisoners. She could hold them in there forever. She wondered vaguely if she might have been a sadistic prison guard in a former life.

Then, she left the door and glided back to her desk as if borne on magic slippers.

"Hey Eric," Brynn grinned as she passed him. He glanced up from Thump It with a little frisson of irritation, blinking rapidly.

"Yes?"

"I'm going to get some air."

"How's that copy coming along?"

"The snippet?"

"Whatever."

"I'm on it."

"By the way," Eric winked at Brynn. "Can you make some coffee on your way out? I don't think Pam's coming in this morning."

"Of course," said Brynn, winking back. "By the way, where's Sid?" she asked, inquisitive as Satan.

"I think he had an early meeting at Ataxia," Eric said, shrugging, not looking up.

"And Randy and Gaylinn?"

"They were going to present some new ideas for an ad campaign."

"That must be where they are then," said Brynn. She walked past the fetid conference room and the reception desk. A lightness perfused her being, though her legs still felt a bit unsteady, as if they were only now being fully used. She barely touched the office door, and it gave way easily, respectfully.

The Monterey Bay was clear and blue after last night's showers, pure in its unrelenting coldness, its chilly kelp forest swaying greenly beneath in blissful indifference to all human pettiness and perversity.

She walked down the office steps and turned onto Del Monte Avenue. The sun sought her eyes, richly warming her hair, loosening her joints. Beside her, traffic seethed in comforting swishes and blatts and groans. Brynn felt protected, anointed, almost holy. The universe seemed to be listening to her at last. She cocked her head upward, and the sky was vast, infinite and inviting.

"I was left out," she spoke aloud into the crisp air. The universe nodded its curved space-time warp kindly. I was handling it, you know, she added, though she knew that was not entirely true. But symmetry had been reestablished. From now on, she knew that everything, everything would be easier. She may not be able to see it yet, but the path ahead lay open.

Euphoric Recall

The affair was over, but her heart remained stuck in its web, a dry and twisting husk. Nights, she lay awake, flayed by insane cravings as her mental eye strained to recreate every detail: the solid breadth of his shoulders, the slight twin depressions just above the buttocks, the tiny mole beneath his right ear. Her mental palm grazed his smooth, damp cheek, redolent of shaving cream. She relived his humid murmurs on her tense, thirsty skin. The affair seemed like an oasis briefly visited in the featureless, arid trek that her life had become.

At the ad agency where she had worked as a copywriter, Brynn had begun to arrive late, looking as if she'd been dressed by psych techs. She analyzed her failed relationship at length to silent, stoic colleagues who had learned that even a slight grimace of sympathy fueled another fifteen minutes of monologue.

"They call it 'euphoric recall," said Camille, an art director. "It's what drug addicts do: romanticize the high and conveniently forget the reality." Brynn said nothing. "The reality being that your guy was a self-obsessed douche not worth a missed cat nap."

Brynn said, "Can we talk about this?"

"No."

They gazed from the agency's front window at Carmel Village, charmingly somnolent under a weak winter sun. Down the street, the beach was deserted but for a tough old lady walking a schnauzer. A keen wind whipped sugary sand through grassy outcroppings and stunted cypress, stirring whitecaps on a Crayola blue ocean. Above, a tiny cumulus perched petlike beside a pallid fingernail of moon.

But the calm was deceptive: Carmel was poised for the onslaught of the AT&T Pro-Am Golf Tournament. Soon, people would pour in by the Mercedes-load, mad to party.

"Your orders," said Cam, "are to get out of your funk and participate. Didn't Maitland Pease invite you to join her at the Hog?

"I don't feel like partying."

"She's a client. Do you feel like being employed?"

"My job is all that's holding me together."

"Who says you're 'together'?" Cam raised a supervisorial eyebrow.

That evening, Brynn descended a narrow stone staircase to the courtyard of the Hog's Breath Inn, Clint Eastwood's own restaurant. He frequently mingled here, regally lanky amid a troop of sycophants nicknamed the "barnacles" by restaurant staff. A sombrero'ed portrait of the High Plains Drifter brooded from the restaurant wall onto a roomful of pardners chewing whisky steak. The painted mouth was thin, the eyes hardened by hundreds of celluloid shootings, dumbly villainous spaghetti extras crumpling in arabesques of agony.

Brynn tried to sweep gracefully into a chair, but her heels skidded on the cobblestones and she landed baggily, with an oof. Her sweater dress of latte cashmere had cost half a month's pay. At her ears were wooden baubles from a tree that had germinated around the year Christ was born. Cowering within her costly exoskeleton, Brynn felt as secure and confident as a newborn crawdad.

All around her, people greeted each other with easy camaraderie amid eddying currents of laughter. Occasionally, men appeared to be heading in her direction but they veered off instead toward the bar, the restroom or another woman, making her feel as if a car had used her driveway to turn around.

"Did I keep you waiting? Poor baby, I heard about your breakup, I won't lie." Maity's glow was a nimbus, illuminating the space around her. People yoo-hoo'ed from across the courtyard. Drinks arrived. "There are five parties tonight," Maity said, flowing into the chair beside Brynn. "The big one is at the Hyatt, celebrity central if you're into such things. I had Clint put us on the guest list." She tossed her head dismissively at Brynn's little gasp.

Maity Pease was the archetypal Pebble Beach post debutante, her mane the blonde of a Krugerrand, her eyes the blue of a Carmel wavebreak. Six feet tall, she could fold herself into a Ferrari Testarossa like a piece of origami.

They had met when the agency handled a charity event for Maity's family trust. Both of their mothers had neglected them; Maity's for Ibiza, an opera tenor and golf; Brynn's for Reno, television and bowling.

Charging toward them, a young man greeted Maity with the excitement of a physicist spotting a new subatomic particle.

"Brynn, meet Bad Bo McPeak. Brynn is in advertising. Bo is in, well, what can I say?"

"In misery, in torment." Bad Bo slapped his head with a rolled up AT&T programme and wriggled onto a bench beside Maity. Seen up close, he did not look so young. He had too much hair. He took and kissed Maity's hand. "Darling, we are free now to run off together any time you wish." He hailed the waitress and spun his index finger once in the air. She nodded and disappeared. "In case you haven't heard, it's over between me and Suze."

"I had no idea," said Maity, her affect level and flat.

"Not much." Bad Bo grinned at Brynn. "Last week I get off a plane and boom! Summons, complaint, restraining order, the whole nine yards." He slapped himself again. "Supposedly I've been squandering the community assets on other women. Excuse me? Whose assets is she talking about? She was sleeping on sofas when I met her."

The waitress appeared with a bottle of Talisker scotch and three glasses. "Robert Louis Stevenson called this the king of drinks," said Bad Bo, pouring them each a stiff shot of the amber fluid with its faint chili-pepper aftertaste. "They keep this here just for me." He winked at nobody in particular.

In deepening twilight, the courtyard took on the hues of a Caravaggio. Fires smoldering in hunched stone pits cast a demonizing glare on the crowd. Blue gas jets overhead radiated a chemical heat; inside the bar, mounted boars' heads menaced the revelers from deep, gloomy corners.

To Brynn, the town, with its Hansel and Gretel architecture, was darkly medieval—a setting for the deadly Pied Piper; for peasant mobs howling after cutpurses and lunatics. Stores resembled cuckoo clocks, double doorways hung canted from their hinges, low ceilings sloped and bulged. A local ordinance banned street lights, so the dark was pitch, broken only by hearths and lamps, and by the endless parade of cars seeking nonexistent parking spaces.

Anthony and Charlotte stopped by to introduce Charlotte's nephew Jason, caddying the AT&T for the first time. Only nineteen, Jason reminded Brynn of a Gothic fairy-tale knight. The arms of an oatmeal golf sweater embraced his neck;

his watch was an array of tiny dials and astronomical symbols. His family, Maity whispered, "owns half of Carmel Valley."

"This *boy*," Anthony indicated Jason with a wicked grin, "needs some experience. An older woman would do nicely."

Deadpan, Jason shook Brynn's hand. "My uncle is out for blood tonight.""Anthony, stop." Charlotte's head shake was meant to be tolerantly affectionate but to Brynn, it looked like an effort to ward something off. Charlotte was one of those thin-skinned aristocratic blondes who populated the pages of *Town and Country*. In repose, her face defaulted quickly into unhappiness; a simple, conventional soul, Brynn guessed, marooned among the zany rich.

"Party at the Lodge tonight," said Anthony, pouring a hefty shot of Bad Bo's scotch into a water glass.

"Bunch of old bores in blue blazers," Maity tossed off. Bad Bo exaggeratedly perused his blue blazer but nobody acknowledged the effort.

"Everybody come over and get in our hot tub," Anthony said.

"What about The Big One?" Brynn asked hopefully.

"That's the last place you want to be tonight, trust me," said Charlotte. "They all bring their wives. Go to the one tomorrow night where they *don't* bring their wives."

"That one will be infested with pros, and I don't mean golfers," said Maity. Clint Eastwood materialized at their fireplace. He hugged and air-kissed Charlotte, then gave Maity a real kiss, prolonged to the point where everybody glanced away.

"You're not hanging out with *that* guy, are you?" said Clint Eastwood, jerking his thumb at Bad Bo, who mimed innocence, rolling his eyes upwards.

"I never learn, do I?" said Maity. Bad Bo and Clint chatted about the tournament while the barnacles migrated toward their table and tourists stared, slack-jawed.

By now, people were jamming the stone steps that led from the street down into the courtyard. The waitresses, good soldiers, hoisted their trays high and squeezed through tiny gaps in the crowd. A light drizzle had begun to fall; the misted hair and faces of the women sparkled as if with tiny diamonds, intensifying the night's fairy tale ambience. The scotch was working, Brynn noticed, effacing and softening her memories. When she tried to recall the face of her lover, she could summon only a mildly pleasant blur.

A man stopped by and introduced himself to Brynn as the mayor of Sunnyvale. He pulled out a press clipping that showed him with Dianne Feinstein at a ribbon-cutting, thrusting it at Brynn's eyes. The clipping grew damp in the mist.

"I believe you. Really," Brynn said, smiling. The mayor suggested that she leave with him and go to his motel.

"I beg your pardon?"

"His honor has a bonner," said Jason. Brynn laughed, and the mayor gave an irritated shrug and moved on through the crowd.

"My political career is over," Jason mourned.

"You'll never eat lunch in Sunnyvale again."

"I just couldn't watch that self-inflated little dick hustle you."

"I think Jason is hustling me," Brynn told Maity in the restroom.

"Unquestionably."

"Tell me about Anthony," Brynn said.

"He graduated from the Naval Academy. He was flying jets when he met Charlotte in the Officers Club at the Naval Postgraduate School. The Trident Room, been there?" Brynn tried to look ignorant. "We've got to go. I'm the biggest pilot groupie on the Peninsula. Anyway, Anthony and Charlotte got in the middle of a brawl that same night and ended up with matching black eyes. The next I hear, they're married."

The ladies' room was perhaps eight feet by twelve, jammed with women. More waited outside, thumping and whacking the door. The mirror was a bouquet of anxious faces, mouths pouting, eyes analytical. Makeup was applied with a precision that hopefully attends all heart transplants. Perfected, the women squeezed out and sallied forth one by one, like young penguins casting off into the Polar sea.

"Tell me about Jason," Brynn said.

"That puppy? Barely paper trained. Anyway, Anthony retired from the Navy when he and Charlotte got married, and Charlotte's dad got him a job as an aide to Senator Rafferty. Everyone expects Anthony to run for State Assembly next term. I think he'd be great."

"Doesn't he miss the cockpit?"

"Probably. But what could he look forward to? Being a bus driver on some commercial airliner for the next thirty years? Now he's married into one of the most prominent families on the Peninsula. They say Charlotte's grandmother had an affair with Bob Hope. Supposedly Charlotte's mother is Bob Hope's love daughter."

"No way."

"Check out her nose when we get back." But instead, Brynn studied Anthony again. In the firelight, his Scott Fitzgerald-handsome face had gone slack, with a disillusioned puffiness around the eyes. Drunk, he became a deadly mimic and made a nuisance of himself. He confessed to Brynn that he had always wanted to be an actor.

"What was it like up there, flying a jet for the first time?" she asked him.

"I got lost," Anthony said, and then stared into the fire, very far away.

"Jason," said Charlotte, "we're going to our place. You bring Brynn."

"Who's coming with me?" asked Bad Bo, and for a long moment nobody replied.

"I'll go with Bo," said Charlotte brightly at last. "And Maity will go with Anthony."

"We don't have to go with them," Jason said, helping Brynn into his BMW. "Anthony keeps juvenilizing me. Fuck him."

"Oh, he's just teasing."

"I wish Charlotte had never met that flyboy. He's dangerous, you know? Dangerously bored. Aunt Charlotte's been getting these panic attacks. And migraines that go on for days." Jason searched for words. "She used to read me fairy tales when I was a kid."

"Eons ago, I'm sure."

"So I'm a little boy to you too?" He grinned. "Think so?" Brynn shrugged.

"Abigail. What kind of a name is that? Sounds like a bratty little girl in braids."

"That's me, all right."

"So what do bratty little girls do for a living?"

"I write ads. I hate it."

"So why do it?" Jason started the car, and they rode in silence for a few minutes. "At least Charlotte lets people know she's miserable," Jason said. "Maity's the real phony. She pretends everything is great, then she goes and tries to kill herself."

"When did she do that?"

"Last year. After Anthony went back to Charlotte. Of course Charlotte took him back, the little fool."

"How does Charlotte feel about Maity now?"

"How does anybody feel about Maity? She's a force of na-ture."

"A Brett Ashley."

"Oh, yeah, *The Sun Also Rises*."

"Good for you. I don't mean to patronize. I just admire literacy in my men."

"Does that mean I'm your man?"

"Slip of the tongue. So what's up with Bad Bo?"

"No fair changing the subject."

"Okay."

"Okay what?"

"Okay don't push your luck." Jason tried to suppress a smile.

"What's the story with Bad Bo?"

"I went to school with his son Boyce Junior, who is gay. Bo doesn't like that getting around, but of course everybody knows. Junior isn't a bad kid. His dad's a dick."

"That makes two dicks I've met tonight. Bad Bo and his honor."

"Want to make it three?" Jason leaned over and kissed her. Against her own sensible but feeble advice, Brynn decided to let herself fall into the hands of this cynical, privileged kid, who represented everything she did not have and could not be. Nor would want to be, she reminded herself.

Jason parked, and they groped their way down the driveway toward Anthony and Charlotte's house. When she grew disoriented, he put his arm around her, and she sud-denly wanted to pour everything out to him—how she felt like a human screen saver, generating meaningless, repetitive patterns until jogged by somebody. How every man she ever knew, including her father, had found her easy to leave. How her childhood dream of writing novels had adjusted itself downward to polishing slogans for shopping malls.

At the edge of the swimming pool, they kissed with abandon, emboldened by the darkness, leaning up against a hedge, which sagged and nearly fractured.

Suddenly Anthony yanked open the front door and flashed a high intensity beam on them.

"Sounded like somebody was in trouble out here." He peered about innocently, swaying a little. Giggling like chastened children, Brynn and Jason followed the beam to the front door.

The house was deceptively modest, a one-story bungalow, but the antiques looked real, as did the elegant Persian carpet. A Neil Young song was playing: "I'm sorry for the things I've done, I've shamed myself with lies." Everyone was drinking champagne except for Bad Bo, who rested a little glass of scotch on a shesham wood table beside his chair. Every so often, he rose and refilled it.

"Laurie 'Cocaine' de Frayne is a congressional aide now?" Maity shook her head; deep blonde waves fell across her face, almost hiding her sham pout. "How does she keep landing those jobs?"

"Are you kidding?" said Anthony. "Best head on the Peninsula."

"I'm going in the hot tub," announced Charlotte quickly. She rose and walked out.

"I mean head for *business*," said Anthony, eyes ingenuously wide. Everybody studied the Persian carpet.

"Come on," said Maity, pulling Bad Bo to his feet. Jason took Brynn's hand and guided her, protesting feebly, toward the rear of the house, to a bedroom furnished in rich Asian décor. Two deep futons were separated by a low, exquisitely lacquered table. A lamp threw shadows on carefully arranged souvenirs: decorative knives and fans, dragon lady posters, books, potions and balsa wood toys, along with Navy insignia and paraphernalia. Brynn realized that this room was Anthony's shrine, a memorial to his former life.

Laughter and talk drifted in from the hot tub outside the window. Above the curtains, the yellow half moon shone in, ragged clouds gliding across her face. Jason's lips were sweetly curved, his teeth perfect. Brynn became depersonalized, watching herself make love with an abandon that seemed quite alien to her. Afterwards, they giggled and gabbed, sipping aquavit from a bottle. When she lay back, her head began to whirl, and she followed the vortex down fearlessly, spinning away into oblivion.

Loud, angry voices woke her—a scream, and then another sound, a soggy punch, delivered hard. Brynn opened her eyes. She was alone in the bed and for a moment, she could not recall how she got there. She sat up, dizzy, covering herself with the sheets.

The lights were on in the bedroom. Everyone stood around, wrapped in bath towels and shouting at each other. Then Brynn saw Bad Bo doubled over at the foot of the other futon, not moving. Anthony, in boxers, stood over him, breathing like a freight train and twitching with rage.

"Anthony," pleaded Charlotte, "he didn't do anything. Leave him alone."

Jason, wearing blue jeans, stepped in front of Anthony. "Don't hit him again."

Anthony turned to Jason and unclenched his fist. "Fuck off, you rich little twit. You fucking caddyboy." He looked at Charlotte. "You paid me back, didn't you?" Bad Bo moaned, and Anthony doubled up his fist again.

"Cut it out," said Jason. "Or you'll kill him. You may have already killed him."

"Hope I did kill his worthless ass." Anthony drew his fist back as if to hit Jason, but bent suddenly instead to grab the too-long hair of Bad Bo, who sagged helplessly in his grasp, batting at the air and trying to wriggle free. Suddenly, his hairpiece ripped loose in Anthony's hand and Bad Bo rebounded onto the floor, his bald scalp red as a burn, flecked with white pieces of glue. Maity let out a whoop, quickly suppressed. Anthony hurled the hairpiece to the floor in disgust.

"Jesus Christ," Brynn shouted. "What's going on here?" Nobody answered. But the tension had been broken by the hairpiece. Everyone suddenly turned away in embarrassment, shifting their bath towels to better cover themselves.

Anthony, very drunk, staggered, caught himself, and said "shit."

Jason sat down beside Brynn. "Pretty little scene. You missed the worst of it, thankfully."

"What happened?"

"Charlotte goes to sleep, so Bo gets out of the hot tub and goes wandering around naked and finds her and just climbs aboard. At least that's the story they're putting out. Anyway, Anthony caught them." He shrugged.

"Anthony," said Maity blurrily, "let's go back in the tub. We need to talk." A towel hung carelessly from her magnificent body, her wet hair plastered across her breasts. Her bloodshot eyes were unfocused. When she dropped her towel and took Anthony's arm, he followed her as tamely and meekly as a little boy. Charlotte sobbed softly from an armchair.

"What about him?" Brynn couldn't believe they were just going to leave Bad Bo bleeding on the floor.

"He's okay," said Maity over her shoulder. "He won't remember a thing in the morning."

"Hey, old buddy," said Anthony to Jason, "run him into the ER for me will you? I'll owe you."

"I'm not your 'old buddy,'" said Jason.

Suddenly, Bad Bo lurched unsteadily to his feet, the blood drying into crusts on his face. "I will take my own self to the hosp'al," he announced with drunken dignity. "Ribs broke. Mus' be fix." He slapped his wig onto his head lopsided, and began to put on Brynn's dress, which Jason ripped out of his hands.

"I'll get him his clothes." Charlotte left and returned with Bad Bo's clothes, dumped them at his feet, and then disappeared. Slowly, painfully, Bad Bo dressed, looking like a bald, naughty baby under Jason's flat gaze. Brynn couldn't tell if the whimpers emanating from the hot tub were of anguish or something else, but Jason smiled sardonically and shook his head.

Hours later, Brynn awakened again to the sound of dripping, misting rain. Night was fading into a gray drizzle, and water had condensed on the bedroom window, rivulets drooling down the pane both inside and out.

Beside her, Jason checked his watch, yawned and rose, pulling on blue jeans and sweater. "Get dressed, and I'll take you to your car. My pro is playing today. I've got to get cleaned up and get out there. They'll start the minute the rain stops."

Brynn found her wadded dress and struggled into it under the covers. They tiptoed out to the front door. The living room was clean—Charlotte must have tidied up—but the grim silence seemed still weighted with the echoes of bloody conflict. Passing a mirror, Brynn saw herself in bleak light, her eyes swollen, black makeup smeared beneath them. The contouring of her cheeks had faded to a blotched film. Her lips, lined in mauve around the cupid's bow, were half erased. Her hair was flattened on one side, giving her head an oddly elliptical shape.

Outside, an icy fog was moving in swiftly. The cypress trees lining the road dripped and swayed in a light wind. Jason started the car and headed into the Del Monte forest. The foggy road was practically invisible, but he took the curves with practiced ease. As they emerged onto the beach road, the rain clouds parted briefly to reveal a cold, brilliant blue sky, the stars still as sharp as needles. Jewellike strands of varicolored lights embraced the dark void of the Monterey Bay like a necklace. Strolling couples, out late or up early, lingered to watch tall, foamy waves emerge and crash against the rocks.

Wordlessly, they drove into deserted Carmel Village and found Brynn's car. As they passed the ad agency's front window, Brynn looked in and saw Cam already working, her back bent over her design table.

Stumbling against Jason in the dark, Brynn giggled like a bimbo. "I hate myself," she mumbled, thinking he could not hear, but he put his arm around her.

"Don't." They kissed like lovers, the keys jingling in her hand. "I'll call you," Jason said, and though he almost certainly didn't mean it, Brynn felt suddenly released and restored. As she watched his retreating figure, the shiny streets seemed to radiate out from him like conduits into another dimension. She was free now to drive home and get into a hot bath, free to euphorically recall everything, and nothing.

The Hundred Thousand Dollar Suit

"I wish the Asteroid would just come and put us out of our misery already," David said, raising his arms to beckon the night sky outside my front door. Because he had failed chemistry yet again, David was willing—eager to curse away our entire four point five billion years of arduous evolution.

I scanned the dark vault above for any chance blazing Armageddons, but the stars hung reassuringly in place. A plane was homing in on San Francisco International Airport, beacons winking. I imagined the dark, cozy cabin stirring with anticipation; travelers bringing their seats to upright, straightening their clothes.

And they, suspended illogically in thin air, were gazing down as giants would, on the fragile Bay Area with its seething, threadlike freeways and lacework bridges. Did the cosmos really care about our gnawing ambitions and torrid little intrigues?

David dreamed of becoming a plastic surgeon, but at age thirty-four, time was not on his side. His stale bachelor's degree was in U.S. history, and he had yet to pass basic chemistry. He had taken the accursed class at junior and state colleges, even at pricey private colleges, but the outcome was always the same: A couple of weeks in, he would begin to falter. The coursework instantly stampeded over him. He missed one lab; then all of them.

But come next year, there he was, backpack bulging with textbooks, cram sheets, tutor lists; a calculator with the power to guide him to Mars—as if the sheer volume of his preparation could somehow propel him through. But for David, chemistry was a skipping record, Ground Hog Day, a Rod Serling script.

When he wasn't occupied with chemistry, David worked at his father's store, Tile Style, in Redwood City. Mere blocks away, Home Depot bulged with ruthlessly underpriced tile; down the road was Color Tile. Across the street was yet another shop that David called Bile Tile. The owner was a former employee whom David's father had denied a small raise, who had then quit and started his own business. Bile Tile grew like a beanstalk, sprouting ingenious new promotions every week. Pretty girls greeted the customers.

After work, David often drove into Palo Alto to visit the Stanford Bookstore on University Avenue. He made a show of perusing books like *Lambda Calculus for Dummies* before ascending to the second floor, where the texts and supplies for the medical school sat on their shelves like religious sacraments.

A female mannequin graced the room, a medical madonna modeling the emblematic white coat, for sale only to the anointed. A stethoscope rested on her pink bakelite bosom; more stethoscopes coiled like whips in a nearby glass case. But all the stethoscopes in the world could not lash David through Chemistry.

He moved reverently among the books, where the trademark nose jobs of the big surgeons were set forth. No tortuous cartilage or bony spur could defeat the cunning scalpels of the Nose Lions. David fantasized a morning of facelifts and liposuctions lined up like monetary jumbo jets on the airstrip. Sixty thousand dollars later, he would usher his trio of svelte receptionists to late lunch at El Becor. A mussel dripping at the end of his tiny fork, he recounted his days in medical school, basking in their rapt, immature gazes. Sometimes for fun on a slow afternoon, he would enhance their lips or breasts for them.

We had met two years ago at a singles mixer in Palo Alto. David's pale face and dark, curly hair had floated on the periphery of the crowd, following me like an unhappy moon seeking an object to orbit. And what had attracted him? My unfocused hazel eyes, defiantly curly hair, gangly legs—and nose job, of course. I invited him over to watch *Quest for Fire*, and he confided his dream. As a copywriter who had been planning a first novel for decades, I understood. When I let him mark up my face and breasts with a felt pen, he fell in love.

I have always thought it an odd coincidence that the day after David summoned the Asteroid, his father's distant cousin Joe arrived from some undivulged parsec. Joe had ruined himself with gambling and cocaine, but for some reason, the family buffered him against the consequences, which would probably fit neatly in a Quentin Tarantino film. They simply passed Joe along, year after year, to whoever currently held the lowest status in the family. Due to Bile Tile, this was now David's father, Sam, whose brothers never tired of reminding him that a raise of *pennies* per hour would have prevented the employee from starting his own tile shop. Sam, dour and thrice-divorced, had to sit and take it. And now he had to take Joe.

It was a balmy Saturday afternoon in Silicon Valley, summer 1999, and you could feel the stock market spiking like a tropical fever. We sat torpid and oblivious in hazy, sunny Mountain View, sipping iced lattes at a sidewalk cafe.

"Here he comes," David said, and added, annoyingly, "Who knows, you might go for him." Because I was three years older than he, David had a habit of verbally unloading me on older men. Whenever he saw a Cadillac with a duffer in doubleknit at the wheel, he would invariably remark, "There's a nice guy for you." He protested that he was only looking out for my long-term happiness.

Joe was about fifty, but his short stature and plumpness gave him an air of juvenility. Tight, glossy, azure blue pants and a cream-colored shirt of what David called "nipple silk" added to the impression that Joe had been dressed by some tasteless Edwardian mama. A gold chain lurked in the graying hairmat of his chest. I smiled into his averted hangdog gaze, and his hand slithered through my grasp like a minnow. His lips were rubbery and moist, as if primed for pleading. He seemed to be wearing a wig, but looking closer, I spotted hot pink scalp through the black curls.

He clambered onto a chair and mumbled into an iced latte: He had a vengeful ex-wife in Queens, an estranged adult son, many creditors, lost decades. He was not a well man.

We gave Joe a tour of Palo Alto, I pointing out the wonders of Silicon Valley ascendant: the House That Sold for A Million Over Asking Price; the startup garages and coffee shops that launched a thousand global enterprises. The Valley was a petri dish for growing wealth, I explained.

I was what the rising tide had lifted—a divorced, disorganized scribbler who had missed every boat. But I felt a goofy, proprietary pride anyway: these were MY entrepreneurs. I breathed the same air as they, walked the same streets, ate the same Vindaloo.

David had made an art of what I called startup-spotting At one intersection, a nondescript, balding man in khaki shorts crossed the street in front of us, holding hands with a small child.

"Oh my God," David cried, pressing his nose against the windshield. "That's Kenneth Lickmoss. He's worth three hundred and fifty million." Sometimes he didn't even know peoples' names: "Twenty million last month," he said, jabbing his finger at a man in blue jeans walking a Chihuahua in Menlo Park.

In the rear view, I saw Joe studying his fingernails, occasionally swooping down on them like a skua. Probably replaying some fateful craps toss, I imagined, or reflecting on his blown life. He must feel terribly inconsequential amid all this florid success, hurling his penury at him. I was feeling indulgent as I maneuvered around white stretch limousines clogging the narrow streets.

"Computers, I don't get 'em," Joe mumbled, shaking his head.

"What *do* you 'get', Joe?" I asked gently.

"Clothes. Everyone understands a good suit." Except you, I thought.

"Believe it or not, he still has some great connections," David said after we dropped Joe at one of the few cheap motels in the area. "Europe. He wants to start a business importing suits. Only the best. Armani, Versace, Canali, Pal Zileri."

"Who wears Italian suits around here?"

"Are you kidding? They'll sell like hotcakes. Men are reaching out for elegance."

"And their idea of elegance is Banana Republic."

"So we'll educate them. This is the perfect time for European style."

"Somehow I can't envision Ken Lickmoss drinking his spirulina smoothie in a Pal Zileri suit."

"You just revealed your paucity of imagination. And that's why you'll never get rich."

"How much Joe is hitting up your father for?" David flinched.

"If you're smart, you'll invest too, "he said.

"I can't. I'm broke. "

"And whose fault is that? Remember I told you to buy Inktomi? Do you know what Inktomi is selling at now?"

"The good thing about being broke is that it keeps away parasitical shirttail relatives."

"And you'll always be a renter. With no stock options, no savings."

"Don't care."

"You ought to care. " The implication, of course, was that I was not getting any younger. But in fact, time was running out on one of us, and it wasn't me: poor, aging, single, female writers are everywhere, while old medical students are rarer than the White Sumatra Rhinoceros.

But suddenly, I understood. For David and his father, Joe's suits were an escape route from their respective hells of Chemistry and Tile Style. If David became an entrepreneur, he could have the income of a plastic surgeon without working another equation, memorizing Gray's Anatomy, or removing impactions from the indigent.

And wasn't this Sam's chance to have the last laugh on his overbearing brothers with their paid-off houses in Great Neck and kids in the Ivies? And was David's ambition any less pathetic than my own secret fantasies of winning the National Book Award or optioning my screenplay to Ridley Scott?

"Joe's got factory contacts—designer suits will cost us a measly seven fifty or so apiece; we wholesale them for fifteen hundred, and the retailer sells them for whatever the traffic will bear. It's all gravy and we take our cut right off the top. All we need now is a name." He looked at me expectantly.

"David, I can't just pull a name out of a hat." But in fact I was doing just that for myriad companies. It was a great era for naming. In the past week alone, I had named eight technology startups. I also named a new commercial development near Half Moon Bay: Paradigm Park—a secluded enclave of luxury suites where dot com executive teams could incubate their forward visions.

So I named the new suit company Zalnizza, a play on their surname, Zalnick. I presented it the next day at the Mountain View café.

"Zalnizza sounds too much like pizza," said David. How about Zalnello." I felt a stab of anger. "Sounds like Jello. Sounds like marshmallow."

"Zalemia."

"Sounds like anemia. "

"You're just bitter," said David. "That somebody else can do what you do."

"Zal Amore. Zalnucopia," said Sam, with an Italian hand swipe.

"I've got it," said David. "Zalnezzia Menswear! I'm a genius."

Face flushed, I offered up my aggressive tag line: "Go ahead, ask me."

"Ask me what?" said Sam, wrinkling up his big nose.

"It doesn't matter," I said, "There's no *what*. Don't be so literal, so concrete."

"It means ask me out," said David.

"It does not," I said.

"But ask me what?" Sam.

"Where this suit came from!" David.

"But that's the one thing they *shouldn't* ask," wailed Sam.

"It means ask me how much this suit cost," said Joe. "I dare you."

"Right, "said David, sticking out his jaw. Sam nodded slowly. I felt a sudden rush of gratitude toward Joe. Maybe he wasn't such a loser after all.

We celebrated that night with sushi; at the next table sat Twenty Million, a pierced and tattooed couple whose baby screamed through the entire meal.

Tile Style occupied a storefront in a nondescript, medium-sized building owned by Sam. Because his three divorces had produced an exponential number of heirs, most not even related to him, Sam's will diced the building into more pieces than a Martha Stewart Gazpacho. Now, Sam took out a second mortgage to capitalize Zalnezzia. This cash went to Joe, who departed immediately for Europe, to make the purchases from his Sources, who would deal only with him.

The next time I dropped by Tile Style, I noticed paper-wrapped bundles the size of elephant calves piled along the back of the building. The inventory of tile had been shuffled off to a remote corner of the lot.

"See?" David pointed triumphantly "And you didn't believe Joe." I said nothing. They're fine suits," said David. strutting past the bundles and slapping them with the flat of his hand.

Within the building's fenced yard lived a number of transients who bathed in the building's restrooms and worked for Sam as handymen and informal watchmen. Whenever a truck pulled up bearing suits, they swarmed out of the bushes from their tents and camper shells to unload it. They worked fast to open the packages, sort the suits by size, and ready them for delivery.

David and Joe traveled the Bay Area together, visiting men's stores and wholesaling for all they were worth. I had never seen the usually laconic and cynical David so energized. He told me the suits were practically jumping off the trucks; so many orders were pouring in that Joe soon had to fly back east to set up a New York branch. This was run by the estranged son, who had managed to resolve his issues with his father.

David compared himself to Levi Strauss, outfitting the Forty-Niners rather than seeking gold himself. Meanwhile, his obsession with plastic surgery seemed to go into remission; the chemistry textbooks lay in a zipped backpack on the floor of my closet.

It only went to show, David claimed with a knowing smile, that in this business climate, a little initiative, a little risk-taking, went a long way.

"So where are your profits?" I asked one day, "if the business is doing so well?"

"Stick to your Victorian novels, "David chuckled indulgently. "You don't know the first thing about running a business. You have to pay your overhead before you take your profit, silly. And your suppliers."

"I thought Joe pays everything up front. So whatever you make from the retailers here ought to be pure gravy, right?" David rolled his eyes.

"Joe is reinvesting it. We have to keep up our inventories." He patted my hand. "I know this is a bit convoluted, but trust me, our ROI is running way out in front of projections. And don't worry yourself about Joe. He actually knows what he's doing. He also knows this is his last chance to make good with the family and with....others." I instantly envisaged a horde of Atlantic City enforcers bearing down on Joe with crowbars, ropes, and gasoline. Somehow, it was not an unpleasant scenario.

"At the rate these suits are selling, we'll be in positive cash flow in no time." About a week later, I encountered David dining in downtown Mountain View with a miniskirted Russian girl. The girl, who couldn't have been more than nineteen, was twined around her chair like some mercenary flowering vine. David waved, smiled weakly, and said something to the girl, who instantly glared me into the Gulag.

He knew better than to call after that, so when my phone rang at seven a.m. a couple of weeks later, I picked it right up, my collection agency sad story at the ready.

David's voice held an edge of panic, muffled, as if he had his hand over the mouthpiece. "I'm in Redwood City, "he said. "Can you please come and get me? Now?"

"What's wrong?"

"The Feds are here," he said.

"The what?"

"The suits," David said, "are counterfeit." He paused. "Who knew?"

"Are you under arrest?"

"Not yet. Will you please get out here?"

"Where's your car?"

"Joe's got it. Look, he probably didn't know they were counterfeit either."

"Of course he didn't. Why don't you call your little Svetlana to pick you up?"

"I'm going to walk out by the slough," David said. "Please, please come get me."

"Where is Joe?"

"He's out of the country."

"With your car?"

"Brynn, I don't know where the car is. I don't know where anything or anybody is. Except me."

I turned off El Camino Real and followed Seaport Boulevard past cement and fertilizer companies until the road dwindled into an untrafficked path beside a small, serene inlet of San Francisco Bay. A few ratty-looking boats swayed on the flat, luminous water, bobbing gently in the wake of a single jetskiier. A sandwich sign outside a moribund seafood restaurant invited local rummies to Happy Hour. Farther on, the parking lot of a nondescript two-story office building reached to the water's edge. There, David stood on the asphalt like the last man on earth, looking out toward his diminished horizon. I pulled up beside him and got out. Down the road a go-cart track buzzed like a nest of faraway hornets. The jetskiier swooped and veered; a small spray of droplets speckled us on a light breeze.

"Asshole," David muttered at him. He didn't turn around right away. "Thanks, "he finally said and climbed into my car. I followed the shore of the slough until the road petered out in a dirt mound. Fishermen cast their lines into the water. Shorebirds jeered.

"He was pocketing everything we gave him, plus what he made from selling the suits," David said. "The Feds think he probably never paid the crooked suppliers either. He told them they would get theirs from what the retailers paid him."

"I'm actually impressed. I didn't think he was capable of cleaning up like that. Sam's money, plus the free suits—even if they were counterfeit—plus cash from the retailers." David didn't answer. "So where did the all the money go?" My mind was working very fast now. "He must have plenty stashed away somewhere."

David sighed. "What didn't go up his nose and his son's nose, he left in Vegas." I shook my head. David's cell phone rang. He flipped it open and listened for a long time as I drove.

I am not, I thought, going to chauffeur him around while he mends fences with a Russian teenager. This I cannot do.

"But they said the suits were counterfeit." David said. He put his hand over the phone. "Joe says it's all a misunderstanding. I'm just giving him a chance to explain." I threw on the brakes in the middle of the road. David lurched forward but kept the phone to his ear.

"I can only put together about eight hundred," I heard him say.

"What!?"

David flapped his hand at me to shut up. "If we can get you fifteen hundred, can you get us one more shipment? You can? Well, that would help." David covered the phone again. "He says he can turn them around inside of a day and get us ten thousand dollars cash." I stared. "Well it's better than nothing. " I felt a kind of awe and almost, oddly, respect. David shifted to one side and groped his wallet out of his pants. "Can you take a credit card?"

I lunged for the phone, and David lost his grip. As we grappled under the seat, my foot slipped off the brake, and the car began to idle toward the shoreline. I wondered how steeply it dropped off, and how our deaths would be reported, and just then I got a grip on the slippery little pod and hurled it out the window into the slough and threw the car into reverse.

"Now you've gone and done it." David looked at me shamefacedly, wallet in hand.

"Tell me you weren't about to give that little bastard your credit card."

"I don't know," said David. "It might have been an honest misunderstanding." We drove in silence around the loop. One of the fisherman had caught a little fish that flopped on the asphalt.

"That's you," I said.

"I guess I owe you," David said. "Do you want to see her picture?"

I could tell from the confident, teasing way the girl wooed the camera that she considered herself irresistible and unattainable.

"I see a great future here for her in lap dancing."

"Why so mean?"

"If I were really mean, I would have let you give that goniff your last dime."

"I've lost it all," said David. "My money and you. Not in that order of course."

Is it not now accepted that certain universal tenets govern outcomes, and no matter how they are flouted, eventually reestablish the conditions most compatible with them?

It is an immutable law that I am to be broke. The fact that at some point my income passed six figures was more disconcerting to the Universe than all the cyclotron revving and nucleus cracking of all scientific researchers combined.

Such an irrational state could not exist, let alone endure in defiance of the Second Law of Thermodynamics. The economy of Silicon Valley instantly broke and deflated, whipped back through time as if on an H.G. Wells contraption.

A month or so later, I declared bankruptcy; by then, everybody I knew was out of work, restaurants and businesses shutting down so fast that the sidewalks were blocked with their furniture. Once, I sat next to a former Inktomi Board Member at a sushi bar. He asked me if I knew of any jobs in marketing.

David finally called again, from New York. He was in law school, and although he was floundering in torts, he had new hope. His father too had moved back to New York. The disaster with Joe had made Sam's brothers remorseful, and they got Sam a job with a cousin, brokering dried fruits and nuts to the Near East.

"If not for being swindled," David told me, "I would never have thought of going to law school. So Joe served a purpose. And by the way," he said, "your bankruptcy isn't the end of the world. It's really just a financial management strategy. I'm learning all about it." I said nothing. After a while David said, "I'm going out tonight. I'm wearing my hundred thousand dollar suit."

"Your what? "

"After the Feds left, we discovered four suits they had overlooked. I figure my father lost four hundred thousand dollars on Zalnezzia Menswear. So that works out to a hundred thousand per suit."

"Is it wearable?"

"Of course it is," said David. "It's a 'Versace'."

"Did you ever hear any more from Joe?"

"I thought I saw him once in San Francisco. I was walking on Union Street, and I looked between two buildings, and there he was. I'm pretty sure it was him, because he ran."

"Did you chase him?"

"Of course I did, but he ducked down an alley and disappeared. If I ever catch him," David said, "I will kill him."

Let That Be a Lesson

Two scenic, twisting mountain roads link Santa Cruz with Silicon Valley—one maddeningly slow, the other lethally fast. People believe that this difficult commute is all that stands between us and the Valley's ravening technology guargantuae, straining to plant their sarmak-campuses amidst our beaches and redwoods.

We're often mocked as throwbacks: Birkenstock-wearing, patchouli-reeking tree-huggers and clove-smoking dietary wackos. But decades ago, a rash of serial killings anointed us the "murder capital of the world." Even now, suspicions linger that our ferny forests and riverbeds conceal yet more quick-limed horrors. Beneath our vintage hippie brand, a collective neurosis hums like background noise.

I returned here to heal, but that wasn't happening. When you flunk out of law school, the consequences waste no time manifesting. My deferred student loans shook off their dormancy like the Spanish flu virus in that corpse frozen since 1918. A torrent of demand letters found me huddled weepily in my bedroom watching sitcom reruns. Their bricklike paragraphs walled me into ruinous debt. My ex-husband Cliff, now on his third marriage, had made himself as elusive as the Higgs boson.

Ghosts of my aborted legal education now trailed in my wake. I spotted "tortious" conduct everywhere. Contracts shook its grizzled, knotted head at agreements I made. I couldn't stop inflicting half-baked legal advice on my friends.

Soon, my home became more prison than refuge. Friends' tentative queries about future plans felt like the mind games of the Spanish inquisitors. My current boyfriend requested some space.

But further humbling was in order: my frantic job search had yielded just one tepid offer—from a law firm. I was hired as an "admin trainee," a serf, to perform the most grueling and menial chores. So much for my conquering hero courtroom fantasies.

Demand letters playing in my head like a repeating tune, I arrived for my first day. The firm occupied a hacienda style building with a low-pitched, glowering solar roof. In place of a lawn, water-sparing sedge grass with razorlike sawteeth undulated thirstily. A door the color of dried blood proclaimed Holland & Sklar, Attorneys at Law, in haughty gold cursive.

In the waiting room, a lighted case displayed a stuffed owl lashed to a gnarled tree limb, its eyes realistically desperate behind the taxidermist's glaze.

At last, a tiny woman nearly buried in a black turtleneck sweater opened a door and cocked a beaky little head at me, obsidian eyes blinking rapidly. I followed her into a large cubicled room whose mushy gray carpet grabbed the soles of my shoes.

"That's you," she said, indicating a wooden table and chair wedged between a pillar and the wall. A flat, dusty computer monitor lay inert on the floor, as if injured.

"I'm Edie," the woman said. "I work for Mr. Sklar. Mr. Holland recently died, and we're disorganizing... I mean *re*organizing the office." She cut off my understanding nod with a knifish glare and turned away.

I hung my jacket on the chair and hoisted the monitor onto the desk. Something about the place reminded me of the aftermath of an earthquake, the wrenched ground shuddering and spasming above the broken strata, the very air reverberating.

"It's a pity you'll never know Harv." A tall woman in her fifties was wheeling over an office chair. "I'm Eleanor," she said, sitting beside me. "I was Harv's secretary."

"I'm... sorry," I said, my voice hoarse with disuse.

"He was on borrowed time, poor thing. A heart infection. They cleared it up finally, but the damage was done." Eleanor tipped her chair back alarmingly to grab a magazine from a file cabinet behind her. "Here he is, the way I like to remember him."

The magazine was at least twenty years old, judging from its garish colors and wacky typeface. On the cover, Harv as a youthful visionary gazed into the future from eyes of blue agate. Streaked blond hair tumbled to his collar, and his regular features radiated a complacent moral purity.

"He had a golden aura, didn't he?" Eleanor said fondly, and I nodded, wondering what the auric Harv had looked like at the end.

A man suddenly appeared, grinned at me with perfect but oddly feral teeth. He loomed above Eleanor, who instantly mugged fear and straightened her back.

"Welcome, Brynn. I'm Tom Sklar. officially senior partner here now. Though of course, our Eleanor will never buy that." He winked at her, and she lifted her chin in mock indignation, exposing a deeply corded neck.

Tom Sklar was one of those men who gets better-looking as he ages; his clipped gray hair flattered him more than the tousled brown mop in the wedding picture on his desk. The years had chiseled the youthful pudginess from his face, and his brown eyes were now a steely gray-blue in their tinted contacts. I looked reflexively at the ring on his finger, and he followed my glance, and our eyes bumped and bounced apart.

"I'm sorry to hear about Mr. Holland," I said. Tom's face morphed instantly into practiced sadness. "We go very far back, Harv and I. Eleanor will fill you in on the whole saga."

"Maybe not the *whole* saga," Eleanor said, and something crackled between them like water hitting hot oil in a frying pan. I felt a sudden urge to run, but the carpet held my feet, and "avoid further legal action" recurred in my brain like a mantra.

As the weeks passed, Eleanor took to hanging out at my desk on the pretext of "training" me, but really for an excuse to talk. She was an encyclopedic authority on all matters Harv, fiercely possessive even of his wraith. The sound of his name summoned her like a pheromone; so that people across the room had to whisper or cover their mouths whenever they mentioned him, or she would arrive and hijack the conversation.

The law was woven through Eleanor's life like a weft. She had grown up in Live Oak, an blue-collar Santa Cruz neighborhood nicknamed "Live Okie." Shy and coltishly tall, she had grown her auburn hair long; somebody had once called it a river of fire she told me proudly.

The river was now dammed up into a brassy bouffant cone, secured with a plastic tortoiseshell dagger and sprayed stiff. Her eyes were large and greenish-gray, still arresting in their iridescent eyeshadow and false lashes, despite the wrinkles. Years of hurrying from desk to lawyer's office; to kitchen, waiting and file rooms had given her a stretch-necked, giraffe-like gait. As the day wore on, her lipstick would migrate into the vertical creases around her mouth.

Desperate to escape her brawling, hard-drinking parents, Eleanor had studied office skills in high school, winning awards for her shorthand and typing. After graduation, she endured interviews with grim, Dickensian office managers and lordly attorneys until, one banner day, she had broken through—a legal secretary at last.

I flashed suddenly on a disruptive young office beauty: the gleaming hair and long limbs and intense, riveted gaze, the blouses silky and revealing above sternly fitted pencil skirts; the awe she radiated, the vulnerability and utter, unquestioning fealty. A wife's perfect nightmare.

I could speculate about the various jobs, inevitable affairs, secret getaways and lingerie and baubles and tears and scenes and abortions. The decades had marched past, and the lovers had aged and retired, and some had died. None had kept their promises. Now she was growing old, cast up like flood detritus on the Santa Cruz riverbank after a storm subsides.

Already a veteran when she joined the staff here, Eleanor had promptly taken the helm. Within a couple of months, any competitors or challengers had resigned, retreated or been fired. "I whipped us into shape," she said of that time. "It wasn't pretty, but I did what I had to. Harv could never assert himself the way he should have."

Now, with her boss gone, the once office queen was reduced to a"floater." Former subordinates ordered her to make copies or coffee, sent her on frivolous errands, and pointedly excluded her from smoking breaks and party planning.

Starving for a friend, Eleanor laid claim to me, hovering with protective solicitude, herding others away like some secretarial sheepdog. I began to suspect that she was grooming me to summit the office hierarchy on her behalf. Armed with my college degree, and (nearly) year of law school, I would seize power, restore hegemony, and dispense retribution, with Eleanor guiding me like some Lord Protector.

But this victorious scenario would require the toppling and vanquishing of Edie, the fierce, tiny avian who had opened the door for me on my first day. As Tom Sklar's secretary, Edie had been Eleanor's chief rival. Harv's death had catapulted her to the throne but hardly settled the feud.

The partners had been assistant district attorneys prior to Cliff's and my arrival; they had inhabited an earlier version of Santa Cruz and saw Cliff's generation of young lawyers as ambitious, pumped up arrivistes. The story was that they were one-time tough competitors in the office who had been assigned as a team to prosecute one of the county's emblematic serial killers. The ordeal had seared away their rivalry and forged a close bond. They left the DA's office soon afterward to form a partnership, fueled by Harv's popularity and Tom's slick aggressiveness.

But the competition that the partners had resolved played out now by proxy in their secretaries, and the friction heated up like roiling magma. Eleanor insisted that Harv was the "brains" of the firm, while Edie called Tom the "engine." Their debates turned into screaming matches. I could imagine Eleanor looming like a T-Rex above the agile, ferocious Edie feinting, dodging and darting away from the heavy verbal bludgeons and catapults.

Because it had been the mere circumstance of Harv's death that had taken down her rival, Edie had been denied the decisive victory over Eleanor that she craved. Even now in her triumphal role of "Administrative Director," she couldn't ignore vigilant Eleanor skulking on the periphery, watching for an opening, any opportunity to take her down. Edie responded by shrinking Eleanor's duties to the most demeaning chores, below even mine.

"How can you stand this?" I asked after Edie had assigned her to clean the office refrigerator. Kneeling before a glass shelf encrusted with ancient yogurt drips and mummified veggies, Eleanor looked up at me, her hands in rubber gauntlets, a damp bronze curl dangling from her forehead.

"Things will change," Eleanor replied savoring the words. "They always do. Besides, I know something very damaging about Edie, and she knows I know."

"What's that?"

Eleanor arched her brows with relish and her nostrils swelled. She fixed me with a look of irrefutable certainty. "She's a witch."

"Edie's a *witch*?"

Eleanor cackled. "She let it slip just once, but it explains everything. I realized one day that she'd been casting spells on all of us for a long time. How could I have missed it? I just didn't put it all together until it was too late. For Harv, that is."

"Eleanor," I said, as gently as I could, "witchcraft isn't a real thing. People just pretend to have power…"

"Oh they have power all right, if they're good. And Edie is good, oh my, so very good. In Harv's case, though, she went too far. And she knows it. She killed him." Eleanor pried a tiny dried carrot from the glass shelf and examined it, turning it over and over.

I reminded myself that in Santa Cruz, no belief system was too exotic or outrageous to have its circle of devotees; in fact, witchcraft was actually quite mainstream compared to some of the cults that flourished in this town. A wave of dismay washed over me: how had I ended up here, babysitting a crazy, superstitious old woman rather than lighting up the law review?

"She leaves tokens for me," Eleanor was saying. "Little twisted pieces of hair and scraps of paper with spells written on them. She plants herbs on the property to use in her spells, so her husband doesn't find them around the house. She knows I know. She tried to make me drink some yarrow tea concoction once that would have made me vulnerable, weakened my defenses. I threw it in the toilet, of course." I shook my head. "She casts on everybody in the office—maybe not you, not yet. But she'll try, just watch her, because she knows you're on my side."

After this, I did my best to tamp down Eleanor's obsession, changing the subject or even ignoring her when she presented "evidence." She showed me a two-inch length of coiled black yarn she had found on the carpet that had not been there the night before. She searched her file drawers each morning and threw out items she swore were new, even an expensive scissors once. A stray push pin, a piece of thread—anything that could bind or immobilize was proof of Edie's mischief. Eleanor checked the kitchen thoroughly for any suspect spices, leaves or roots. She would walk past Edie's cubicle, catch my eye and point surreptitiously inside, or jerk her head to alert me that Edie was concocting spells rather than working on office business.

The magazine with Harv's picture came to rest permanently in my inbox. Somehow I couldn't bring myself to return it to the dark obscurity of the file cabinet. I would look into the optimistic blue gaze and wonder what he now must know in his current incarnation.

Whenever I hear people talk of how children enrich one's life, it sets me thinking in just the opposite direction—how thoroughly children can destroy a life. The local wisdom was that Harv's endocarditis was only a secondary cause of his death. The true mortal blow had been struck by Harv's delinquent son, Erik, age 15.

Harv's fate was proof that a life spotlessly and ethically lived can veer off to an outcome so rotten as to turn any observer into a deep and bitter cynic. Nothing you did in life mattered because if there could be Erik, then there was no justice, no order, no sense. Harv's fate became a rationale for indulging any impulse or fancy that struck one: ditching a spouse, buying a sports car, taking revenge.

Erik's latest run-in with the law had been an assault on the high school boys' locker room. He and his accomplice, Fred Pettingast, a judge's son, were caught in the act by the janitor.

This wasn't mere drunken teenage vandalism, but an orgy of demolition. Swastikas were etched and painted everywhere, along with anti-Semitic phrases in Gothic blackletter and caricatures of Jews, blacks and Mexicans. They had pulverized the lockers, crumpling and piercing the metal beyond repair. Benches were splintered, the plumbing in the showers destroyed with corrosive acid, and the tiles shattered into powder. The paint they used in the graffiti was so toxic that it required professional disposal of everything it had touched.

Fred insisted that Erik had been the instigator, while Erik, of course, claimed otherwise. Judge Pettingast must have leaned hard on somebody so that both boys would be undercharged and given probation, and the incident downplayed in local press.

Erik's locker room exploit was not an isolated incident, either. He invaded, rather than attended school; entrepreneurial talent made him a major drug dealer by his junior year. His grades were good, shored up by cheating, bribery and intimidation.

When it all became too much to take, Harv would drop into Tom's office and open his heart to the only person he could trust with his anguish.

"The kid's sowing a few wild oats, so what?" Tom Sklar would comfort his partner. "Hey, I could tell you things I did at his age, you probably wouldn't want to live in the same town with me, let alone practice with me."

"I couldn't make it without you, brother," Harv would choke up.

"Hang in there; you'll get through this just fine, all of you will." Tom would come around his desk, and the two would close in a hug, with a few mutual thwacks on their Barney's jackets.

Eleanor's adoration of her boss had also spawned a proportional hatred for Harv's German-born wife, Helga. Tireless digging into Helga's background revealed a relative who had been a Nazi official in Bavaria, prominent enough to be hanged by the British after the war. Now, although Helga was a dedicated vegan, grammar school teacher, and Democratic party worker, in Eleanor's eyes she was the Beast of Belsen.

Helga must have been beautiful once, but life's stresses were aging her. Her skin was taut over her cheekbones. Her eyes, which Eleanor described as "Nazi blue," sometimes widened alarmingly when she spoke, a sort of tic.

"Come with me," Eleanor said, leading me to the closet of cleaning supplies behind the restroom. She showed me that if you stood in just the right place, you could hear everything going on in Tom's office. She had also used an ice pick to create herself a neat pinhole for discreet peeping.

"Some hot stuff goes on in there," Eleanor said, fanning her face. "Helga and Tom. Yes, right under Harv's nose. For years. They do their nasty here in the office. Tom, the big family man. And Helga with her animal rights and eco-activism. Sometimes I was sure they knew I was here. It was like they were daring me to tell Harv."

"Did you?"

Eleanor closed her eyes and shuddered. "I finally couldn't stand it any more." A vision of Harv at the end suddenly invaded my mind, his face gaunt with disillusionment and betrayal, his eyes now sunken, riddled with bitter self-doubt.

"He got sick right afterwards, one of Edie's spells, I'm sure. She went too far that time. They were all jealous because Harv was a great man. I was the only one who really tried to protect him."

For months, Harv battled every complication his disease could throw at him, surfacing at last, weakened and wearied, from an ocean of antibiotics. His eyes had gone dull and pale, with brownish hollows beneath; his legs, once firm and tanned from the tennis he loved, were now thin and unsteady. The first thing he did was to file for divorce from Helga. The second was to retire.

To everyone's surprise, the sickly, divorced Harv took on a sexual allure that the healthy, monogamous version had lacked. Women began to flock, stalk, and proposition him; even women he had sent to jail offered themselves. Everybody wanted to care for him, to heal him from the inside out. Lock up your daughters, friends would rib him when Harv entered a room. But this stage could not last: like an incandescent bulb, Harv flared into a bright, final burn and then blinked out.

Late last Friday night, the phone rang. I was having a stiff scotch from the half-gallon bottle of Glenlivet that a friend had bought me to celebrate my acceptance into law school. I told myself that when the bottle was empty, I would put the whole experience behind me.

"I'm sorry to bother you at home, Brynn, but I had to tell you. I finally did it. "

"Did what?" My stomach gave a hard jump.

"I told Tom about Edie and her witchcraft. I waited until everyone left tonight, and then I went in and showed him all the evidence. Every single piece was marked with a date and catalogued. Tom always says the chain of evidence is the most critical part of a case. Edie was nailed!"

From my bedroom window, I saw the slate-dark, drizzling sky, and for some reason, I pictured Eleanor out in the rain, the upswept hairdo soaked and collapsing of its own weight, sagging comically to one side like a duffel bag, the false lashes flapping wetly above the livid slash of lipstick.

"When you try to straighten things out," Eleanor said, "and they keep getting twisted up again, you know there's a powerful force working against you. I told Tom I'd tried to fight it for a long time, but her magic was getting stronger and he needed to take action now or it would be too late, the way it was with Harv. If he didn't get rid of Edie, she would turn on him too and tell his wife and kids about the affair. Or else try to take *you* over. Edie is a very dangerous woman."

I couldn't bring myself to speak, so I tossed back the rest of the scotch, which seared a raw, welcome swath all the way down, burning through the hopeful lies; the presumptions and facades and well-worn excuses we employ to shore up our dwindling dreams.

"Oh I had her, all right. I even went out in the garden and pulled the plants she uses in her spells—star anise and bay leaves and lavender and rosemary and about a dozen more, and are they ever potent! They almost burned my hands. Let her try to explain that away when Tom confronts her."

"What did Tom say?"

"He was trying to look unshockable, you know him. He said, "Well, Eleanor, it looks like you've done your homework.

I know how much you care about the office, and I'm grateful for your work all these years."

"That's what he said?"

"Yes, and he *should* be grateful."

My silence must have summoned back Eleanor the careerist. "It's so considerate of you to hear me out, Brynn. I apologize for calling on a weekend, but I did this for you too. Things will be different from now on, you'll see."

When I arrived at work on Monday morning, Edie met me in the waiting room, the stuffed owl observing us with its astute, remorseless stare.

"Brynn, you should know that Tom had to fire Eleanor. She won't be here anymore."

"Tom fired Eleanor?"

"He was only keeping her on here out of pity, anyway, long past the time when there was no work for her. She lost important files and client information, and she was a handful for all of us—including you, I'm sure." Transfixed by Edie's pointed gaze, I said nothing. "Between you and me," Edie said, "she was a disaster waiting to happen. I'm amazed at Tom's patience. He felt terrible, of course, but he had to take the additional step of getting a restraining order to keep her from harassing us. So you let me know if she bothers you."

As I turned away, Edie added that despite anything Eleanor may have told me, Tom was the most faithful of husbands and had always been a loyal friend to his partner. She hoped this whole unfortunate incident would not cause me to think of leaving the firm. In fact, Tom had even mentioned sending me to classes that would prepare me for another try at law school.

When my messages to Eleanor's phone went unreturned, I drove out to her small bungalow in Live Oak and knocked on the door. There was no response, though I sensed movement within, and I either glimpsed or imagined huge, haunted green eyes peering at me from a slat in the blinds.

Last week Edie moved me out of my cramped quarters and gave me Eleanor's roomy corner cubicle. She and Tom even held a little ceremony with cake and tea to mark my elevation to legal research associate. They presented me with all new office furniture and a new computer, and Edie even graced my office with a charming miniature spice garden under its own fluorescent lamp.

Shortly afterwards, my once boyfriend called to ask if I would consider giving our relationship another chance; he had missed me. He sounded more ardent than he ever had.

As I drive to work now, it occurs to me that each street, house and building in town holds its own story, and that these are sometimes very bizarre ones. I remind myself that this must be true of every hamlet in the world.

The Discarded

The empty cubicles of the Discarded remain untouched, their gray, padded walls still displaying the cartoons, awards, and post-it notes of their late occupants. Computers stand inert beside telephones patiently blinking undelivered messages. Ads announcing revolutionary product launches droop from their push pins.

I walk among these cubicles thinking of Heisenberg's living dead cats. If an employee is terminated but unaware of it, does the Cosmos consider him employed or unemployed? I tiptoe past the deserted cubicle of Herman Brandwine, a pale, broad-hipped software analyst with a frizzy hairline. Herman had seemed to visit the restroom on the same schedule as I did, homing in on his forked male symbol with an urgent, duck-footed gait. Several times, he and I had nearly collided.

Penny Dahlen, an accounts payable clerk, has left behind the wolf posters that decorated her cubicle. The yellow eyes of the abandoned wolves track passersby with a cornered, territorial glare. Penny had had a lopsided grin and long, oily blonde hair. Her nasty ex-husband Royal had stalked her, lurking in the bushes outside the building or in the parking lot, ranting of betrayal, orgies and child neglect.

These Silicon Valley firms sometimes self-destruct, I am discovering, much like supernovae: a period of instability will suddenly culminate in a massive ejection of employees, accompanied by a spewing of gaseous press releases. In the coming months, a smaller, denser entity will emerge, composed of odd particles and hierarchies. Or the company might continue to decay, vanishing at last into a sort of black job hole, pulling other firms into its vacuous heart.

To me though, the layoffs seem more ethnic cleansing than cosmic event. Secret cadres meet, rumors fly. Work grows random, minimal. Everywhere, people gather in tense, whispering little knots, exchanging questioning looks and shrugs. A pervasive sense of helplessness causes some to grow feverishly self-indulgent, wasting money on frivolities and sauntering in late from lunch, as if to beckon fate. Others, bitter, declare themselves unappreciated, conspired against. Most simply wait numbly. Every end is a beginning they remind one another, without conviction.

When the fatal day arrived, many simply disappeared with Stalinesque suddenness. Others were plucked away in mid-task by their managers, never to reappear. From my window, I watched blank-faced security guards escort dazed former colleagues through the parking lot, ducking their heads like mob informants.

My group, Marketing Communications, had warred with Corporate Communications. Now, outmaneuvered in the boardroom, we fell, our Director banished to the Gulag of Systems Administration, our functions outsourced. I alone survived, shielded perhaps by my indifference.

Nobody really plans a career in Marcom anyway. Marcom is, rather, where we end up—aspiring actors and singer-song-writers, shell-shocked English teachers, addled psychology majors, law school dropouts and starving would-be novelists like myself. We churn out content, as they call it—or worse, text. We serve the insatiable need of technology to be understood, to be *felt*; to speak in the human tongue even as it eclipses us with its own spate of languages.

The company's latest slogan is "Reaching New Horizons." In the advertisements, server hardware glows amid towering cumulus or hangs in a star-littered cosmos. Back on earth, heroic disk drives conquer Half Dome or rest atop Venezuelan tepuis. I can hardly watch a sunset without imagining some computer part imposed on it.

Tall, thin, and dark-haired, with round hazel eyes, I look like a Modigliani but yearn to be a Klimt—sensual, powerful, profane. I paint my eyes into an upward slant and affect a Klimtish hairstyle, but a vague, rather mournful visage persists.

Day after day, I type away listlessly at an email intended to rebuild morale: The layoffs have so lightened the company, I write, that it has gone airborne, soaring into profitability! I assure myself that nobody will actually read this clatfart, and even if they do, will not believe it.

To preserve my sanity, I surf the Web blatantly, reading *Moby Dick*, and visiting a message board for survivors of Strep A, the flesh-eating bacteria. Some of its victims had merely barked their shins or pricked a finger before being half-devoured by the opportunistic germ. White whale, seamstress or marcom, our fates await the agenda of some other creature.

"This is going to hurt, Brynn," warned Ron, "but I have to tell you. I've met someone." The air between us sagged under the weight of his confession. "You don't know her. She's in my chemistry class. I didn't plan this."

"I was going to move to San Jose anyway," I lied. "The commute is killing me."

He blinked. "When were you planning to tell me?"

"I... was just waiting for the chance."

Every morning I drove from Santa Cruz to San Jose over Highway 17, a sinuous black python winding through mountains of oak and redwood. The highway is poorly engineered, with blind curves, precipices, and straight descents that terminate in tight loops. Commuters share the road with double-jointed gravel trucks and gasoline tankers. An inattentive, complacent, or inexperienced driver might round a curve to see (perhaps the last thing he ever did see) the rear end of an elephantine cement tub complete with girlie mudflaps and "Higher Powered" bumper sticker, toiling along at ten miles per hour in his lane. Intent on survival, I grip the steering wheel, my eyes darting about with primal alertness evolved over millions of years, called upon now to help me dodge not leopard or lion but Audi; not charging aurochs but careening Range Rover.

"You won't last six weeks in Silicon Valley," Ron said, with the confidence of a FBI agent talking terrorism on CNN. "You're so not the type."

But despite the layoffs, I have come to feel oddly secure here. Silicon Valley's numeral world persists as usual within its teeming chips and raceways, obeying its Boolean logic. In contrast, the corporeal world has come to seem lumpy and chaotic, as unsettling as the gaze of a doomsday prepper.

Marooned now in my empty department, I am grateful when Kevin, the Information Technology guy shows up at my cubicle. In the wake of the layoffs, he is as welcome as an old acquaintance in a refugee camp.

"Thought I'd check your memory while I'm in the neighborhood," he sings out, as if nothing in the world is wrong. He slides into the chair beside me before I can protest that my memory was only recently upgraded.

At first I feel a little violated as he deftly accesses my applications and probes my extensions, not even bothering to ask my password. Under his coaxing, hidden recesses of my hard drive yield themselves, responding to his touch with odd screens and prompts. I feel myself succumbing to the intimacy of a shared monitor as our eyes merge onscreen, fingers tapping the keyboard in hesitant unison. A manual lies open across our laps, our knees touching intermittently beneath its discreet mantle. Once, when we both reach for the mouse, his hand inadvertently covers mine.

Kevin shakes his head and murmurs, "You need some new memory, girl." And yes, that is exactly what I need. Take away those stale and depleted histories: the bullies of middle school; my academic rejections and irrational fears and social gaffes. Wipe the damaged sectors, and don't stop there. Take the wars too, the lies and genocides, unavenged murders and race hatred, the profiteering and exploitation...

The voice comes out of nowhere. Kevin looks past me, and following his gaze, I see Royal Dahlen, Penny's psycho ex-husband, as incredible and out-of-place here as a Venusian. Royal's belly sags over a silver and turquoise belt buckle; a buckknife is strapped to his bluejeaned leg. The obligatory wizard tattoo peeps from his sleeveless undershirt, and his lower arms bear cruder tattoos—a skull and crossbones, a knife dripping blood, and, of course, the swastika. His hair, thick and gray-streaked brown, hangs past his shoulders.

"I said, where's Penny? Where's my wife?"

"She's gone," I finally blurt. "She was laid off days ago."

"Lies and more lies," Royal says. "Will you never learn?"

I do not see the gun in his hand until it speaks. Kevin suddenly cries out and slumps over my keyboard like a marionette whose strings have been cut. A small red spot on his back widens rapidly into the weave of his blue shirt.

Royal bends to study my face. He reeks of alcohol. "The govermint's gonna plant computer chips in our brains," he says. "That's what you're helpin' it do." The air molecules around me suddenly expand chaotically and reverberate, and I am thrown backward in my chair. Royal turns and walks away, disappearing among the cubicles like a flea in a dog's coat. I hear more gun blasts, oddly muffled, as if fired through layers of carpeting.

Only now do I think to run, and my shaking legs somehow carry me through the maze of cubicles, down the stairs and through the front door. Outside, giant ferns offer their stalks to my grasping hands. The sun, occluded with little cloudlets, drops suddenly behind the polished angular wedge of a nearby building, leaching the warmth from the air around me. But the sun has not dropped; rather, I am lying prone on the wet shore of a fountain-fed lake. Close up, a dead water skater floats past, others attacking its corpse. During the heyday of the dinosaurs, opportunistic vermin hid among them, awaiting their call to destiny. Swarming from their recesses, an inconceivable plague of mammals overwhelmed the rotting earth. The veil parts, and behind it I now see, at last, what it all was. What it was.

Acknowledgements

"Home Like a Shadow" appeared in The Piltdown Review and was anthologized in *Modern Shorts: 18 Short Stories from Fiction Attic Press,* 2014. It was also anthologized in Best New Writing 2011.

"Let That Be a Lesson" was published in The Writing Disorder.

"A Season of Turbulence" was published in the Conium Review in 2012 and online in Eclectica.

"Sunnyside" was published in Pulse Magazine.

"A Journey From Which Many Do Not Return" was published in print in Able Muse and nominated for a 2016 Pushcart Prize.

"A Shoo-In" was published in Word Riot.

"A Suitable Poison" was published in Black Denim Lit.

"The Hundred Thousand Dollar Suit" was published in Adelaide Magazine. Year II, Number 7, Volume II, June 2017

"The Shakes" was published in Zineweb as "Cataclysm" and also as a podcast in Bound Off

"The Discarded" was published in Blunderbuss Magazine.

About the Author

Linda Boroff graduated from UC Berkeley with a degree in English and currently lives and works in Silicon Valley. Her fiction and non-fiction have appeared in *McSweeney's, Crack the Spine, Writing Disorder, The Piltdown Review, 5:21 Magazine, Thoughtful Dog, Gawker, The Guardian, Hollywood Dementia, In Posse Review, Adelaide Magazine, Word Riot, Hobart, Ducts Magazine, Blunderbuss Magazine, Storyglossia, Able Muse, The Pedestal Magazine, The Furious Gazelle, Eyeshot, JONAH Magazine, The Boiler, In Posse Review, Epoch, Bound Off (podcast), Fiction Attic Press, Black Denim Lit, Stirring, Drunk Monkeys, Fictive Dream* and others.

Linda was nominated for a 2016 Pushcart Prize for fiction and won first prize in the Writing Place fiction competition. She wrote the feature film, *Murder in Fashion Review in New York Times.* Her short story "Light Fingers" and its script adaptation are under option to director Brad Furman and Sony. Linda adapted the biography of film noir actress Barbara Payton, with producer Don Murphy.

www.ingramcontent.com/pod-product-compliance
Lightning Source LLC
Chambersburg PA
CBHW021437020726
47499CB00006BA/2044